Garfield ®

TROUBLE IN PARADISE

BY JIM DAVIS

ROSS RICHIE CEO & Founder • MATT GAGNON Editor-in-Chief • FILIP SABLIK President of Publishing & Marketing • STEPHEN CHRISTY President of Development • LANCE KREITER VP of Licensing & Merchandising • PHIL BARBARO VP of Finance • ARUNE SINGH VP of Marketing
BRYCE CARLSON Managing Editor • SCOTT NEWMAN Production Design Manager • KATE HENNING Operations Manager • SPENCER SIMPSON Sales Manager • SIERRA HAHN Senior Editor • DAFNA PLEBAN Editor, Talent Development • SHANNON WATTERS Editor
ERIC HARBURN Editor • WHITNEY LEOPARD Editor • CAMERON CHITTOCK Editor • CHRIS ROSA Associate Editor • MATTHEW LEVINE Associate Editor • SOPHIE PHILIPS-ROBERTS Assistant Editor • GAVIN GRONENTHAL Assistant Editor • MICHAEL MOCCIO Assistant Editor
AMANDA LaFRANCO Executive Assistant • KATALINA HOLLAND Editorial Administrative Assistant • JILLIAN CRAB Design Coordinator • MICHELLE ANKLEY Design Coordinator • KARA LEOPARD Production Designer • MARIE KRUPINA Production Designer
GRACE PARK Production Design Assistant • CHELSEA ROBERTS Production Design Assistant • ELIZABETH LOUGHRIDGE Accounting Coordinator • STEPHANIE HOCUTT Social Media Coordinator • JOSÉ MEZA Event Coordinator • HOLLY AITCHISON Operations Coordinator
MEGAN CHRISTOPHER Operations Assistant • RODRIGO HERNANDEZ Mailroom Assistant • MORGAN PERRY Direct Market Representative • CAT O'GRADY Marketing Assistant • CORNELIA TZANA Publicity Assistant • LIZ ALMENDAREZ Accounting Administrative Assistant

kaboom!

GARFIELD: TROUBLE IN PARADISE, September 2018. Published by KaBOOM!, a division of Boom Entertainment, Inc. Garfield is © 2018 PAWS, INCORPORATED. ALL RIGHTS RESERVED. "GARFIELD" and the GARFIELD characters are registered and unregistered trademarks of Paws, Inc. KaBOOM!™ and the KaBOOM! logo are trademarks of Boom Entertainment, Inc., registered in various countries and categories. All characters, events, and institutions depicted herein are fictional. Any similarity between any of the names, characters, persons, events, and/or institutions in this publication to actual names, characters, and persons, whether living or dead, events, and/or institutions is unintended and purely coincidental. KaBOOM! does not read or accept unsolicited submissions of ideas, stories, or artwork.

BOOM! Studios, 5670 Wilshire Boulevard, Suite 400, Los Angeles, CA 90036-5679. Printed in China. First Printing.

ISBN: 978-1-68415-237-7, eISBN: 978-1-64144-099-8

CONTENTS

"TROUBLE IN PARADISE"
WRITTEN BY SCOTT NICKEL
ILLUSTRATED BY ANTONIO ALFARO
COLORED BY LISA MOORE

"LOUIE'S LASAGNA CLUB"
WRITTEN BY MARK EVANIER
ILLUSTRATED BY DAVE ALVAREZ
COLORED BY LISA MOORE

"GARFIELD THE BARBARIAN"
WRITTEN BY SCOTT NICKEL
ILLUSTRATED BY KYLE SMART

LETTERED BY JIM CAMPBELL

COVER BY ANDY HIRSCH

DESIGNER KARA LEOPARD
ASSOCIATE EDITOR CHRIS ROSA
EDITOR WHITNEY LEOPARD

GARFIELD CREATED BY
JIM DAVIS

SPECIAL THANKS TO JIM DAVIS AND THE ENTIRE PAWS, INC. TEAM.

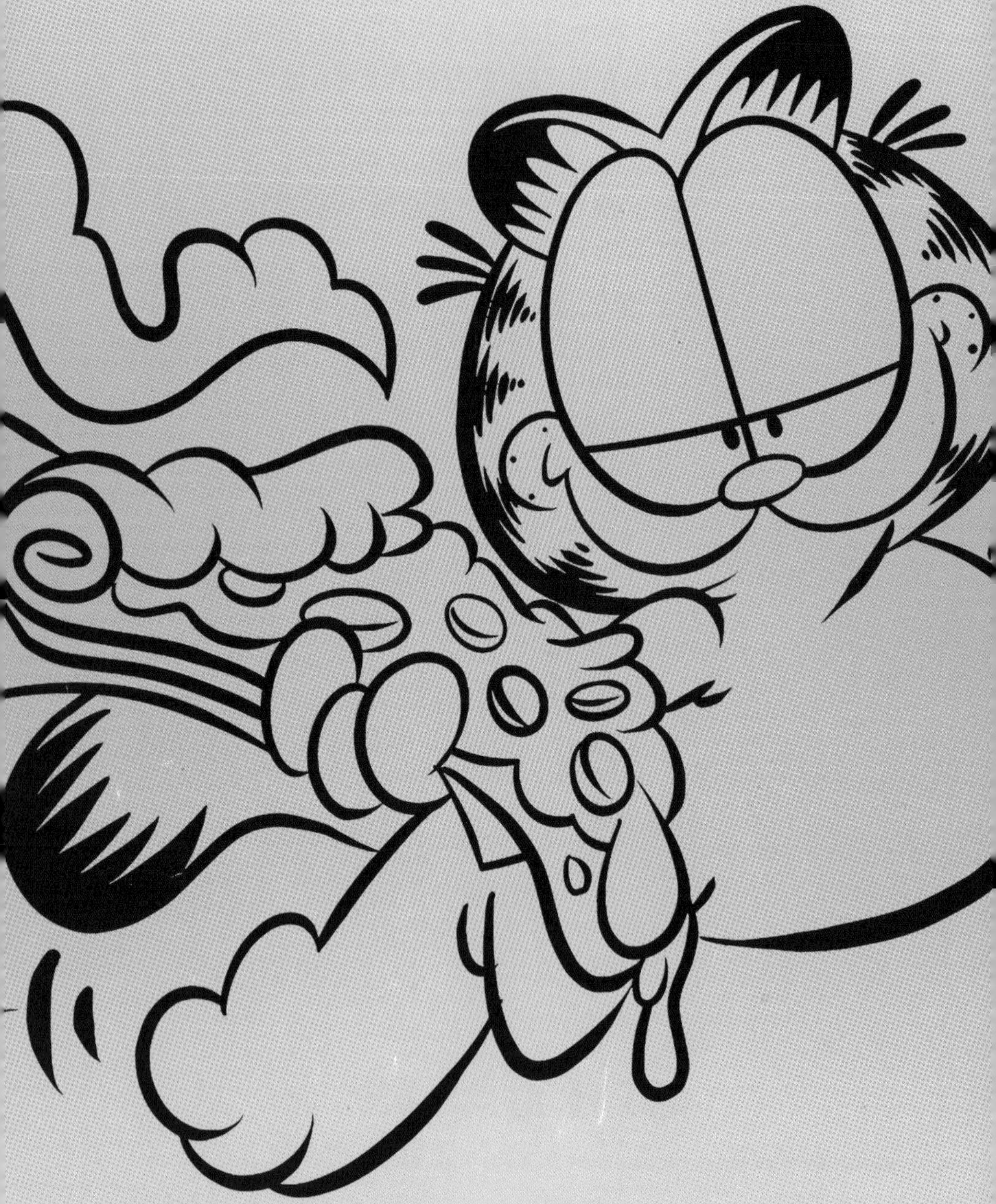

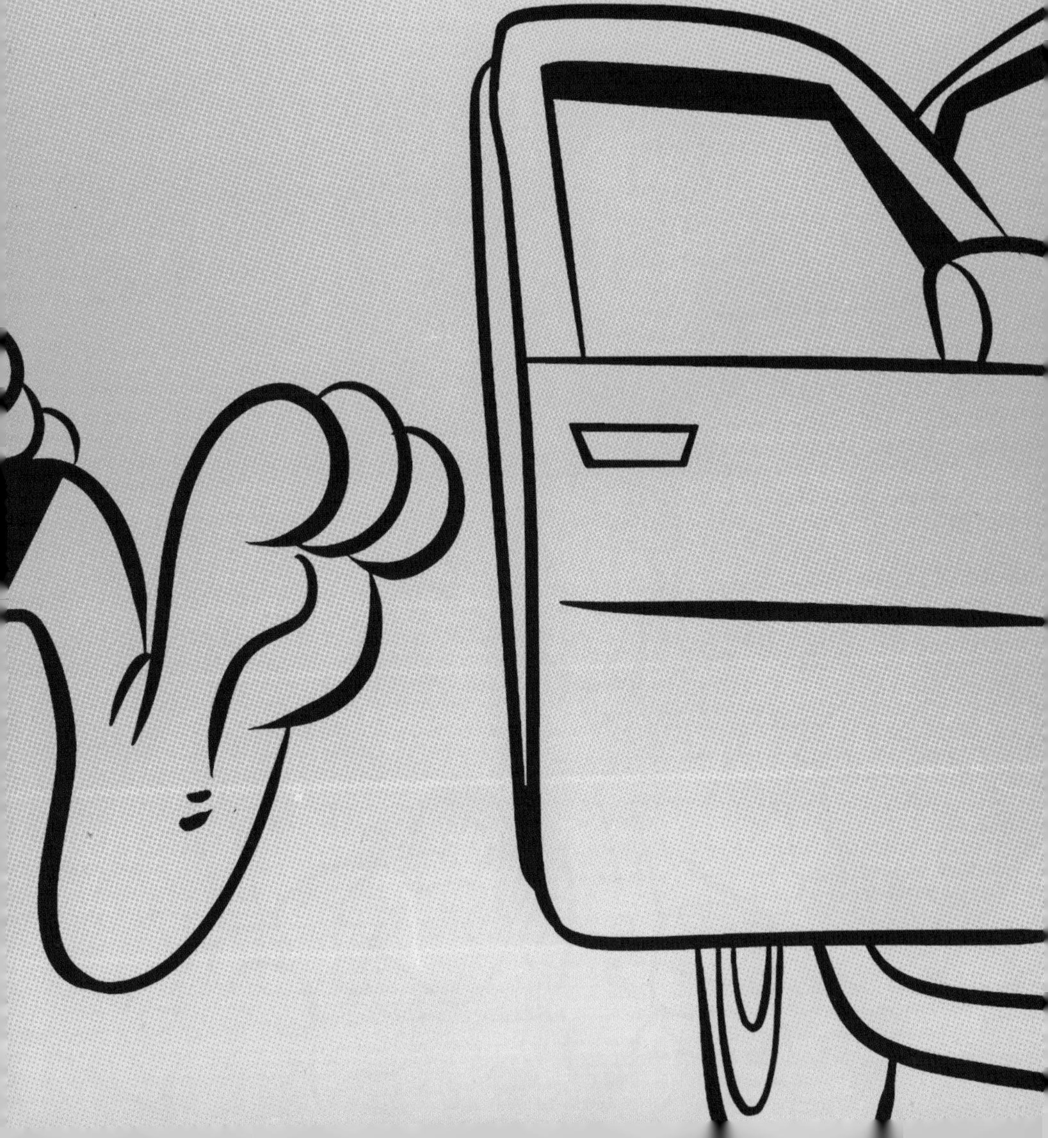

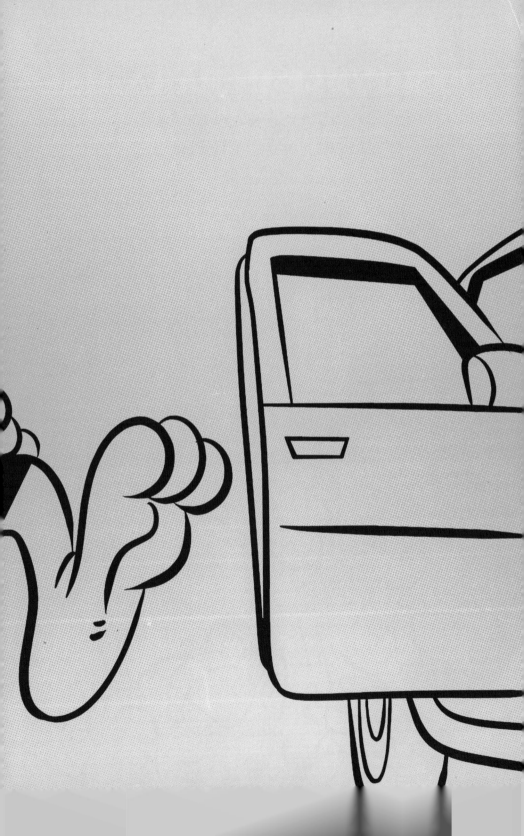

"TROUBLE IN PARADISE"

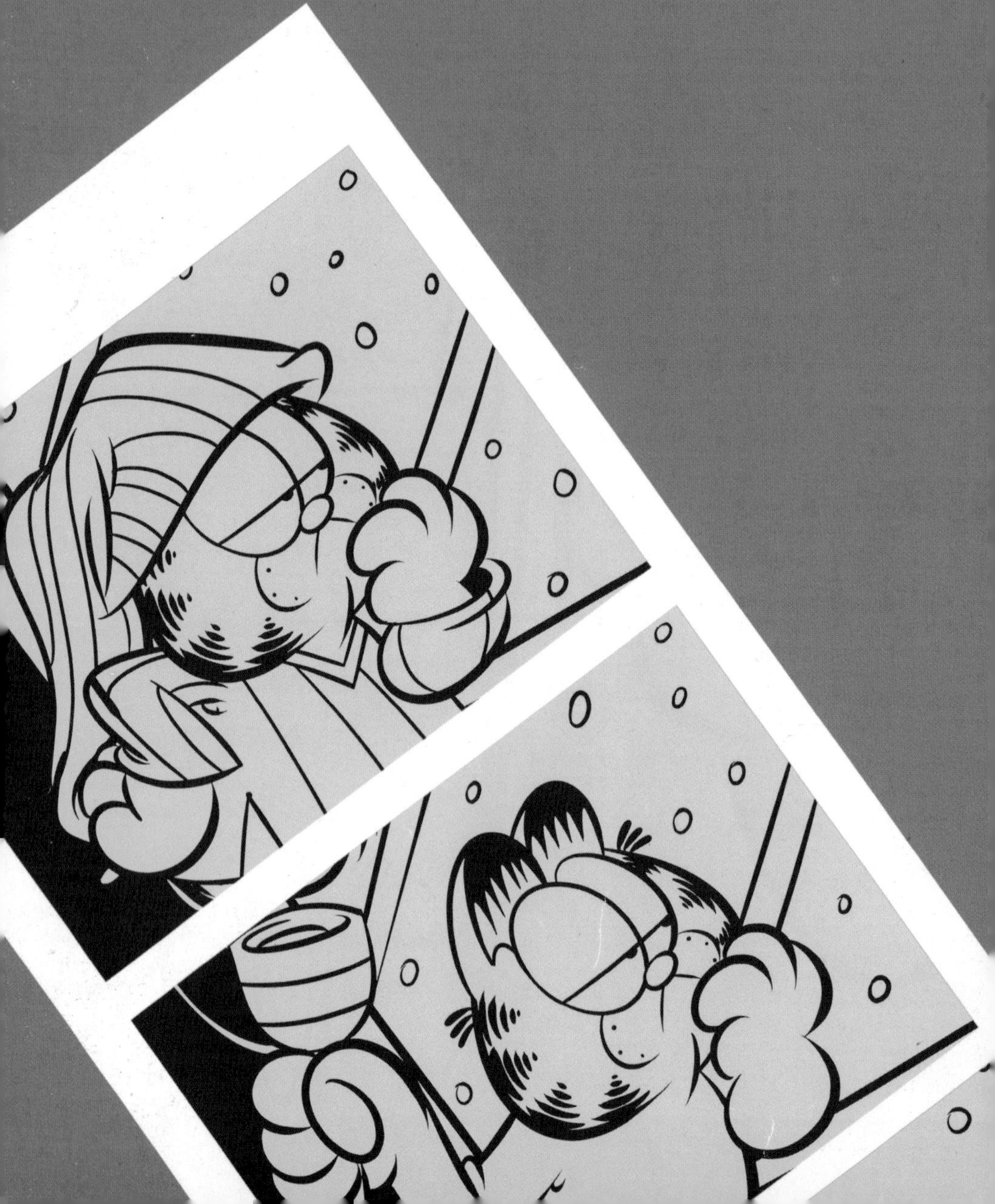

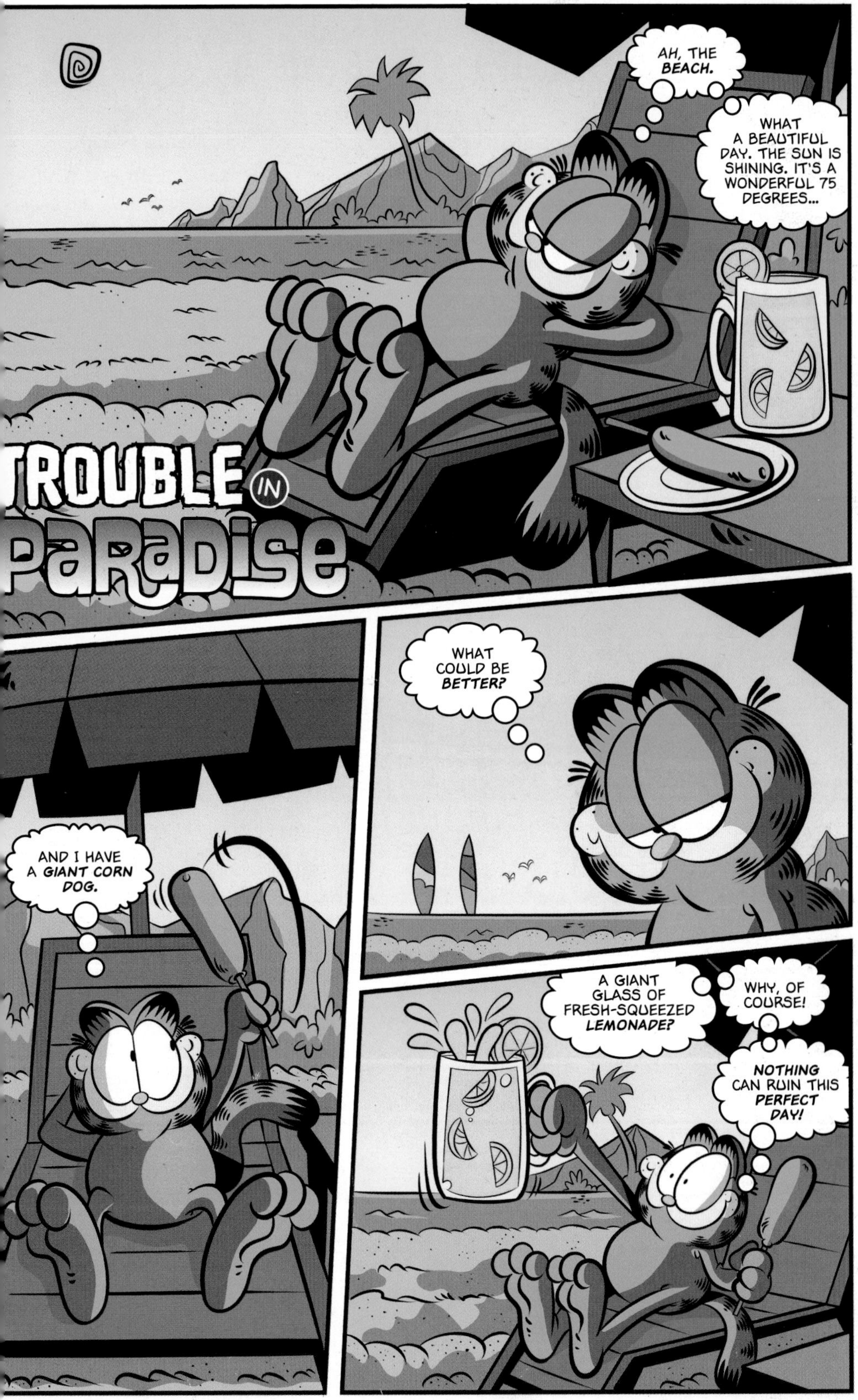
AH, THE BEACH.
WHAT A BEAUTIFUL DAY. THE SUN IS SHINING. IT'S A WONDERFUL 75 DEGREES...
TROUBLE IN PARADISE
AND I HAVE A GIANT CORN DOG.
WHAT COULD BE BETTER?
A GIANT GLASS OF FRESH-SQUEEZED LEMONADE?
WHY, OF COURSE!
NOTHING CAN RUIN THIS PERFECT DAY!

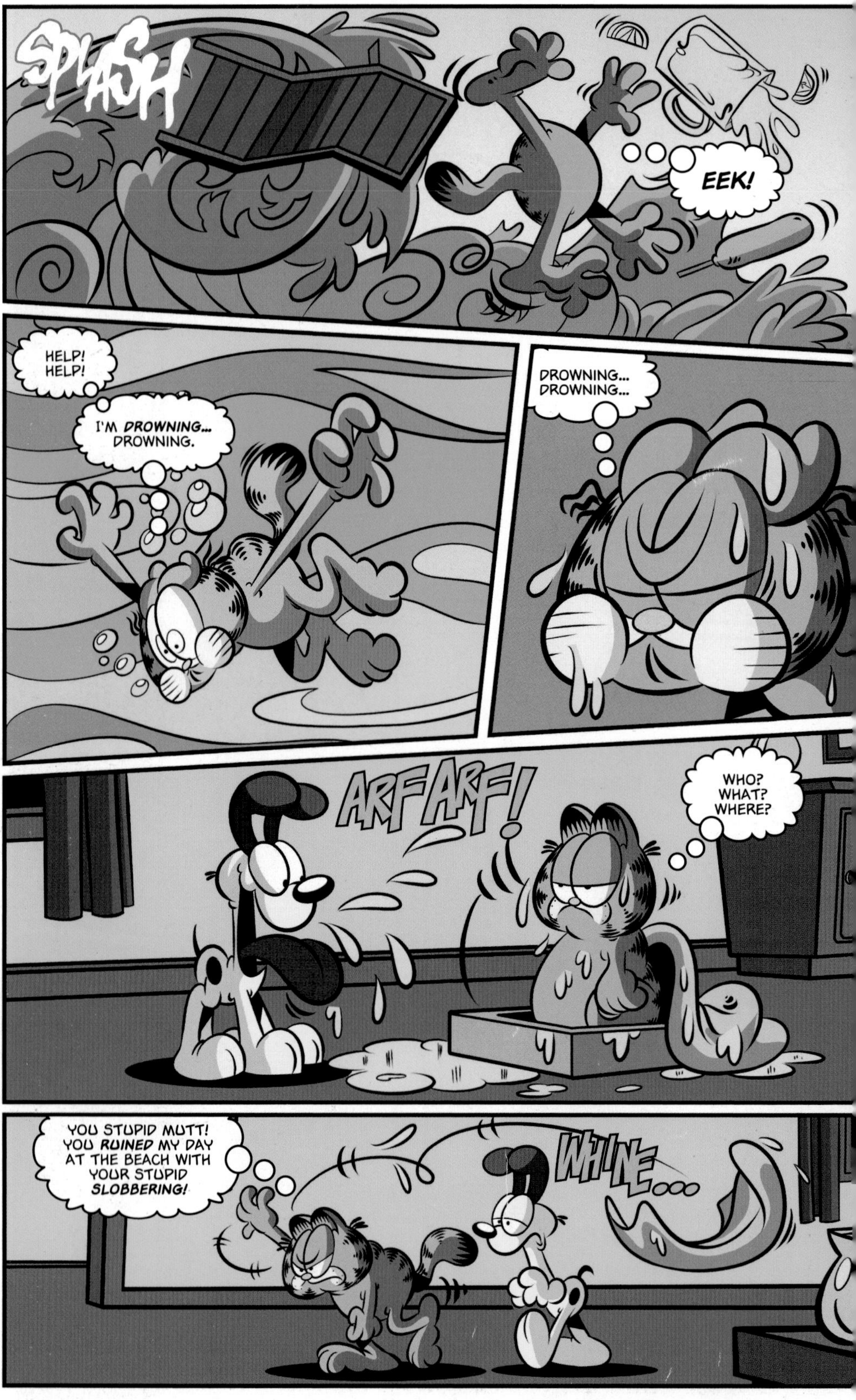
SPLASH
EEK!
HELP! HELP!
I'M DROWNING... DROWNING.
DROWNING... DROWNING...
ARF ARF!
WHO? WHAT? WHERE?
YOU STUPID MUTT! YOU RUINED MY DAY AT THE BEACH WITH YOUR STUPID SLOBBERING!
WHINE...

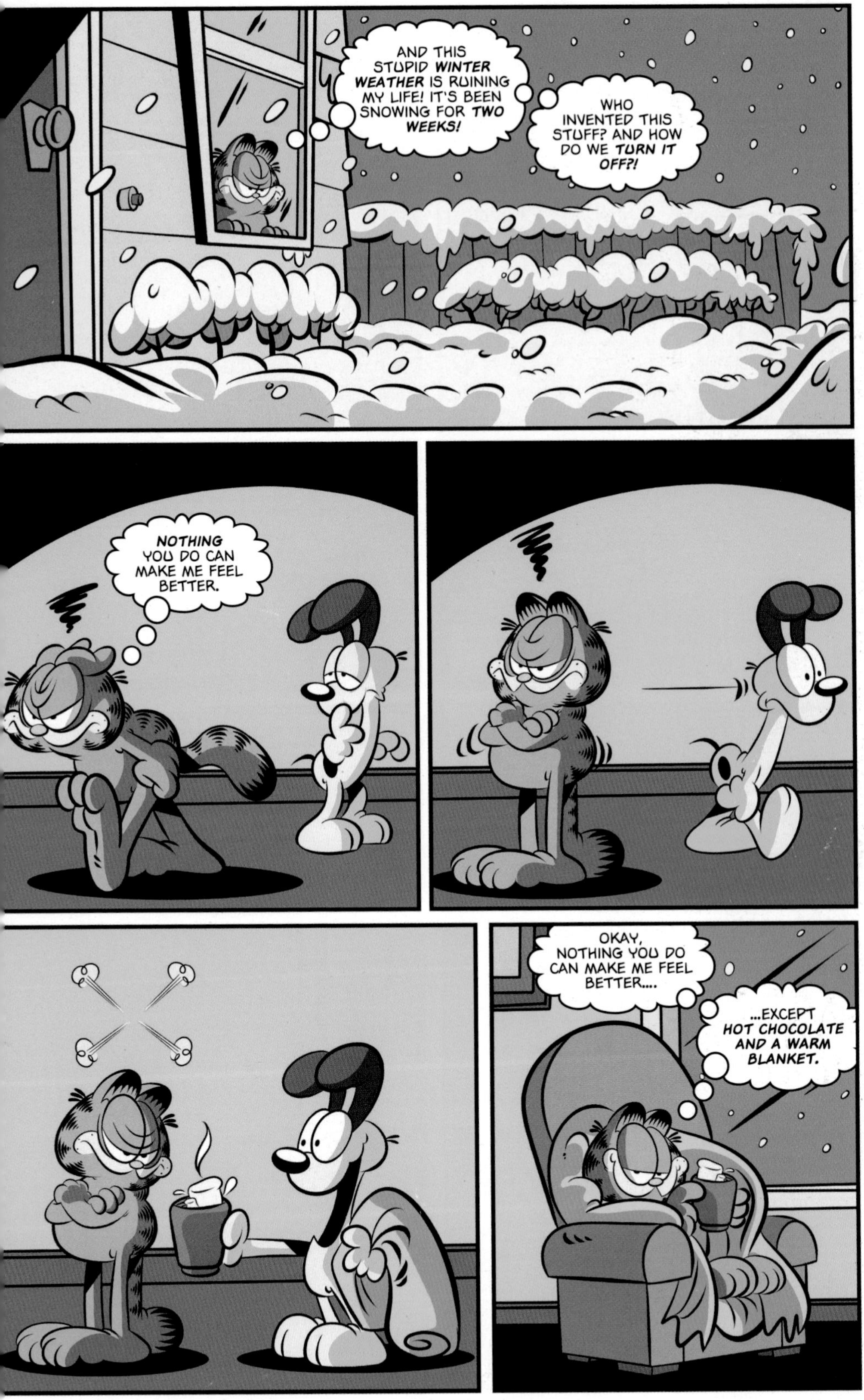

AND THIS STUPID WINTER WEATHER IS RUINING MY LIFE! IT'S BEEN SNOWING FOR TWO WEEKS!
WHO INVENTED THIS STUFF? AND HOW DO WE TURN IT OFF?!
NOTHING YOU DO CAN MAKE ME FEEL BETTER.
OKAY, NOTHING YOU DO CAN MAKE ME FEEL BETTER....
...EXCEPT HOT CHOCOLATE AND A WARM BLANKET.

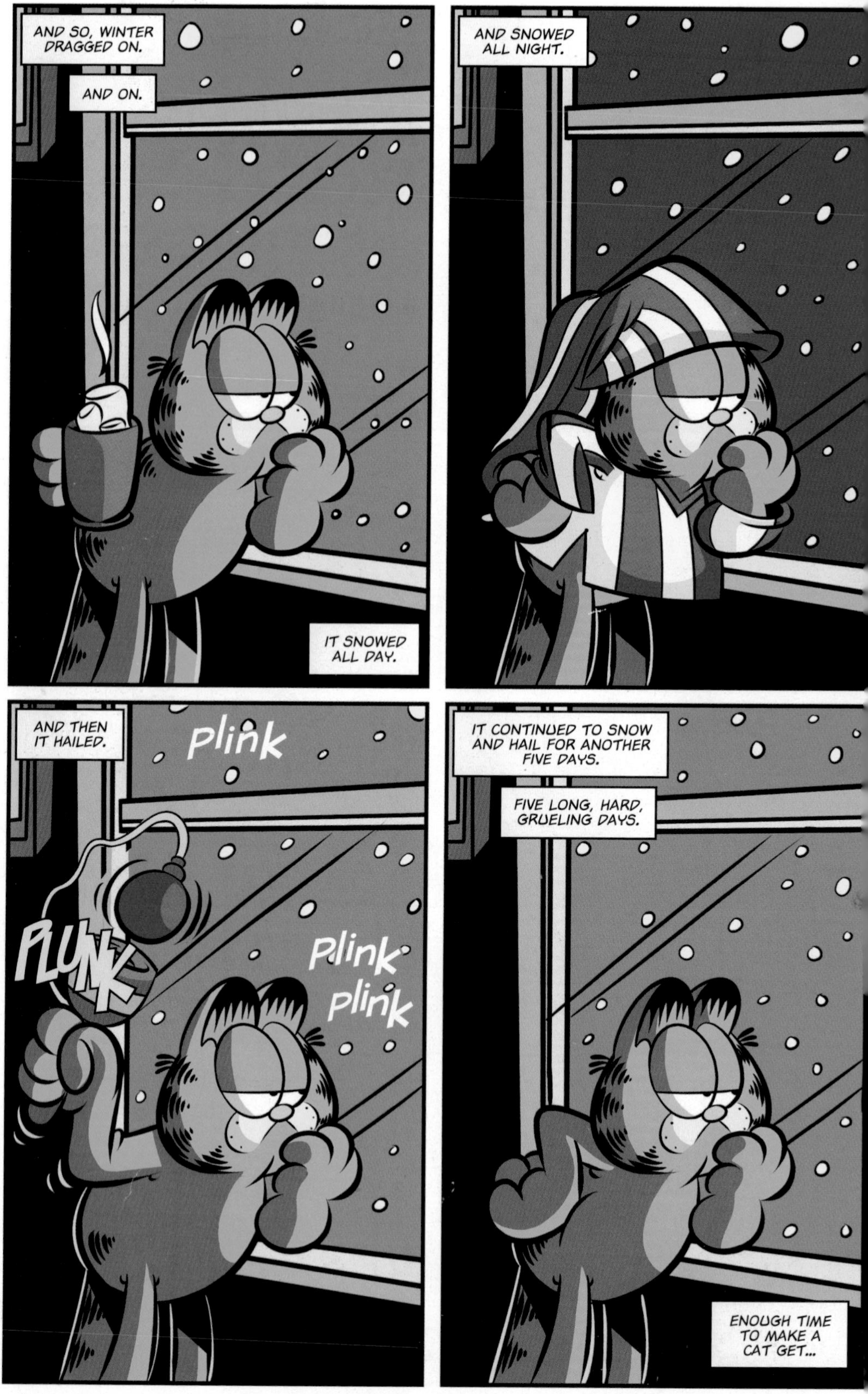
AND SO, WINTER DRAGGED ON.
AND ON.
IT SNOWED ALL DAY.
AND SNOWED ALL NIGHT.
AND THEN IT HAILED.
Plink
PLUNK
Plink
plink
IT CONTINUED TO SNOW AND HAIL FOR ANOTHER FIVE DAYS.
FIVE LONG, HARD, GRUELING DAYS.
ENOUGH TIME TO MAKE A CAT GET...

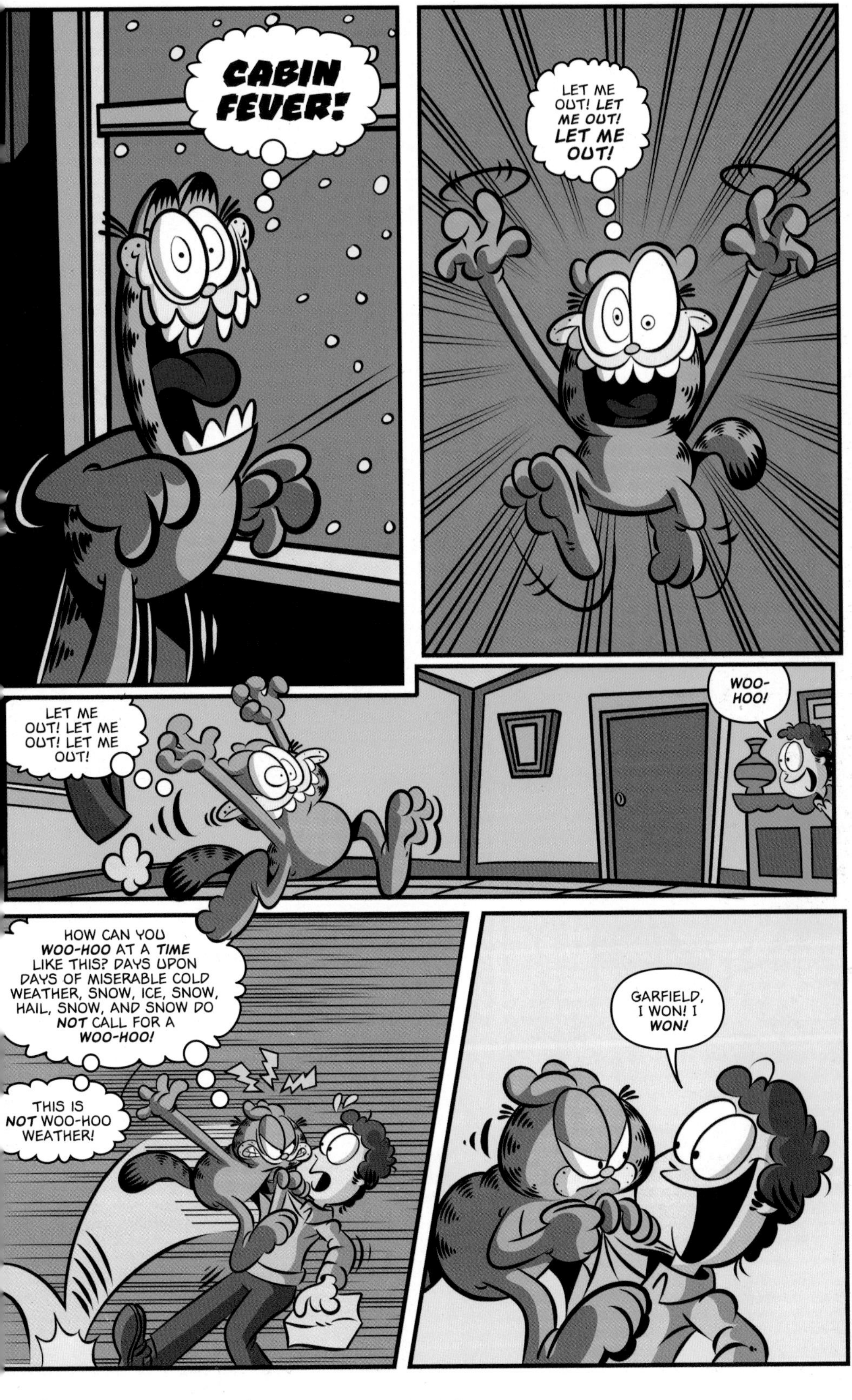
CABIN FEVER!
LET ME OUT! LET ME OUT! LET ME OUT!
LET ME OUT! LET ME OUT! LET ME OUT!
WOO-HOO!
HOW CAN YOU WOO-HOO AT A TIME LIKE THIS? DAYS UPON DAYS OF MISERABLE COLD WEATHER, SNOW, ICE, SNOW, HAIL, SNOW, AND SNOW DO NOT CALL FOR A WOO-HOO!
THIS IS NOT WOO-HOO WEATHER!
GARFIELD, I WON! I WON!

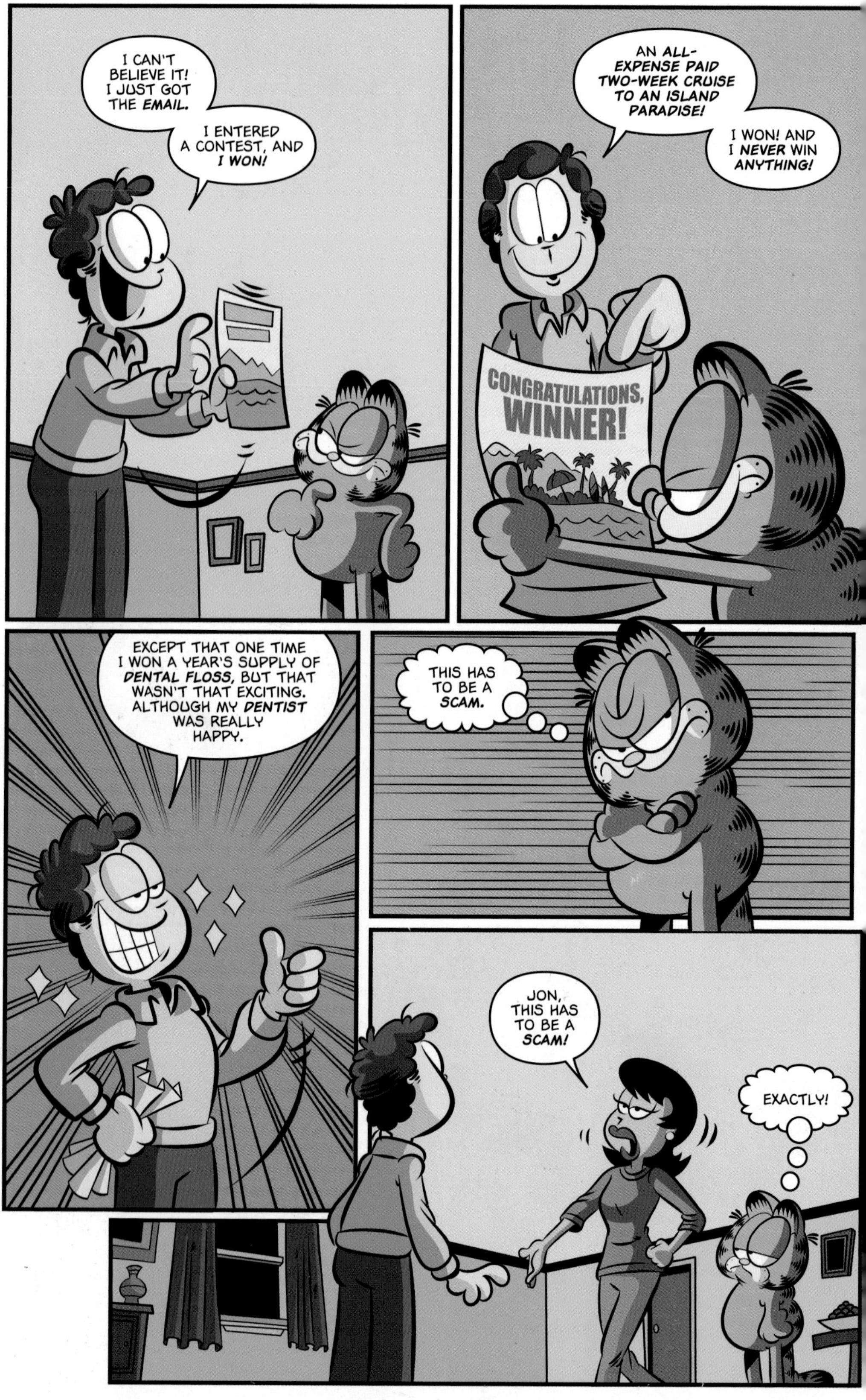
I CAN'T BELIEVE IT! I JUST GOT THE EMAIL.
I ENTERED A CONTEST, AND I WON!
AN ALL-EXPENSE PAID TWO-WEEK CRUISE TO AN ISLAND PARADISE!
I WON! AND I NEVER WIN ANYTHING!
CONGRATULATIONS, WINNER!
EXCEPT THAT ONE TIME I WON A YEAR'S SUPPLY OF DENTAL FLOSS, BUT THAT WASN'T THAT EXCITING. ALTHOUGH MY DENTIST WAS REALLY HAPPY.
THIS HAS TO BE A SCAM.
JON, THIS HAS TO BE A SCAM!
EXACTLY!

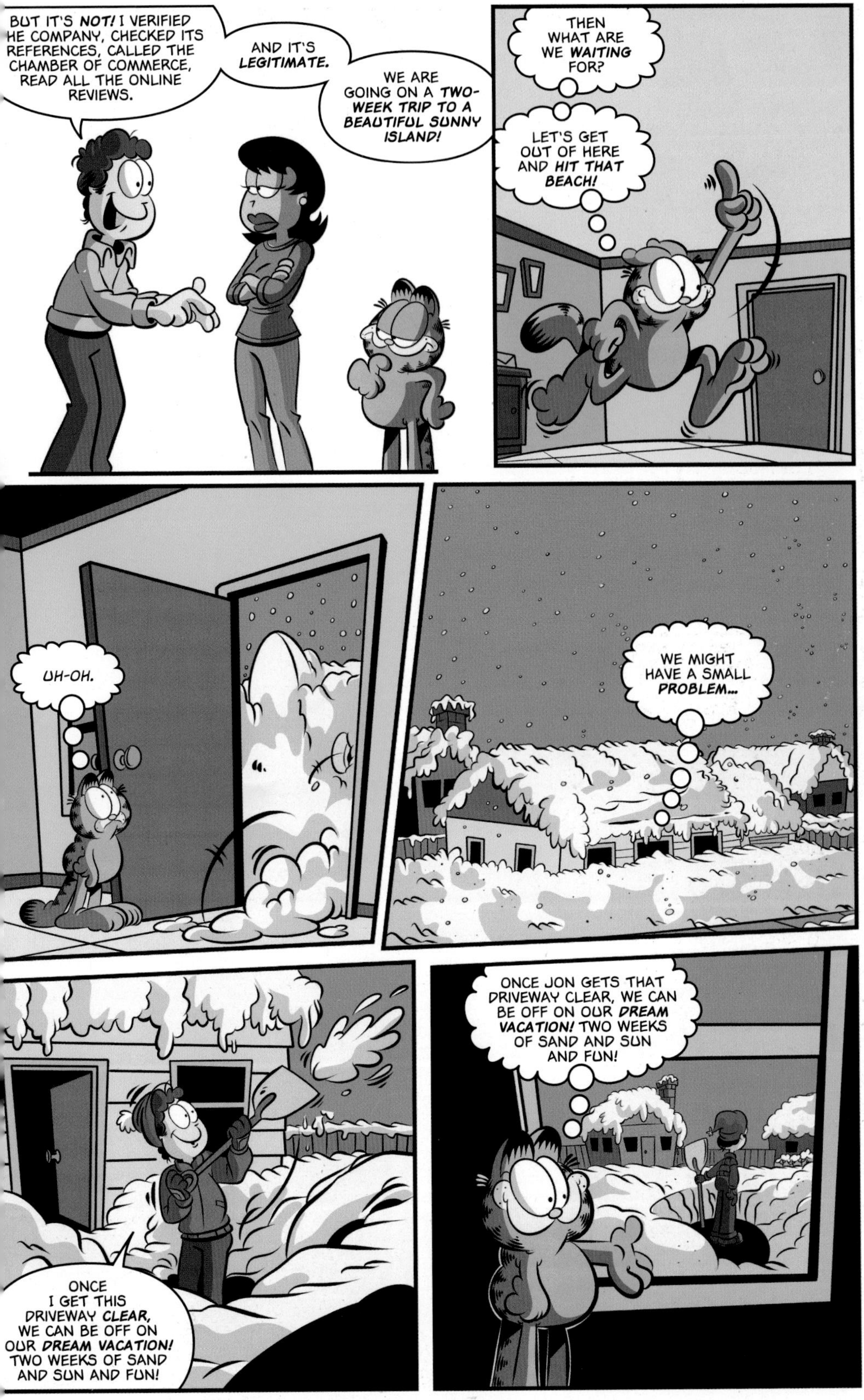
BUT IT'S NOT! I VERIFIED HE COMPANY, CHECKED ITS REFERENCES, CALLED THE CHAMBER OF COMMERCE, READ ALL THE ONLINE REVIEWS.
AND IT'S LEGITIMATE.
WE ARE GOING ON A TWO-WEEK TRIP TO A BEAUTIFUL SUNNY ISLAND!
THEN WHAT ARE WE WAITING FOR?
LET'S GET OUT OF HERE AND HIT THAT BEACH!
UH-OH.
WE MIGHT HAVE A SMALL PROBLEM...
ONCE I GET THIS DRIVEWAY CLEAR, WE CAN BE OFF ON OUR DREAM VACATION! TWO WEEKS OF SAND AND SUN AND FUN!
ONCE JON GETS THAT DRIVEWAY CLEAR, WE CAN BE OFF ON OUR DREAM VACATION! TWO WEEKS OF SAND AND SUN AND FUN!

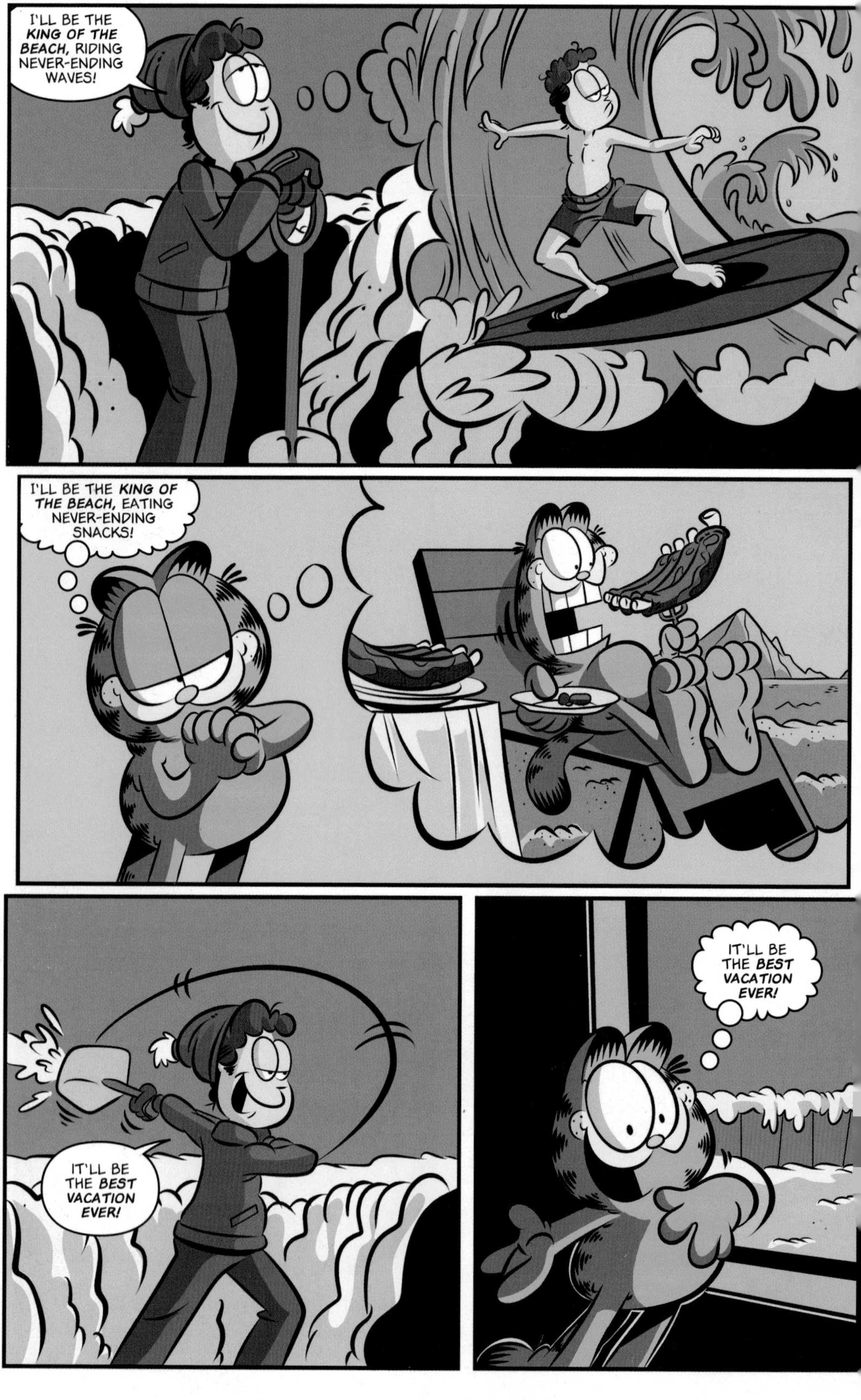
I'LL BE THE KING OF THE BEACH, RIDING NEVER-ENDING WAVES!
I'LL BE THE KING OF THE BEACH, EATING NEVER-ENDING SNACKS!
IT'LL BE THE BEST VACATION EVER!
IT'LL BE THE BEST VACATION EVER!

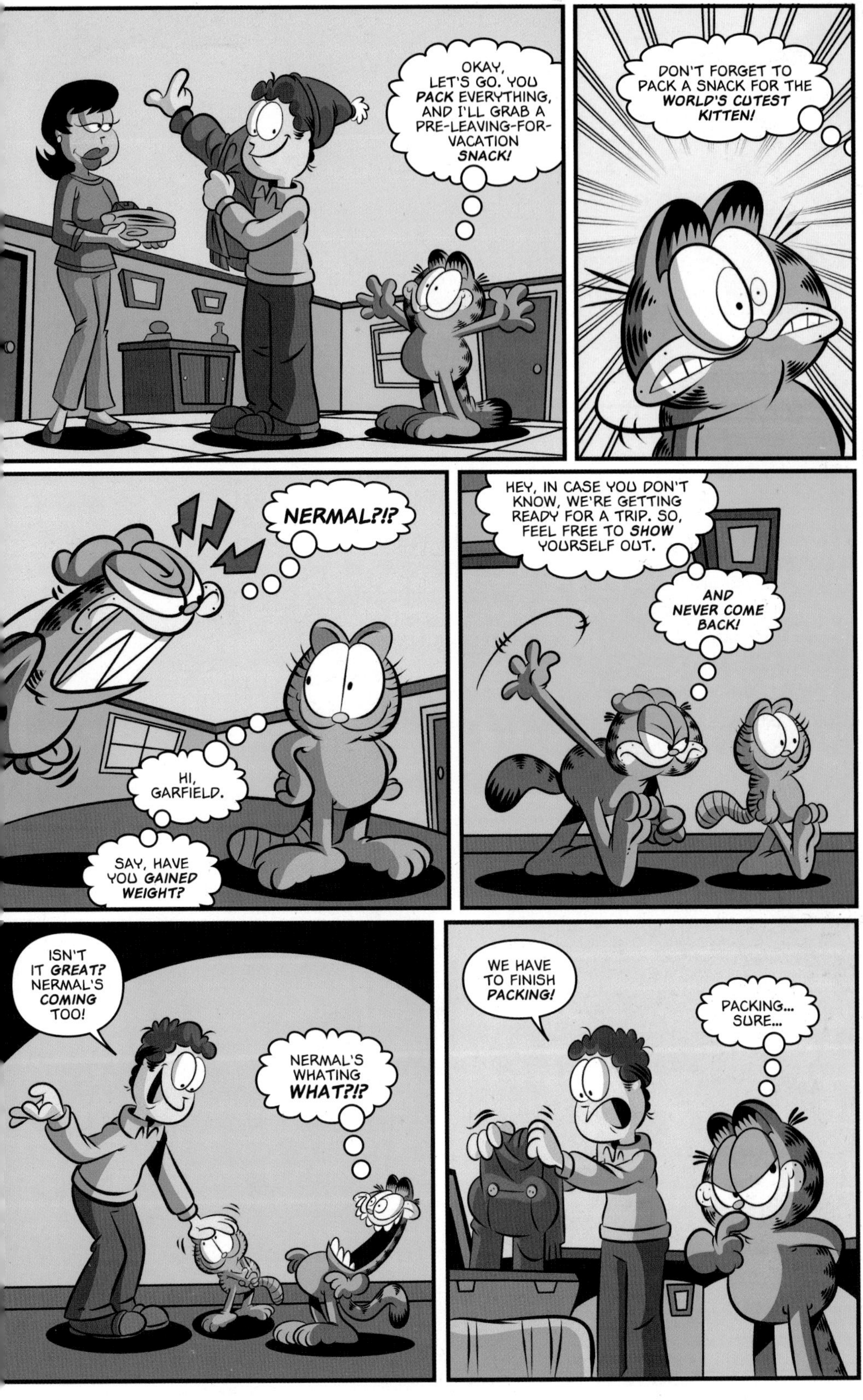

OKAY, LET'S GO. YOU PACK EVERYTHING, AND I'LL GRAB A PRE-LEAVING-FOR-VACATION SNACK!
DON'T FORGET TO PACK A SNACK FOR THE WORLD'S CUTEST KITTEN!
NERMAL?!?
HI, GARFIELD.
SAY, HAVE YOU GAINED WEIGHT?
HEY, IN CASE YOU DON'T KNOW, WE'RE GETTING READY FOR A TRIP. SO, FEEL FREE TO SHOW YOURSELF OUT.
AND NEVER COME BACK!
ISN'T IT GREAT? NERMAL'S COMING TOO!
NERMAL'S WHATING WHAT?!?
WE HAVE TO FINISH PACKING!
PACKING... SURE...

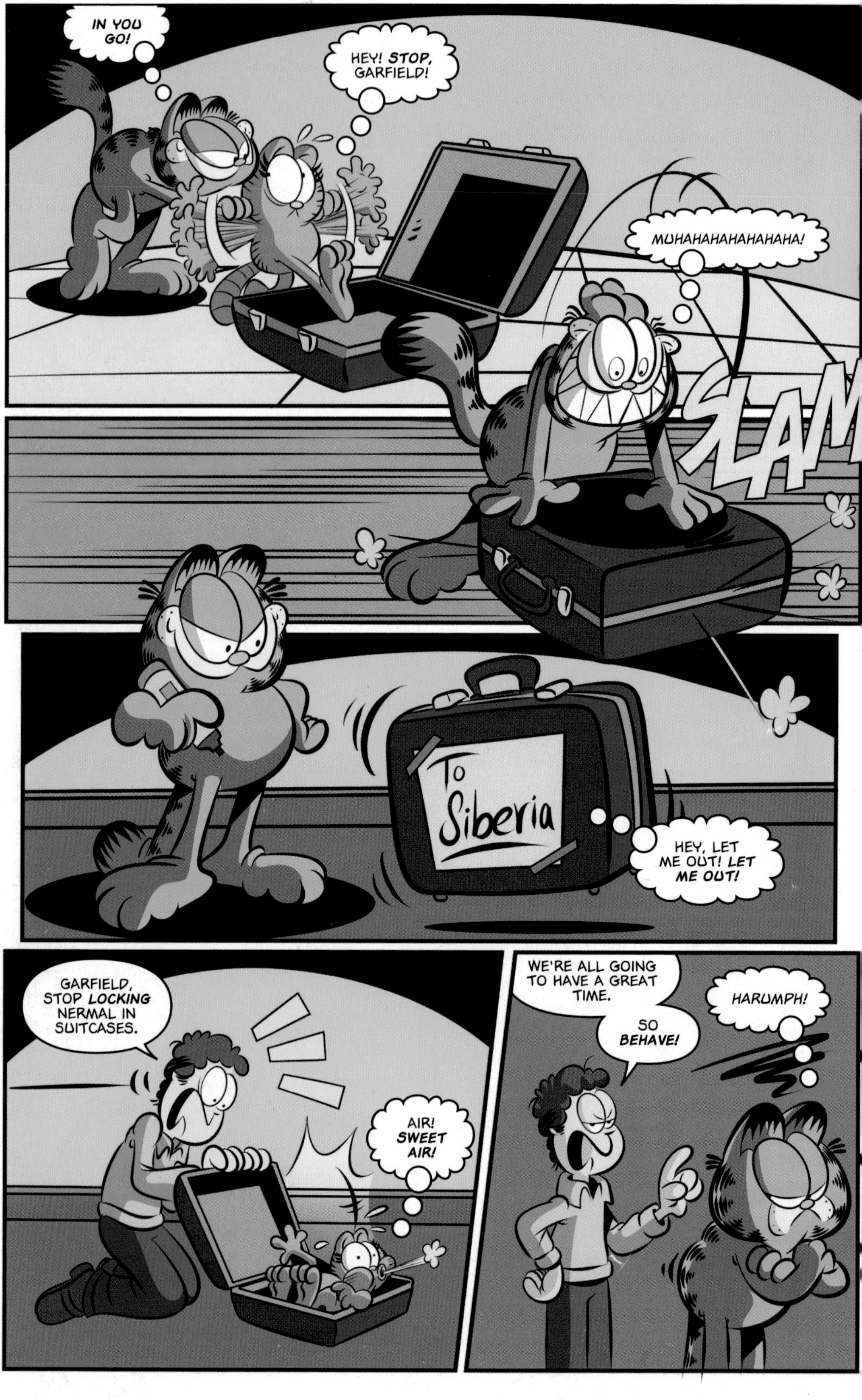
IN YOU GO!
HEY! STOP, GARFIELD!
MUHAHAHAHAHAHAHA!
SLAM
To Siberia
HEY, LET ME OUT! LET ME OUT!
GARFIELD, STOP LOCKING NERMAL IN SUITCASES.
AIR! SWEET AIR!
WE'RE ALL GOING TO HAVE A GREAT TIME.
SO BEHAVE!
HARUMPH!

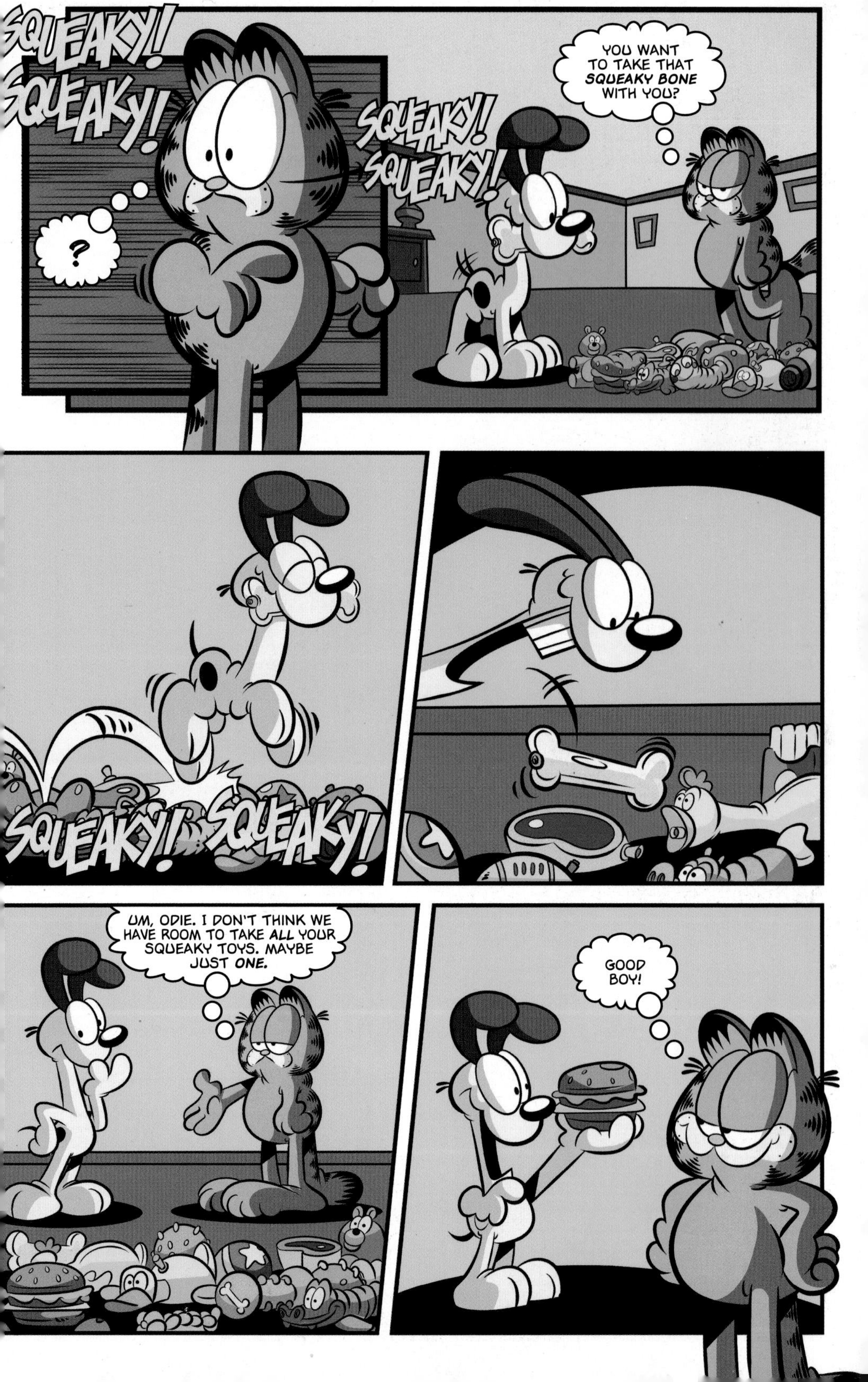
SQUEAKY! SQUEAKY!
?
SQUEAKY! SQUEAKY!
YOU WANT TO TAKE THAT SQUEAKY BONE WITH YOU?
SQUEAKY! SQUEAKY!
UM, ODIE. I DON'T THINK WE HAVE ROOM TO TAKE ALL YOUR SQUEAKY TOYS. MAYBE JUST ONE.
GOOD BOY!

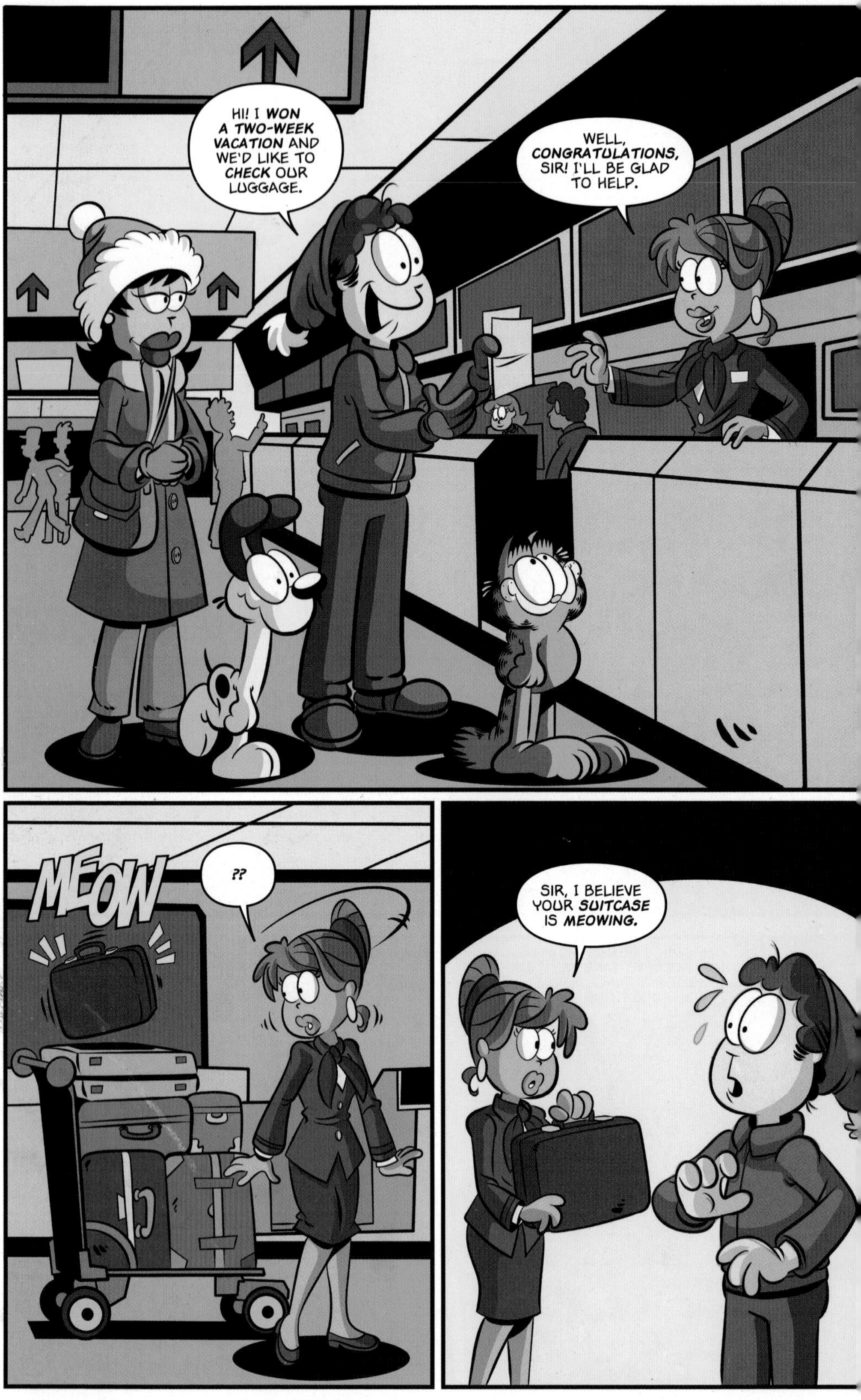
HI! I WON A TWO-WEEK VACATION AND WE'D LIKE TO CHECK OUR LUGGAGE.
WELL, CONGRATULATIONS, SIR! I'LL BE GLAD TO HELP.
MEOW
??
SIR, I BELIEVE YOUR SUITCASE IS MEOWING.

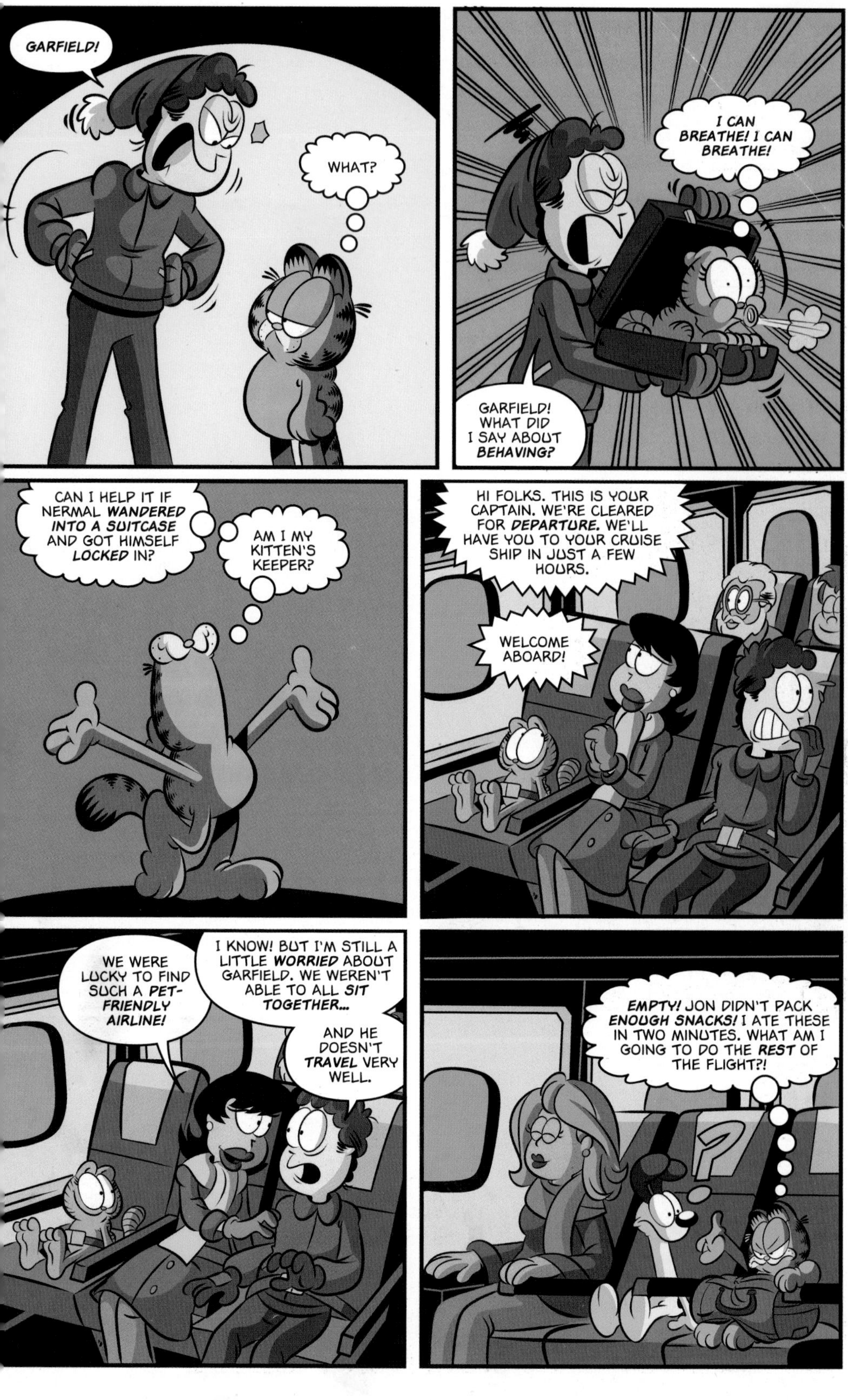
GARFIELD!
WHAT?
I CAN BREATHE! I CAN BREATHE!
GARFIELD! WHAT DID I SAY ABOUT BEHAVING?
CAN I HELP IT IF NERMAL WANDERED INTO A SUITCASE AND GOT HIMSELF LOCKED IN?
AM I MY KITTEN'S KEEPER?
HI FOLKS. THIS IS YOUR CAPTAIN. WE'RE CLEARED FOR DEPARTURE. WE'LL HAVE YOU TO YOUR CRUISE SHIP IN JUST A FEW HOURS.
WELCOME ABOARD!
WE WERE LUCKY TO FIND SUCH A PET-FRIENDLY AIRLINE!
I KNOW! BUT I'M STILL A LITTLE WORRIED ABOUT GARFIELD. WE WEREN'T ABLE TO ALL SIT TOGETHER...
AND HE DOESN'T TRAVEL VERY WELL.
EMPTY! JON DIDN'T PACK ENOUGH SNACKS! I ATE THESE IN TWO MINUTES. WHAT AM I GOING TO DO THE REST OF THE FLIGHT?!

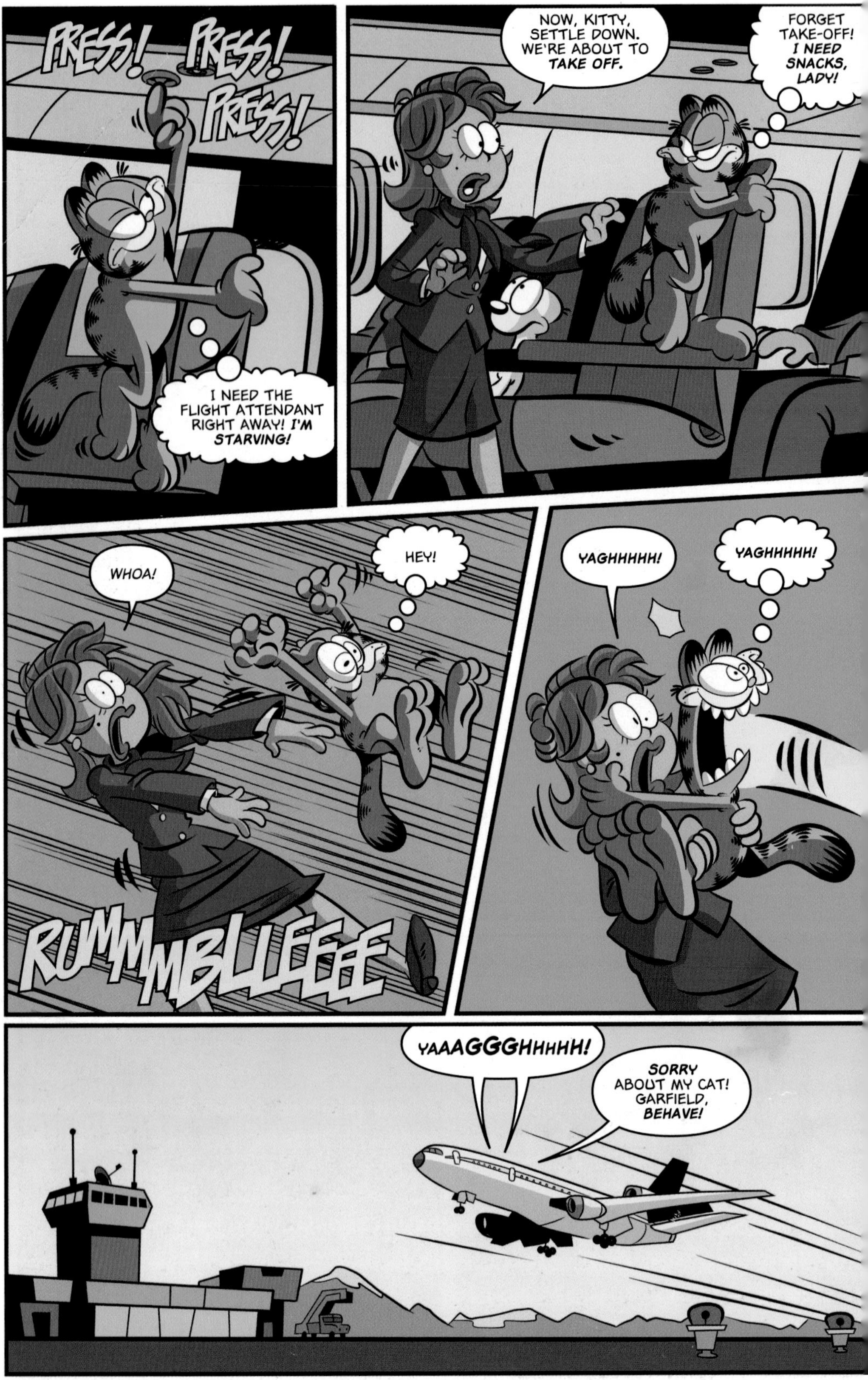
PRESS! PRESS! PRESS!
I NEED THE FLIGHT ATTENDANT RIGHT AWAY! I'M STARVING!
NOW, KITTY, SETTLE DOWN. WE'RE ABOUT TO TAKE OFF.
FORGET TAKE-OFF! I NEED SNACKS, LADY!
WHOA!
HEY!
RUMMMBLLEEEE
YAGHHHHHH!
YAGHHHHHH!
YAAAGGGHHHHH!
SORRY ABOUT MY CAT! GARFIELD, BEHAVE!

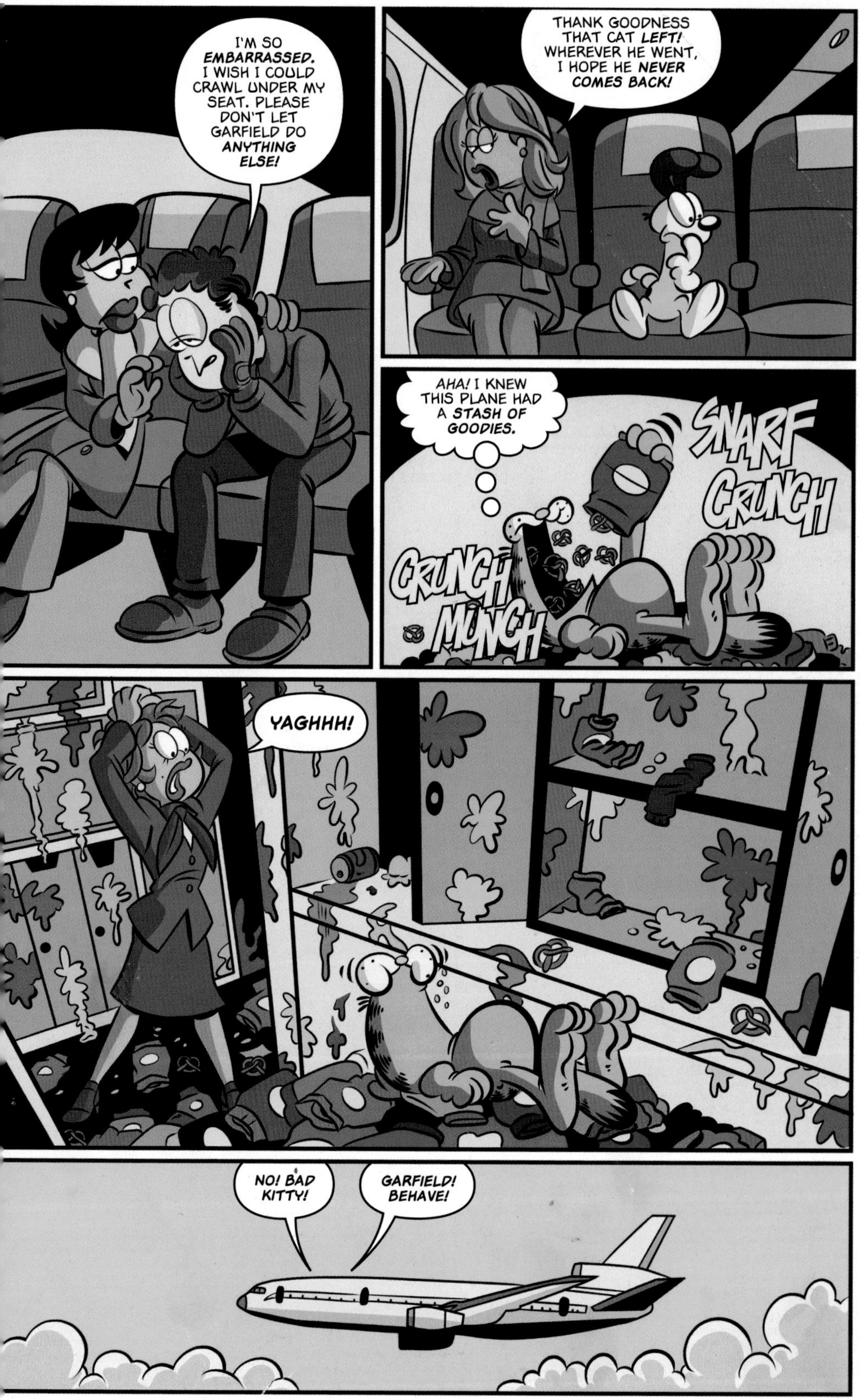

I'M SO EMBARRASSED. I WISH I COULD CRAWL UNDER MY SEAT. PLEASE DON'T LET GARFIELD DO ANYTHING ELSE!
THANK GOODNESS THAT CAT LEFT! WHEREVER HE WENT, I HOPE HE NEVER COMES BACK!
AHA! I KNEW THIS PLANE HAD A STASH OF GOODIES.
SNARF
CRUNCH
CRUNCH
MUNCH
YAGHHH!
NO! BAD KITTY!
GARFIELD! BEHAVE!

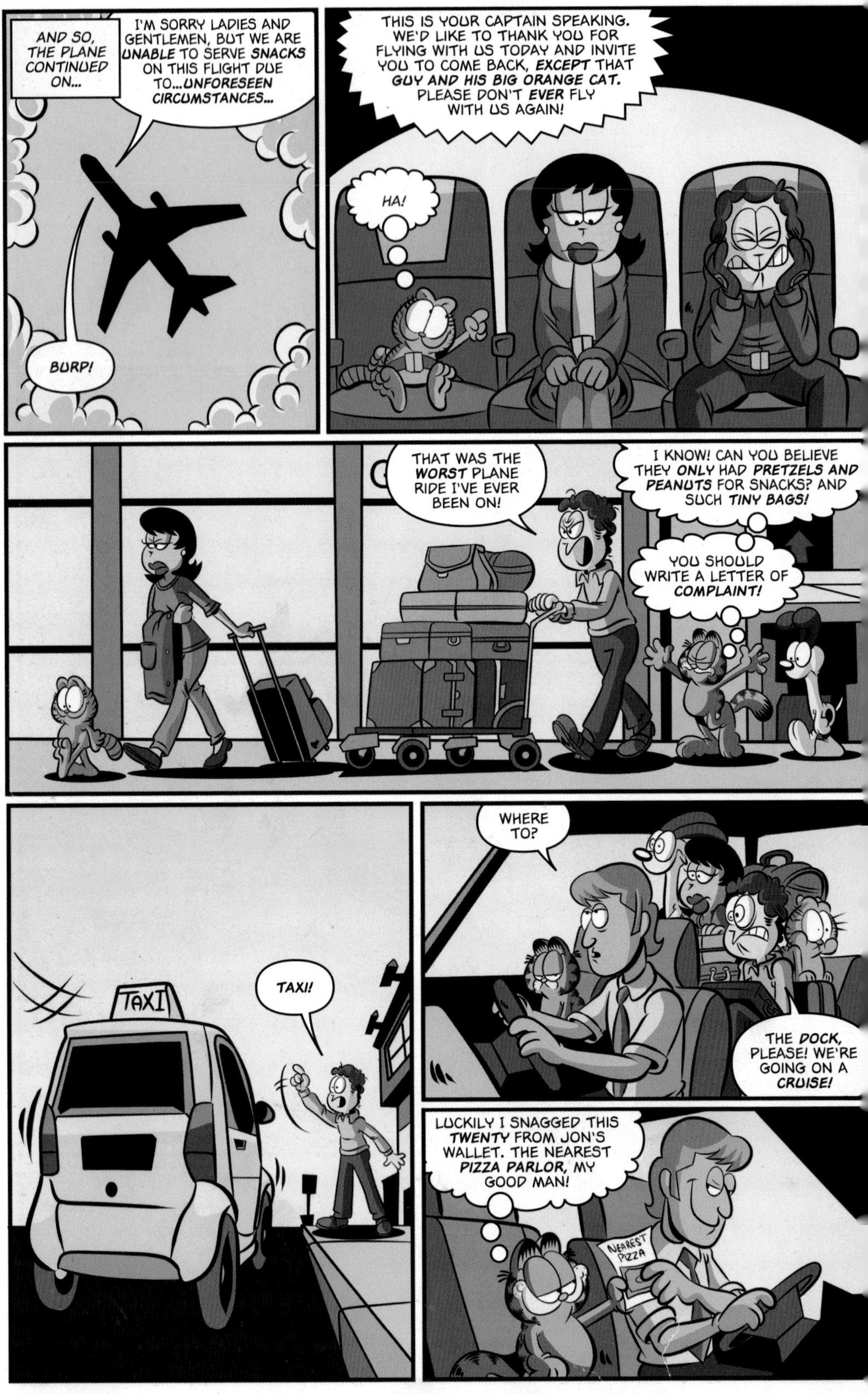
AND SO, THE PLANE CONTINUED ON...
I'M SORRY LADIES AND GENTLEMEN, BUT WE ARE UNABLE TO SERVE SNACKS ON THIS FLIGHT DUE TO...UNFORESEEN CIRCUMSTANCES...
BURP!
THIS IS YOUR CAPTAIN SPEAKING. WE'D LIKE TO THANK YOU FOR FLYING WITH US TODAY AND INVITE YOU TO COME BACK, EXCEPT THAT GUY AND HIS BIG ORANGE CAT. PLEASE DON'T EVER FLY WITH US AGAIN!
HA!
THAT WAS THE WORST PLANE RIDE I'VE EVER BEEN ON!
I KNOW! CAN YOU BELIEVE THEY ONLY HAD PRETZELS AND PEANUTS FOR SNACKS? AND SUCH TINY BAGS!
YOU SHOULD WRITE A LETTER OF COMPLAINT!
TAXI
TAXI!
WHERE TO?
THE DOCK, PLEASE! WE'RE GOING ON A CRUISE!
LUCKILY I SNAGGED THIS TWENTY FROM JON'S WALLET. THE NEAREST PIZZA PARLOR, MY GOOD MAN!
NEAREST PIZZA

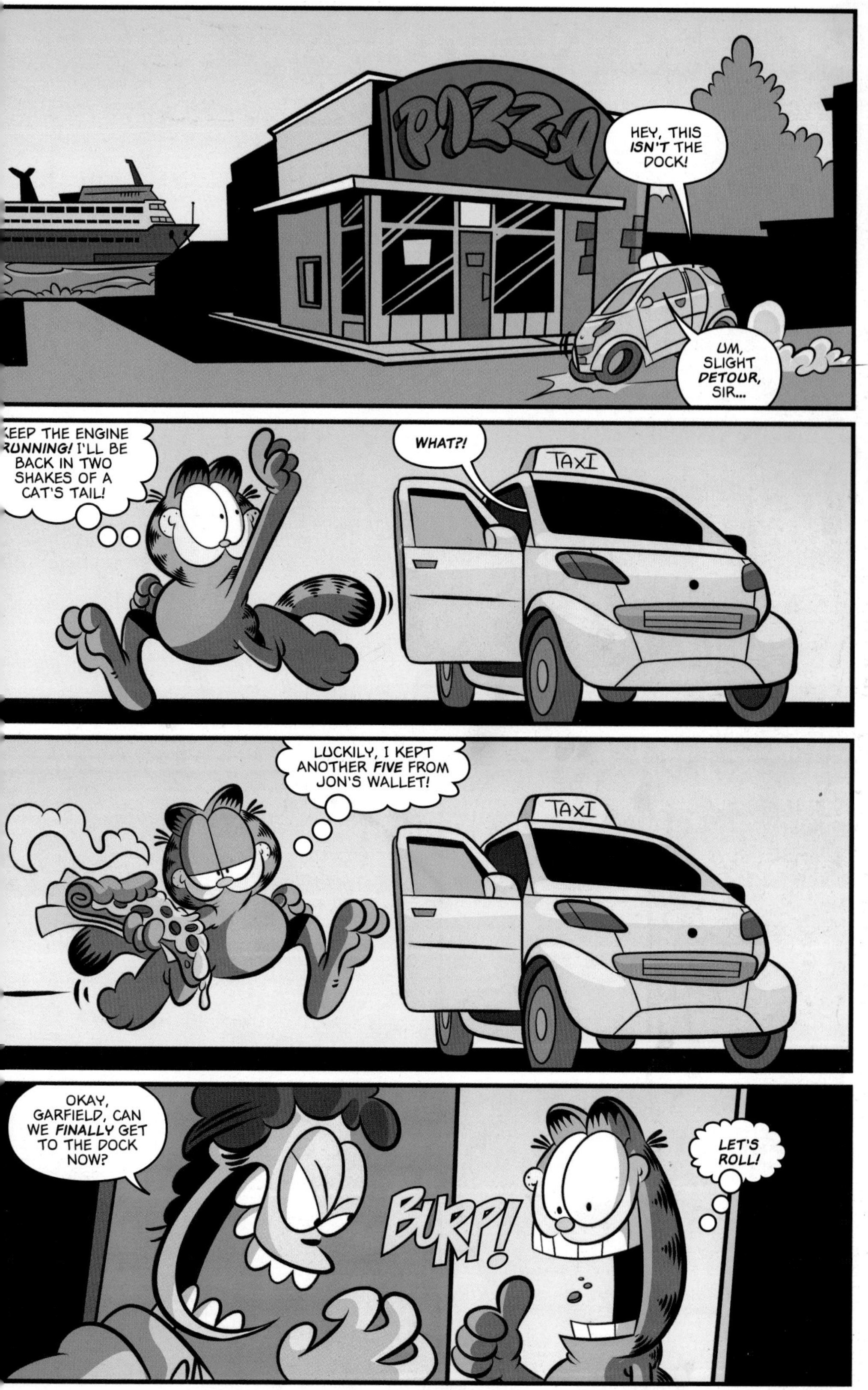
PIZZA
HEY, THIS ISN'T THE DOCK!
UM, SLIGHT DETOUR, SIR...
KEEP THE ENGINE RUNNING! I'LL BE BACK IN TWO SHAKES OF A CAT'S TAIL!
WHAT?!
TAXI
LUCKILY, I KEPT ANOTHER FIVE FROM JON'S WALLET!
TAXI
OKAY, GARFIELD, CAN WE FINALLY GET TO THE DOCK NOW?
BURP!
LET'S ROLL!

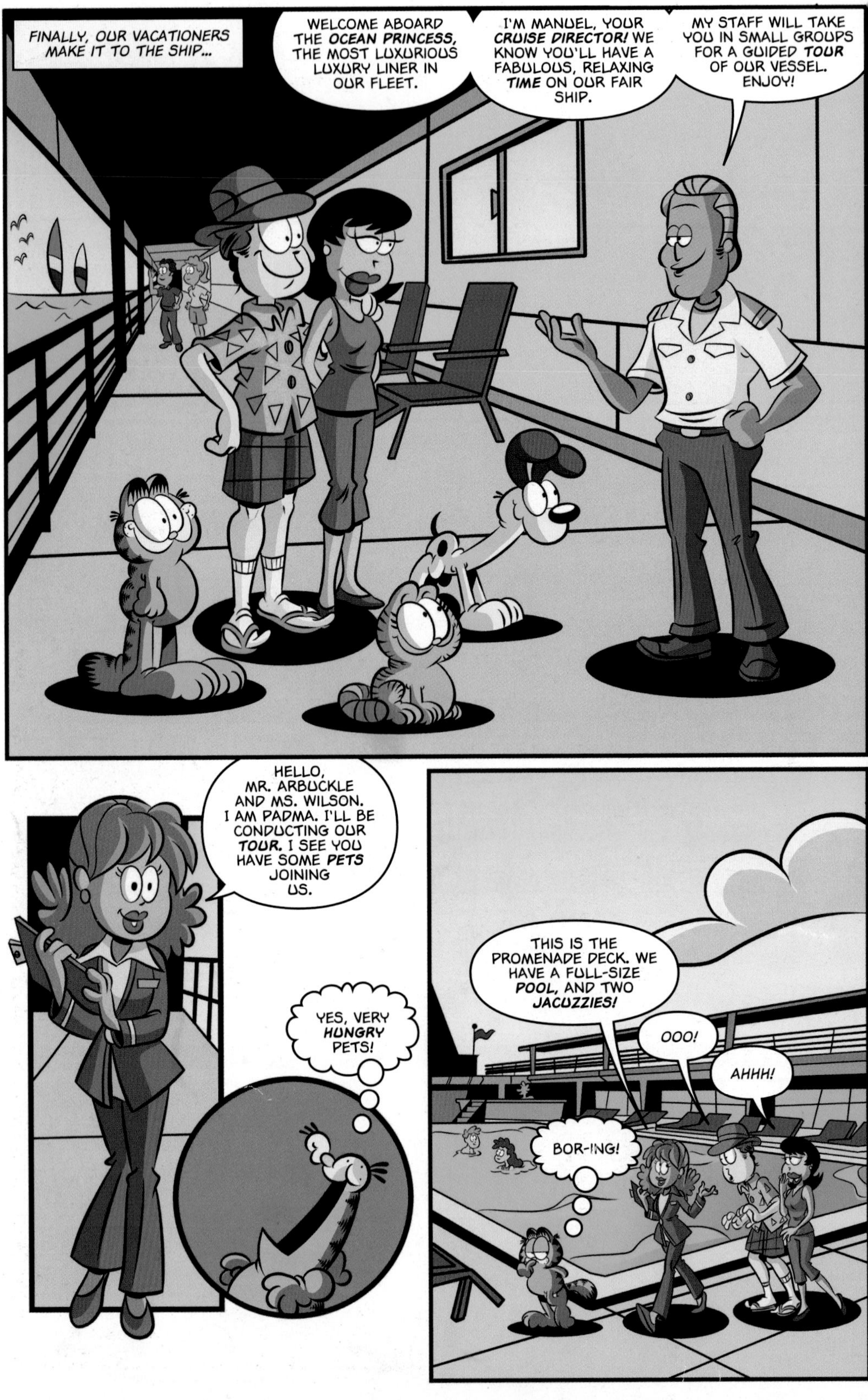
FINALLY, OUR VACATIONERS MAKE IT TO THE SHIP...
WELCOME ABOARD THE OCEAN PRINCESS, THE MOST LUXURIOUS LUXURY LINER IN OUR FLEET.
I'M MANUEL, YOUR CRUISE DIRECTOR! WE KNOW YOU'LL HAVE A FABULOUS, RELAXING TIME ON OUR FAIR SHIP.
MY STAFF WILL TAKE YOU IN SMALL GROUPS FOR A GUIDED TOUR OF OUR VESSEL. ENJOY!
HELLO, MR. ARBUCKLE AND MS. WILSON. I AM PADMA. I'LL BE CONDUCTING OUR TOUR. I SEE YOU HAVE SOME PETS JOINING US.
YES, VERY HUNGRY PETS!
THIS IS THE PROMENADE DECK. WE HAVE A FULL-SIZE POOL, AND TWO JACUZZIES!
OOO!
AHHH!
BOR-ING!

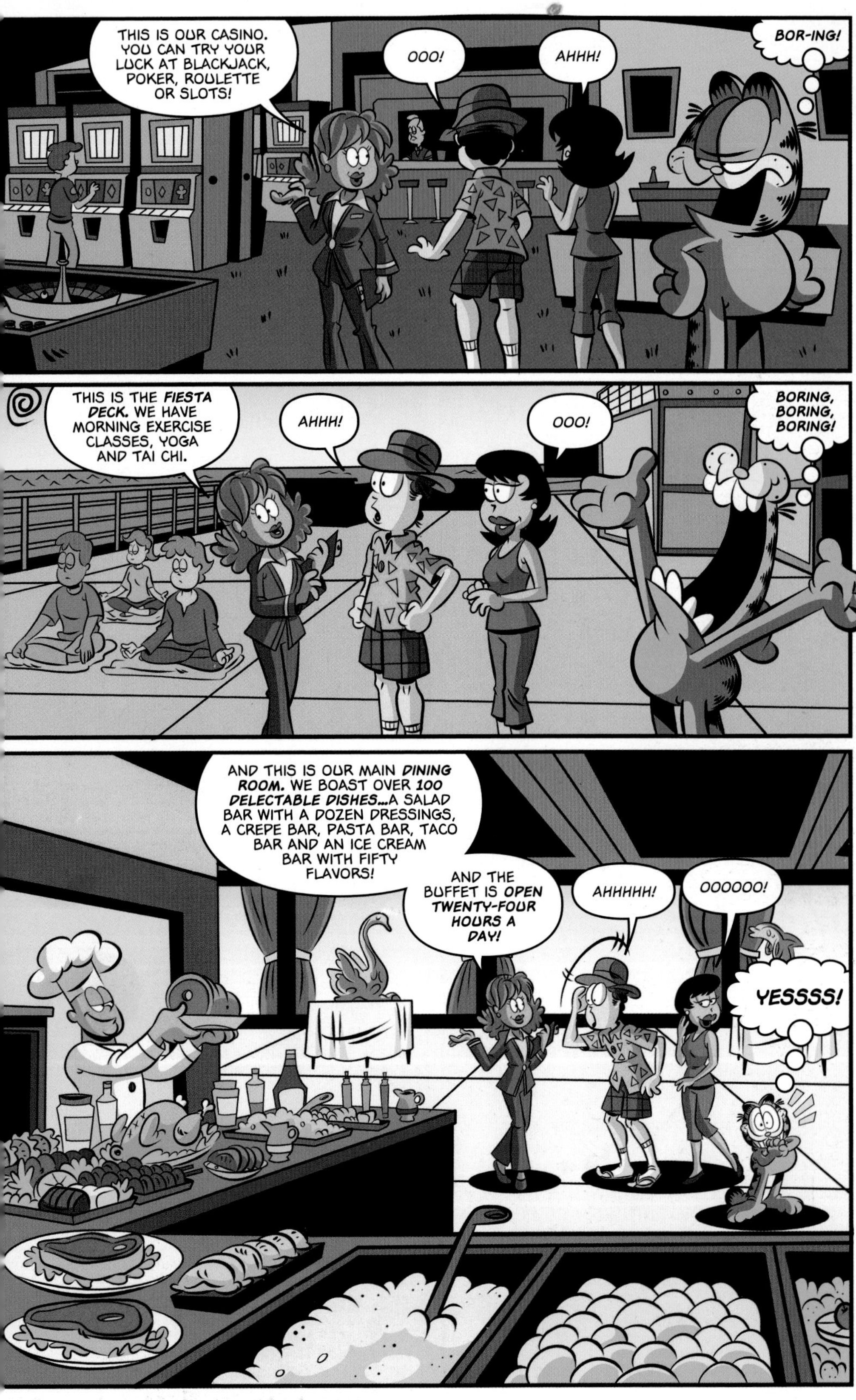
THIS IS OUR CASINO. YOU CAN TRY YOUR LUCK AT BLACKJACK, POKER, ROULETTE OR SLOTS!
OOO!
AHHH!
BOR-ING!
THIS IS THE FIESTA DECK. WE HAVE MORNING EXERCISE CLASSES, YOGA AND TAI CHI.
AHHH!
OOO!
BORING, BORING, BORING!
AND THIS IS OUR MAIN DINING ROOM. WE BOAST OVER 100 DELECTABLE DISHES...A SALAD BAR WITH A DOZEN DRESSINGS, A CREPE BAR, PASTA BAR, TACO BAR AND AN ICE CREAM BAR WITH FIFTY FLAVORS!
AND THE BUFFET IS OPEN TWENTY-FOUR HOURS A DAY!
AHHHHH!
OOOOOO!
YESSSS!

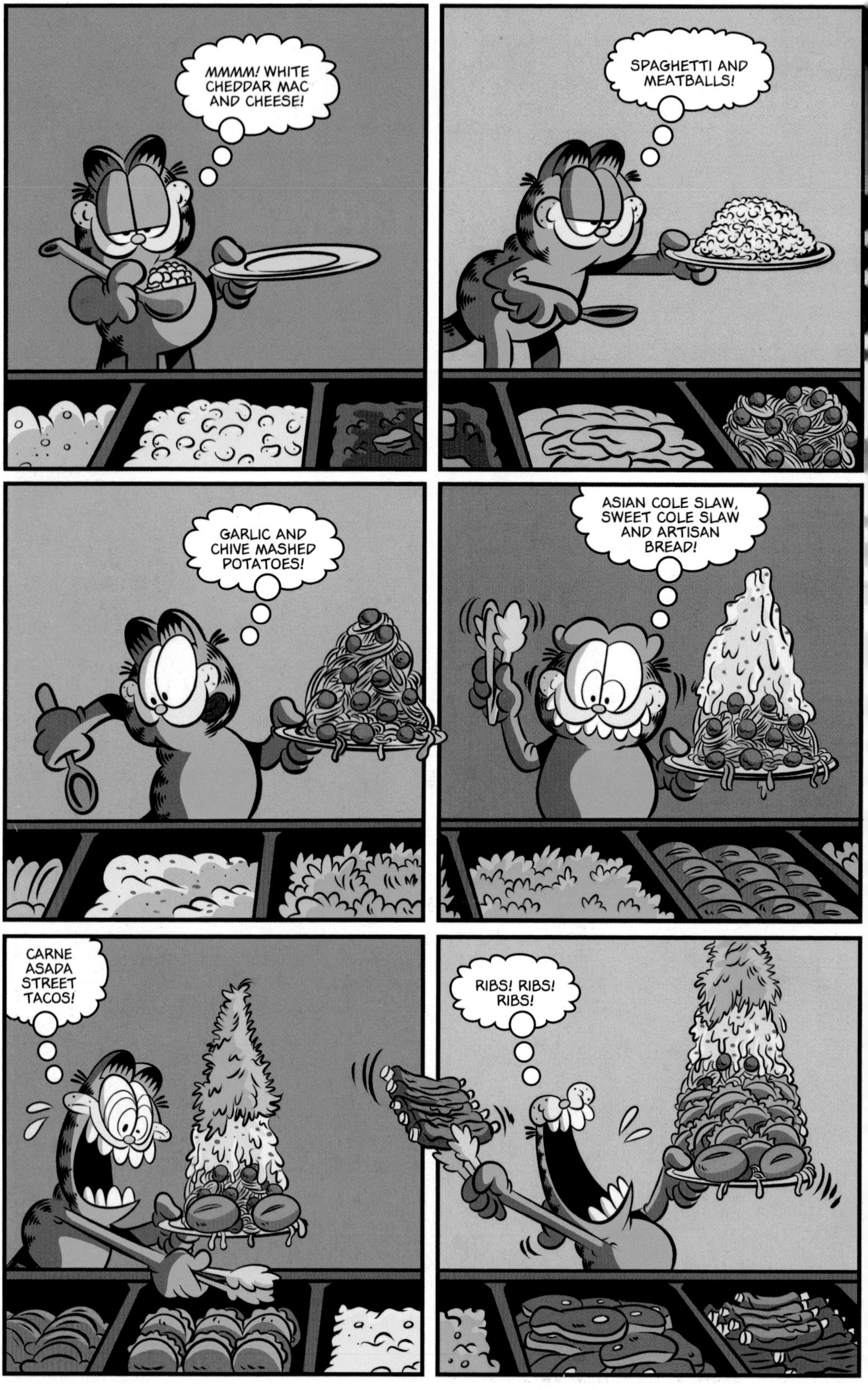
MMMM! WHITE CHEDDAR MAC AND CHEESE!
SPAGHETTI AND MEATBALLS!
GARLIC AND CHIVE MASHED POTATOES!
ASIAN COLE SLAW, SWEET COLE SLAW AND ARTISAN BREAD!
CARNE ASADA STREET TACOS!
RIBS! RIBS! RIBS!

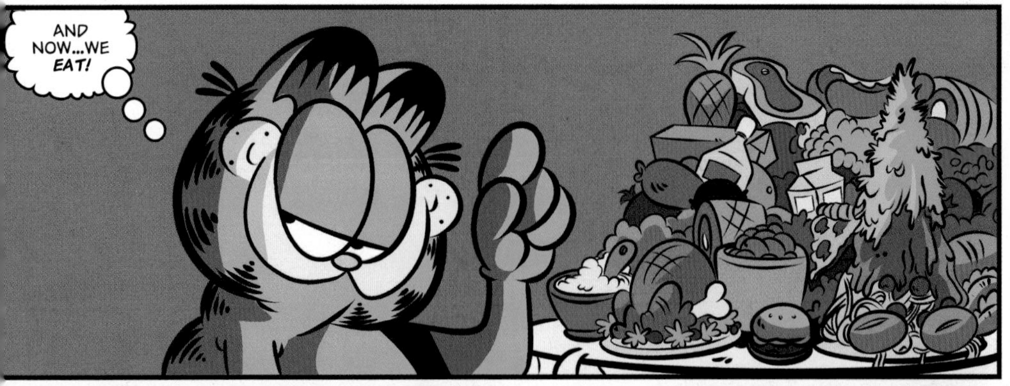
AND NOW...WE EAT!

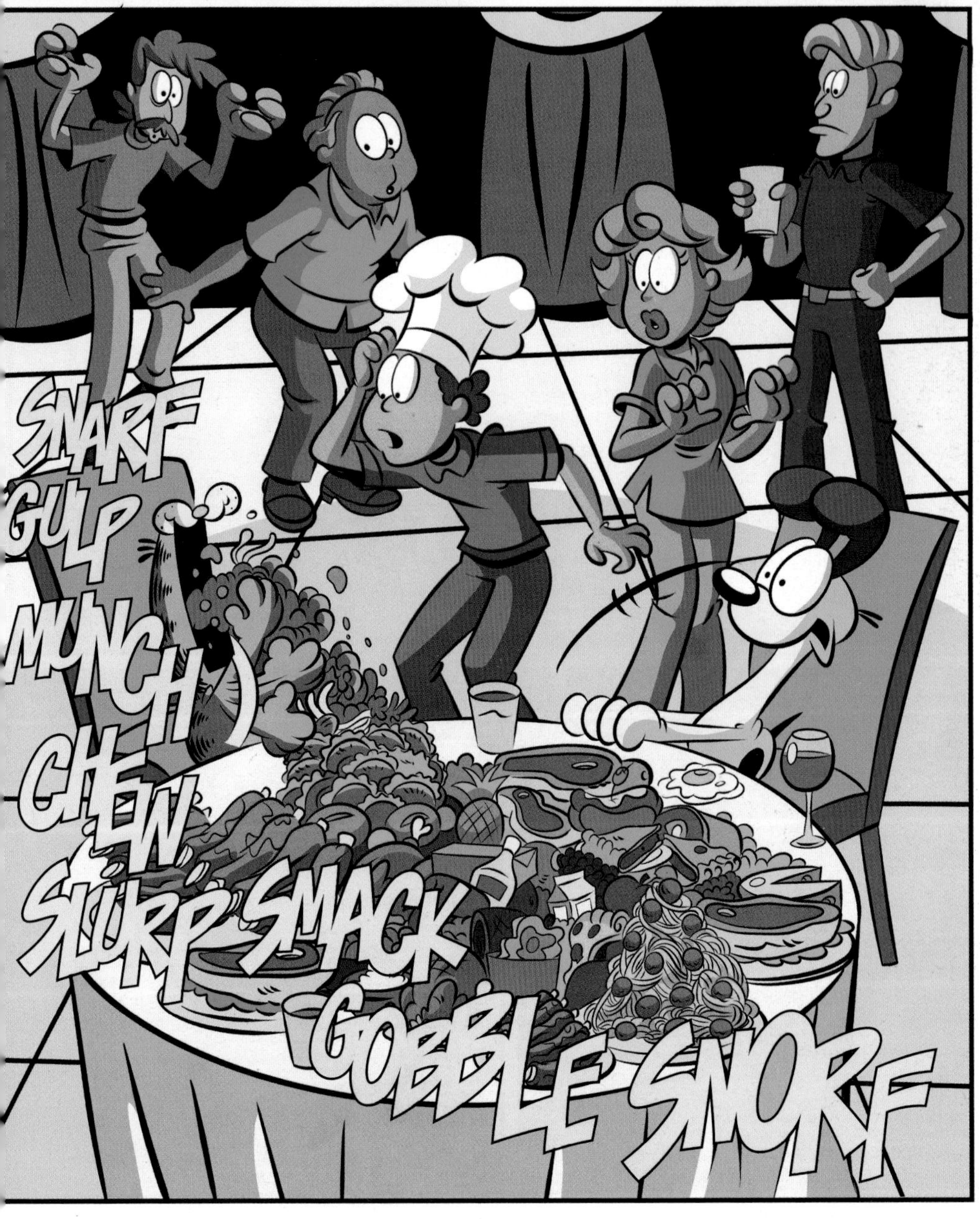
SNARF
GULP
MUNCH
CHEW
SLURP
SMACK
GOBBLE
SNORF

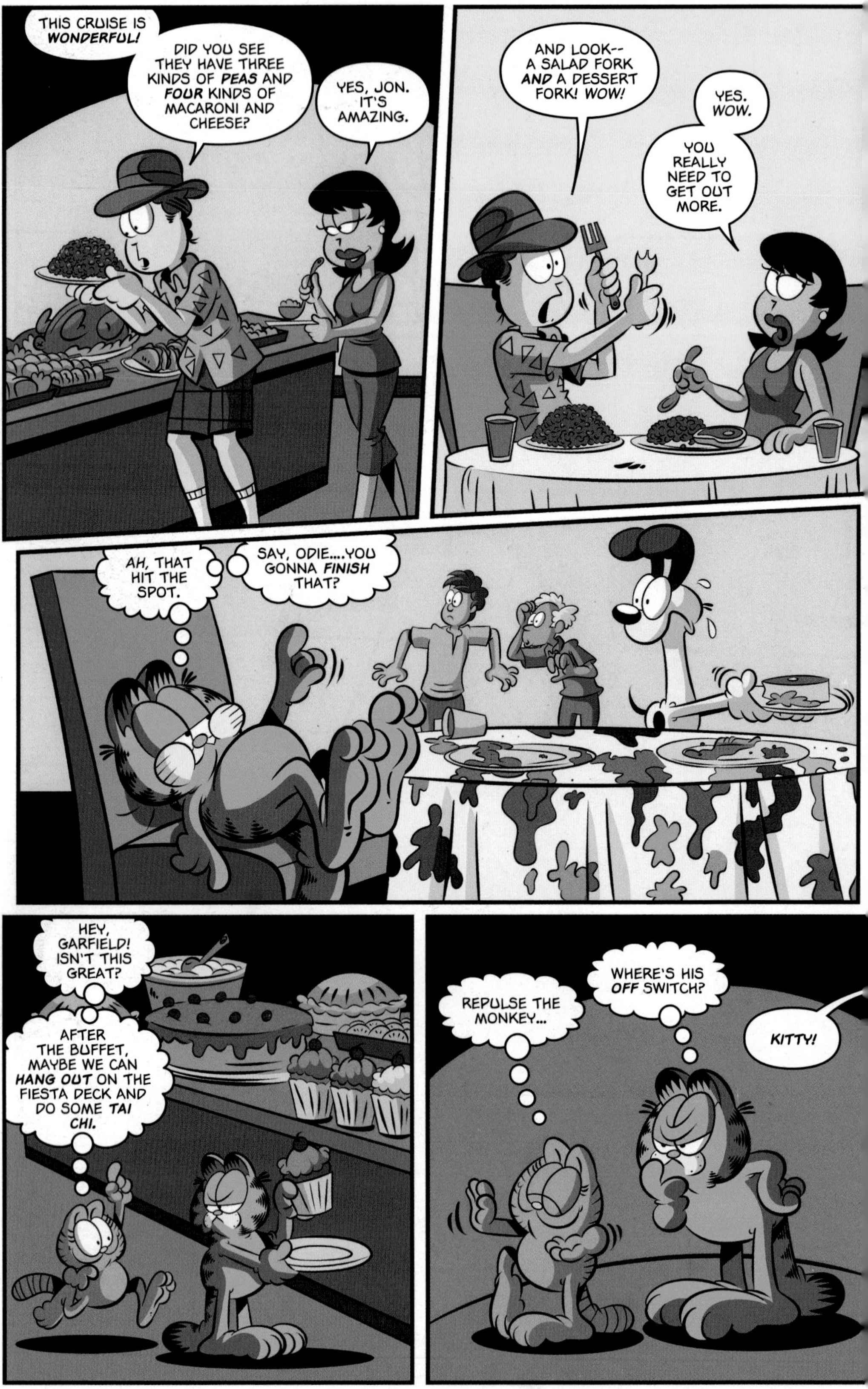
THIS CRUISE IS WONDERFUL!
DID YOU SEE THEY HAVE THREE KINDS OF PEAS AND FOUR KINDS OF MACARONI AND CHEESE?
YES, JON. IT'S AMAZING.
AND LOOK-- A SALAD FORK AND A DESSERT FORK! WOW!
YES. WOW.
YOU REALLY NEED TO GET OUT MORE.
AH, THAT HIT THE SPOT.
SAY, ODIE....YOU GONNA FINISH THAT?
HEY, GARFIELD! ISN'T THIS GREAT?
AFTER THE BUFFET, MAYBE WE CAN HANG OUT ON THE FIESTA DECK AND DO SOME TAI CHI.
REPULSE THE MONKEY...
WHERE'S HIS OFF SWITCH?
KITTY!

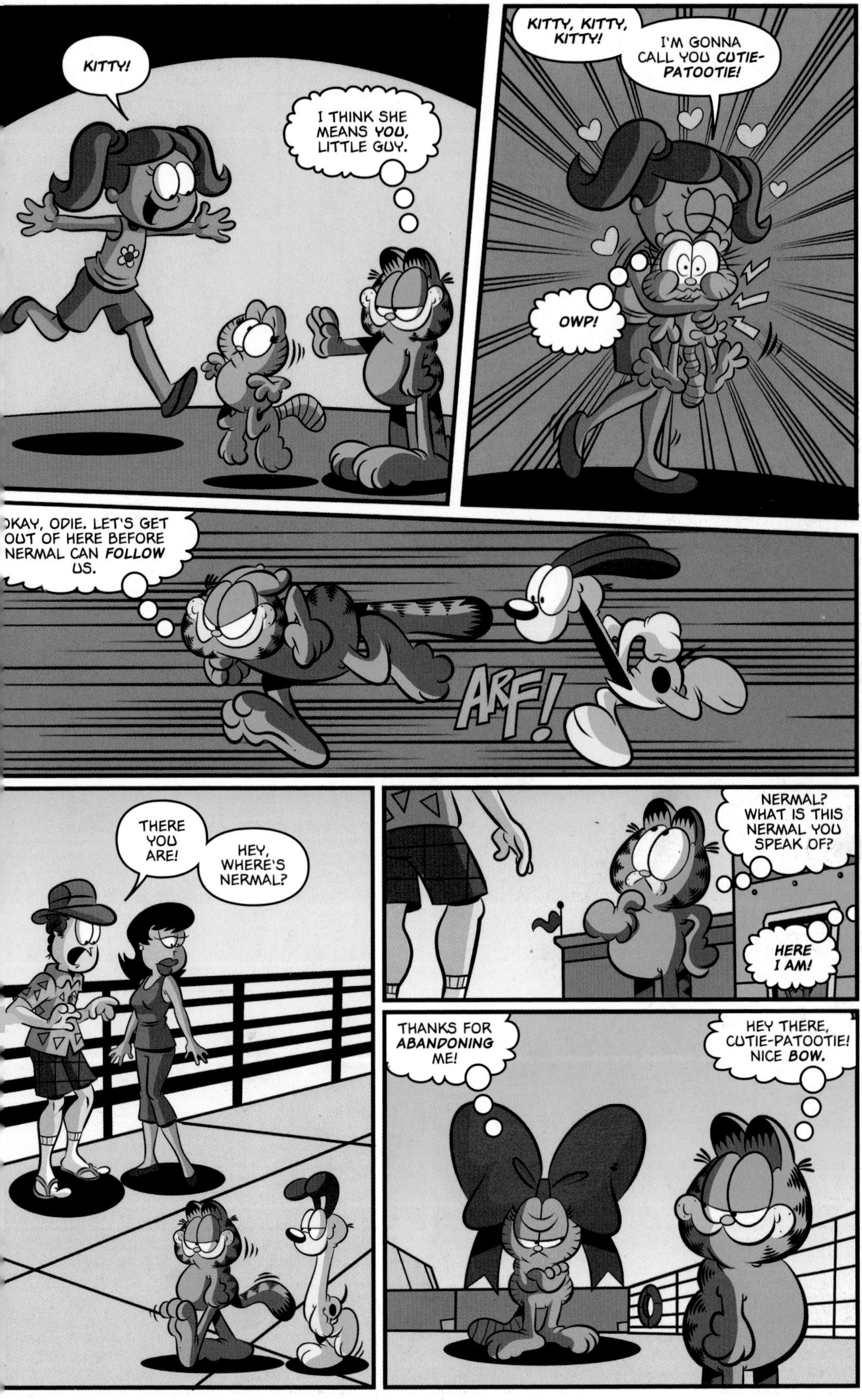

KITTY!
I THINK SHE MEANS YOU, LITTLE GUY.
KITTY, KITTY, KITTY!
I'M GONNA CALL YOU CUTIE-PATOOTIE!
OWP!
OKAY, ODIE. LET'S GET OUT OF HERE BEFORE NERMAL CAN FOLLOW US.
ARF!
THERE YOU ARE!
HEY, WHERE'S NERMAL?
NERMAL? WHAT IS THIS NERMAL YOU SPEAK OF?
HERE I AM!
THANKS FOR ABANDONING ME!
HEY THERE, CUTIE-PATOOTIE! NICE BOW.

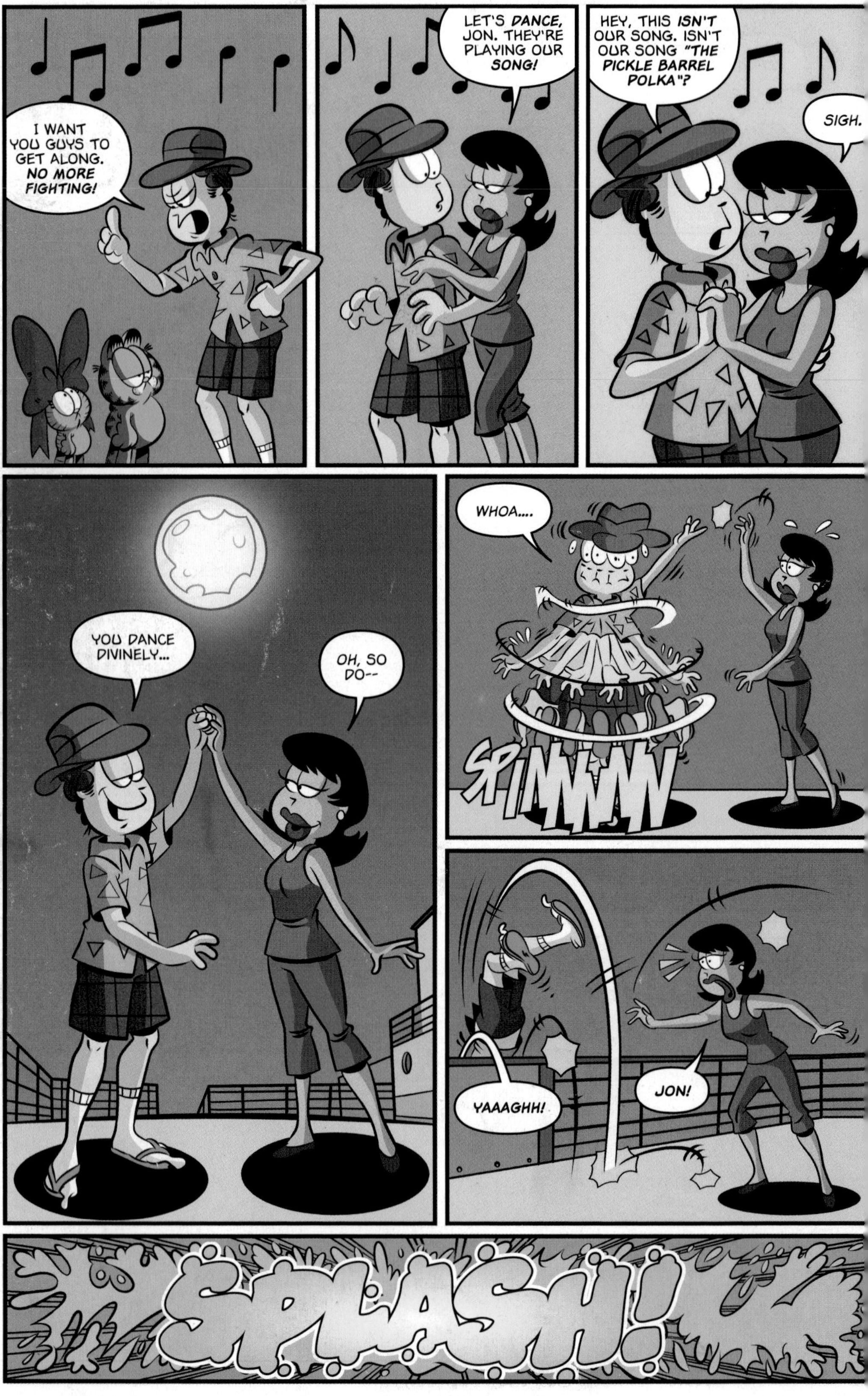
I WANT YOU GUYS TO GET ALONG. NO MORE FIGHTING!
LET'S DANCE, JON. THEY'RE PLAYING OUR SONG!
HEY, THIS ISN'T OUR SONG. ISN'T OUR SONG "THE PICKLE BARREL POLKA"?
SIGH.
YOU DANCE DIVINELY...
OH, SO DO--
WHOA....
SPINNNNN
YAAAGHH!
JON!
SPLASH!

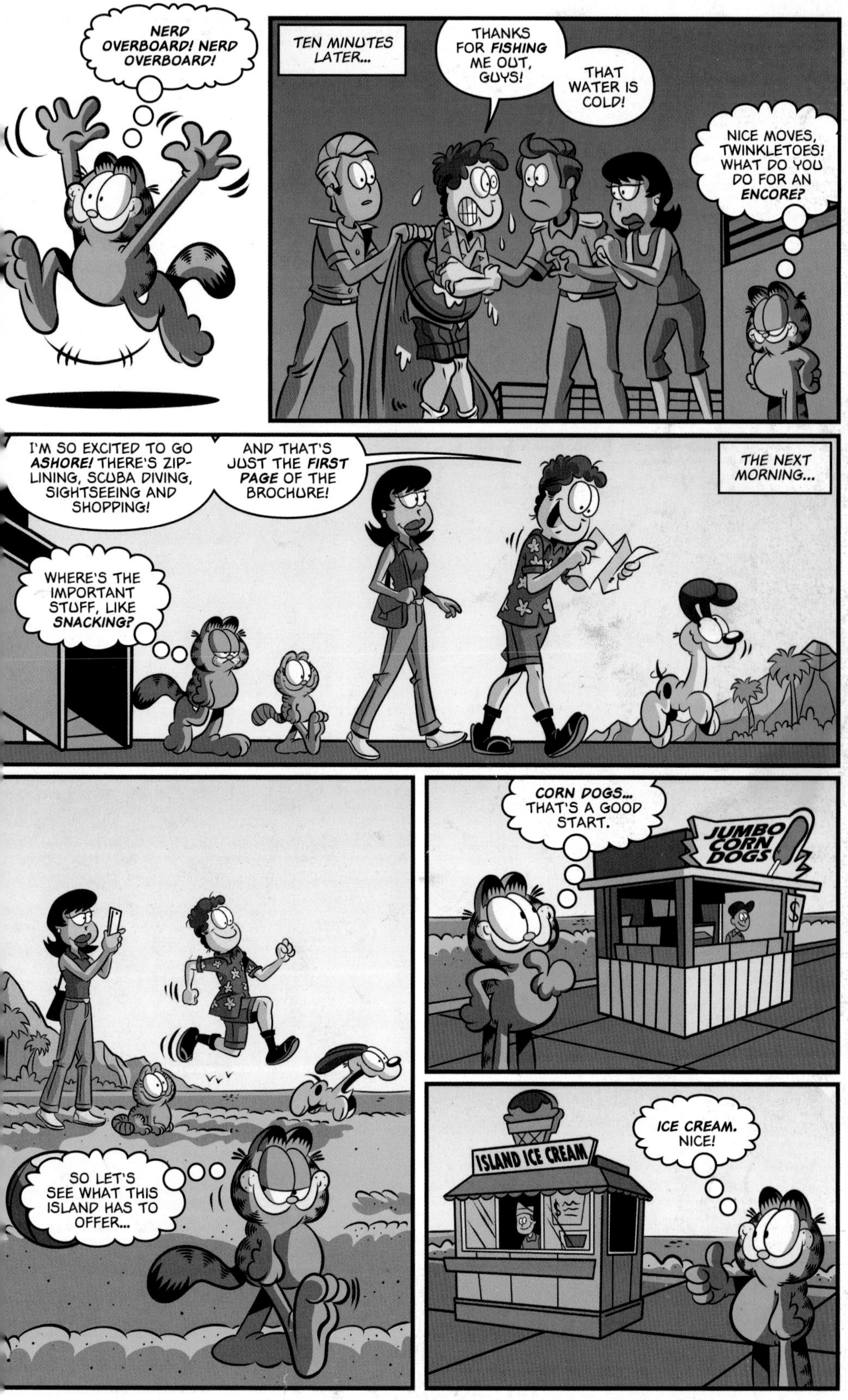
NERD OVERBOARD! NERD OVERBOARD!
TEN MINUTES LATER...
THANKS FOR FISHING ME OUT, GUYS!
THAT WATER IS COLD!
NICE MOVES, TWINKLETOES! WHAT DO YOU DO FOR AN ENCORE?
I'M SO EXCITED TO GO ASHORE! THERE'S ZIP-LINING, SCUBA DIVING, SIGHTSEEING AND SHOPPING!
AND THAT'S JUST THE FIRST PAGE OF THE BROCHURE!
THE NEXT MORNING...
WHERE'S THE IMPORTANT STUFF, LIKE SNACKING?
SO LET'S SEE WHAT THIS ISLAND HAS TO OFFER...
CORN DOGS... THAT'S A GOOD START.
JUMBO CORN DOGS
ISLAND ICE CREAM
ICE CREAM. NICE!

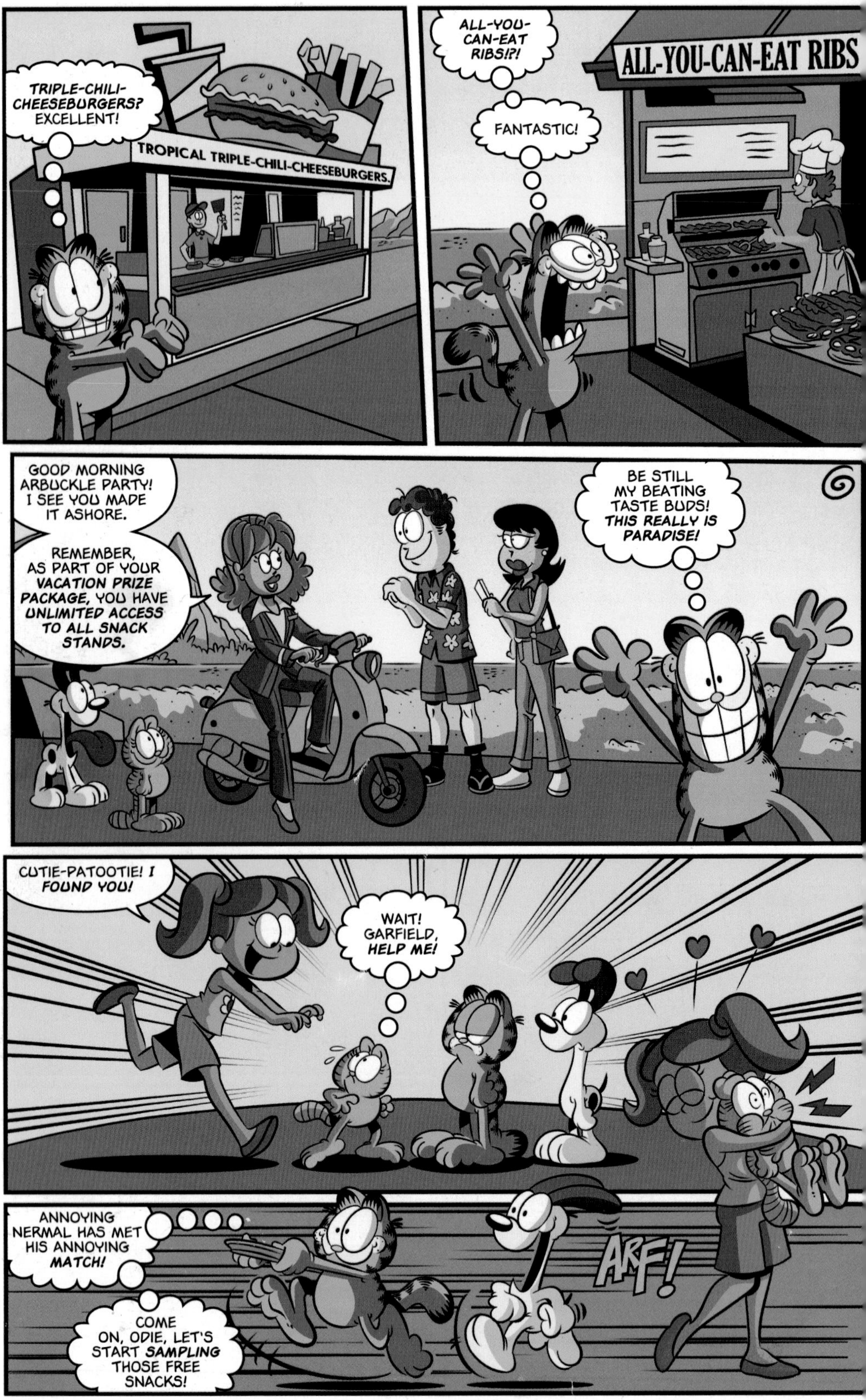

TRIPLE-CHILI-CHEESEBURGERS? EXCELLENT!
TROPICAL TRIPLE-CHILI-CHEESEBURGERS.
ALL-YOU-CAN-EAT RIBS!?!
ALL-YOU-CAN-EAT RIBS
FANTASTIC!
GOOD MORNING ARBUCKLE PARTY! I SEE YOU MADE IT ASHORE.
REMEMBER, AS PART OF YOUR VACATION PRIZE PACKAGE, YOU HAVE UNLIMITED ACCESS TO ALL SNACK STANDS.
BE STILL MY BEATING TASTE BUDS! THIS REALLY IS PARADISE!
CUTIE-PATOOTIE! I FOUND YOU!
WAIT! GARFIELD, HELP ME!
ANNOYING NERMAL HAS MET HIS ANNOYING MATCH!
COME ON, ODIE, LET'S START SAMPLING THOSE FREE SNACKS!
ARF!

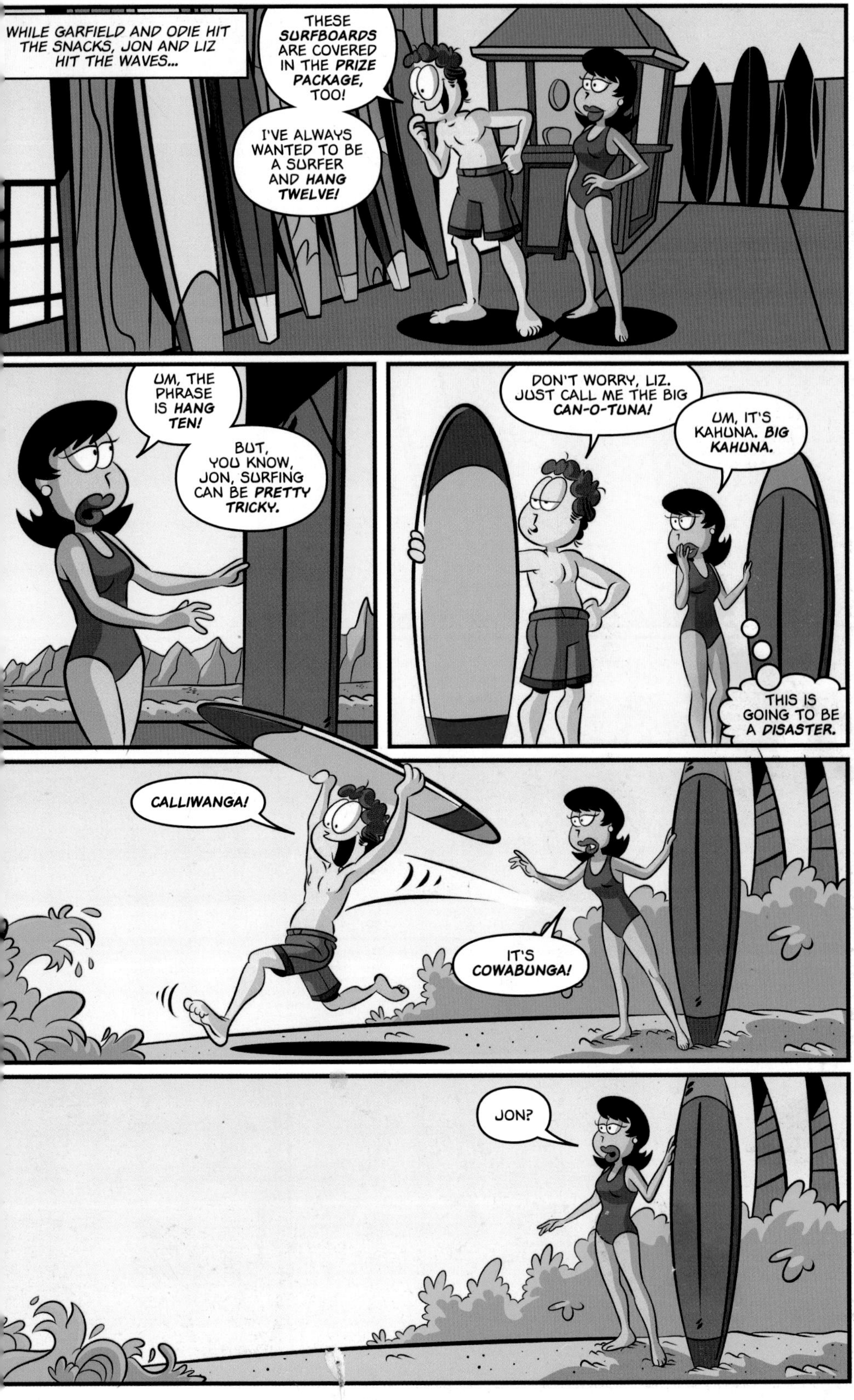
WHILE GARFIELD AND ODIE HIT THE SNACKS, JON AND LIZ HIT THE WAVES...
THESE SURFBOARDS ARE COVERED IN THE PRIZE PACKAGE, TOO!
I'VE ALWAYS WANTED TO BE A SURFER AND HANG TWELVE!
UM, THE PHRASE IS HANG TEN!
BUT, YOU KNOW, JON, SURFING CAN BE PRETTY TRICKY.
DON'T WORRY, LIZ. JUST CALL ME THE BIG CAN-O-TUNA!
UM, IT'S KAHUNA. BIG KAHUNA.
THIS IS GOING TO BE A DISASTER.
CALLIWANGA!
IT'S COWABUNGA!
JON?

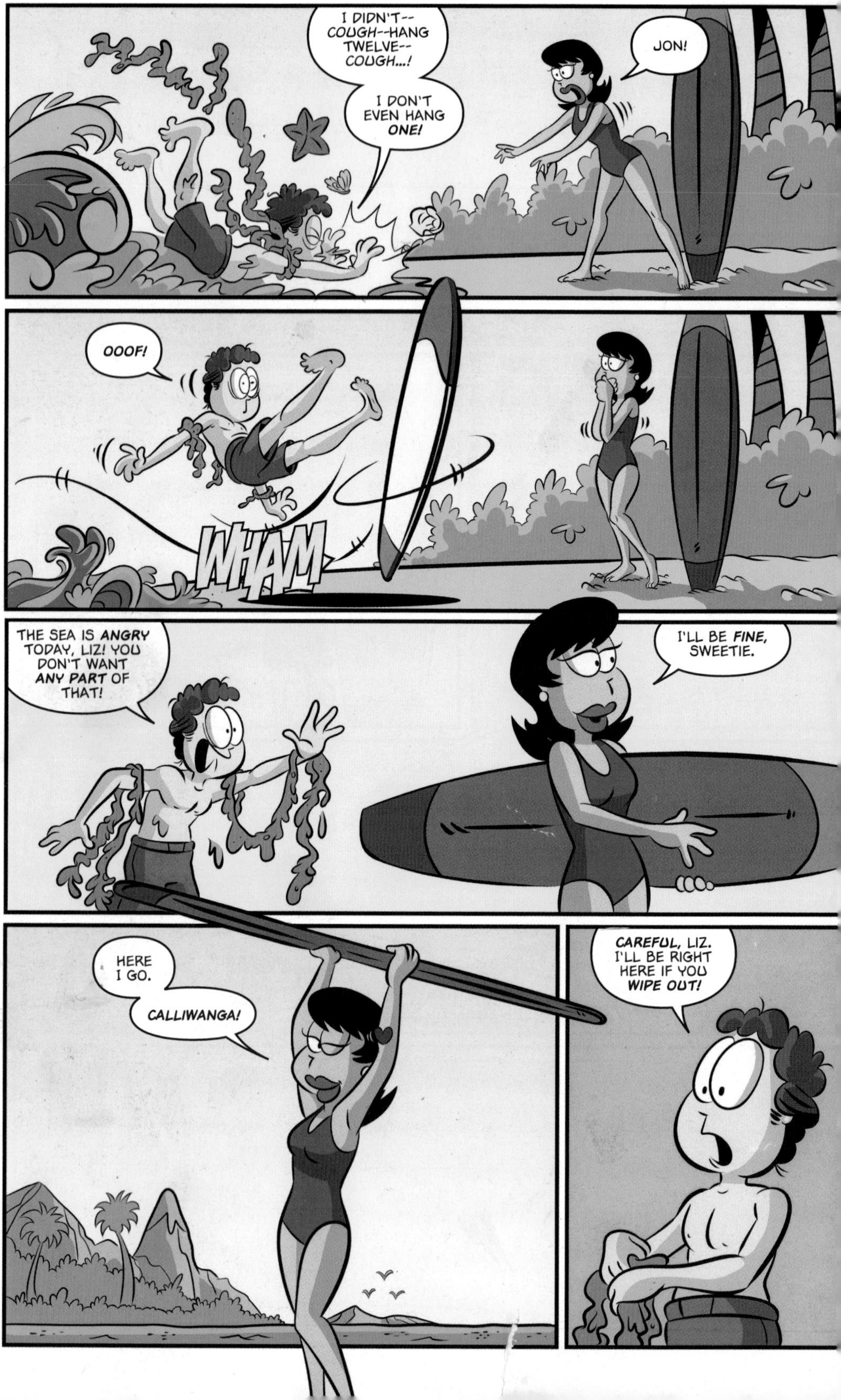
I DIDN'T--COUGH--HANG TWELVE--COUGH...!
I DON'T EVEN HANG ONE!
JON!
OOOF!
WHAM
THE SEA IS ANGRY TODAY, LIZ! YOU DON'T WANT ANY PART OF THAT!
I'LL BE FINE, SWEETIE.
HERE I GO.
CALLIWANGA!
CAREFUL, LIZ. I'LL BE RIGHT HERE IF YOU WIPE OUT!

WOO-HOOO!

THIS IS AWESOME!

JUST CALL ME THE *BIG CAN-O-TUNA!*

I GUESS THAT SUMMER IN COLLEGE I SPENT IN *HAWAII* IS STILL PAYING OFF!

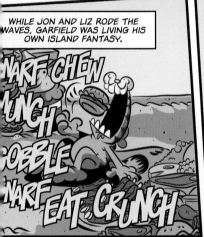

WHILE JON AND LIZ RODE THE WAVES, GARFIELD WAS LIVING HIS OWN ISLAND FANTASY.

NARF. CHEW MUNCH GOBBLE NARF EAT. CRUNCH

LIZ! LIZ! ARE YOU *OKAY?* DO YOU NEED MOUTH-TO-MOUTH? THE HEIMLICH? SHOULD I CALL AN *AMBULANCE?*

WHAT? I'M FINE. DIDN'T YOU *SEE* ME OUT THERE?

TO TELL THE TRUTH, I *COULDN'T LOOK.* I HAD MY EYES *CLOSED.* DID YOU *WIPE OUT* REALLY BAD?

NO! I RODE THE WAVES LIKE A *PRO!*

BUT I THOUGHT--HEY, WHY IS THE SKY SO *DARK* ALL OF A SUDDEN?

A *STORM* MUST BE COMING.

PING PING PING

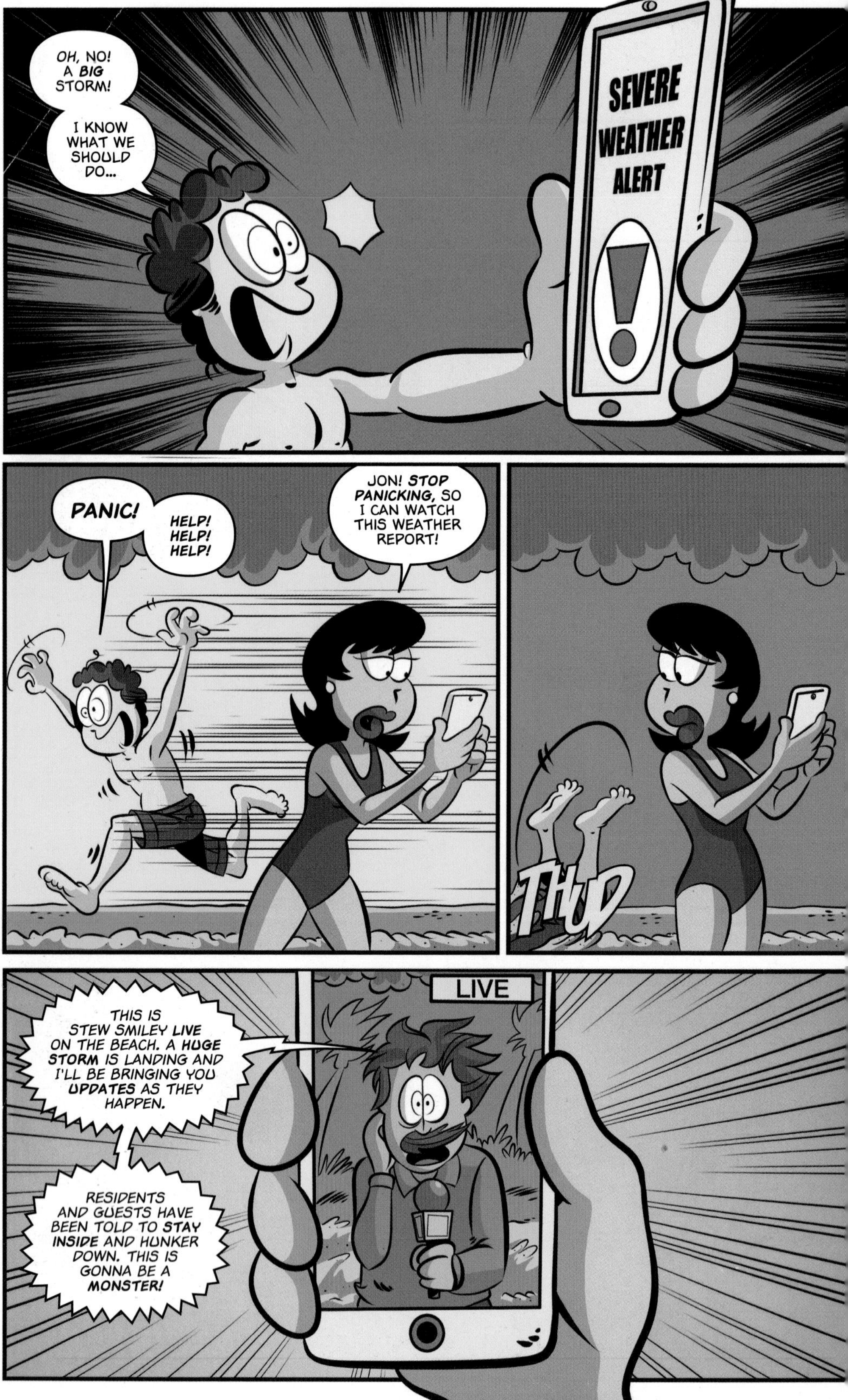

OH, NO! A BIG STORM!
I KNOW WHAT WE SHOULD DO...
SEVERE WEATHER ALERT
PANIC!
HELP! HELP! HELP!
JON! STOP PANICKING, SO I CAN WATCH THIS WEATHER REPORT!
THUD
LIVE
THIS IS STEW SMILEY LIVE ON THE BEACH. A HUGE STORM IS LANDING AND I'LL BE BRINGING YOU UPDATES AS THEY HAPPEN.
RESIDENTS AND GUESTS HAVE BEEN TOLD TO STAY INSIDE AND HUNKER DOWN. THIS IS GONNA BE A MONSTER!

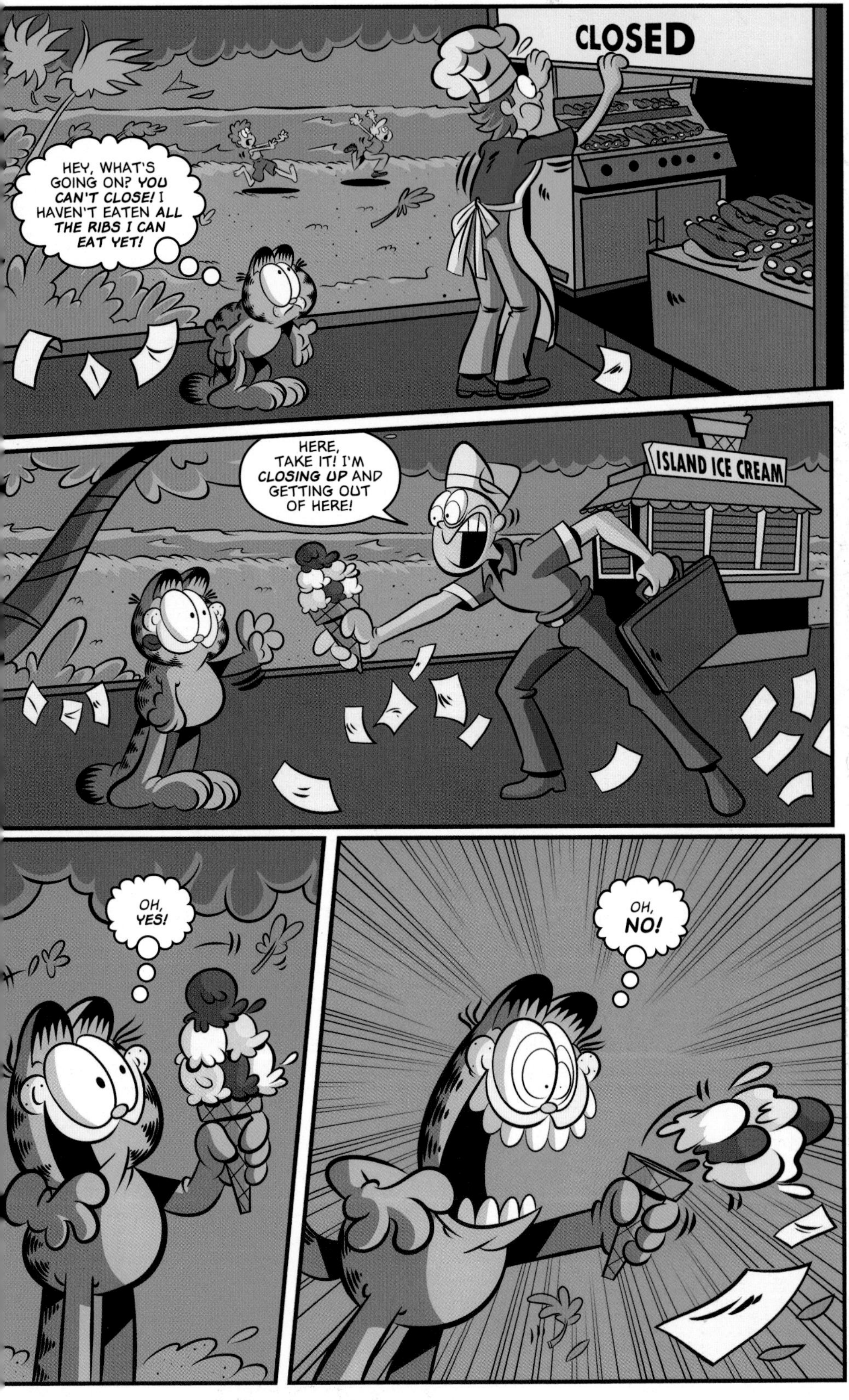
CLOSED
HEY, WHAT'S GOING ON? YOU CAN'T CLOSE! I HAVEN'T EATEN ALL THE RIBS I CAN EAT YET!
ISLAND ICE CREAM
HERE, TAKE IT! I'M CLOSING UP AND GETTING OUT OF HERE!
OH, YES!
OH, NO!

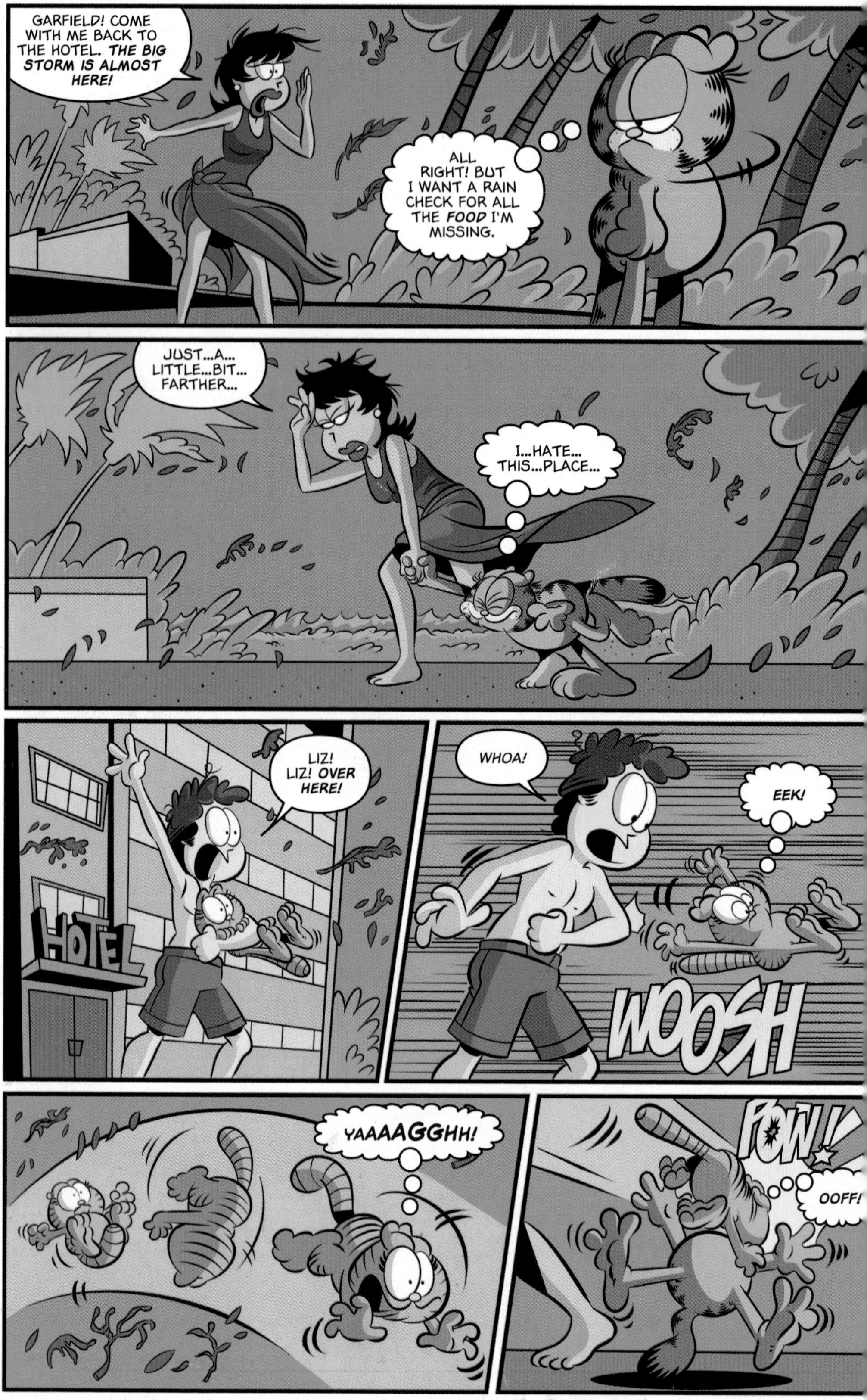

GARFIELD! COME WITH ME BACK TO THE HOTEL. THE BIG STORM IS ALMOST HERE!
ALL RIGHT! BUT I WANT A RAIN CHECK FOR ALL THE FOOD I'M MISSING.
JUST...A... LITTLE...BIT... FARTHER...
I...HATE... THIS...PLACE...
LIZ! LIZ! OVER HERE!
HOTEL
WHOA!
EEK!
WOOSH
YAAAAGGHH!
POW!
OOFF!

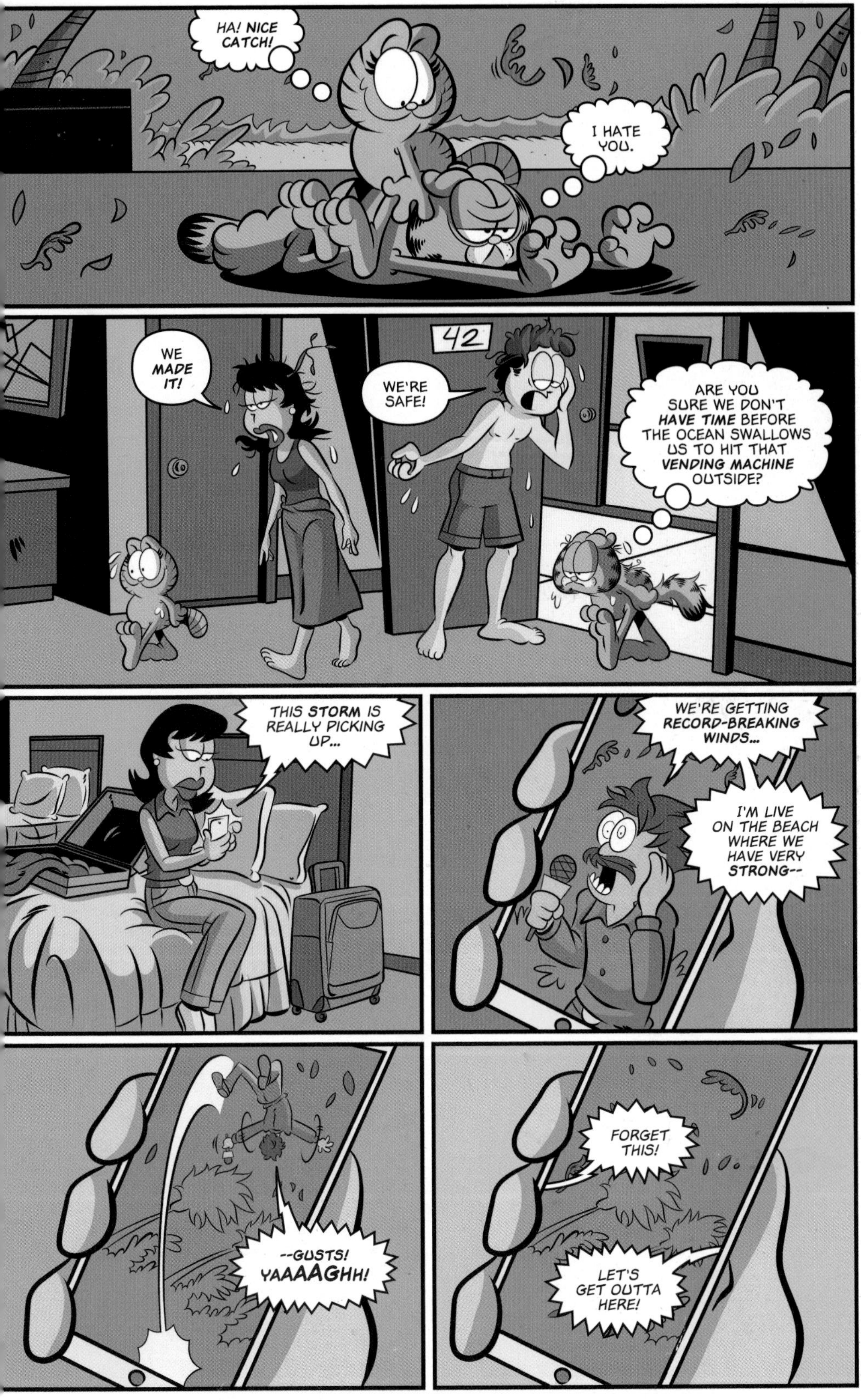
HA! NICE CATCH!
I HATE YOU.
WE MADE IT!
WE'RE SAFE!
ARE YOU SURE WE DON'T HAVE TIME BEFORE THE OCEAN SWALLOWS US TO HIT THAT VENDING MACHINE OUTSIDE?
42
THIS STORM IS REALLY PICKING UP...
WE'RE GETTING RECORD-BREAKING WINDS...
I'M LIVE ON THE BEACH WHERE WE HAVE VERY STRONG--
--GUSTS! YAAAAGHH!
FORGET THIS!
LET'S GET OUTTA HERE!

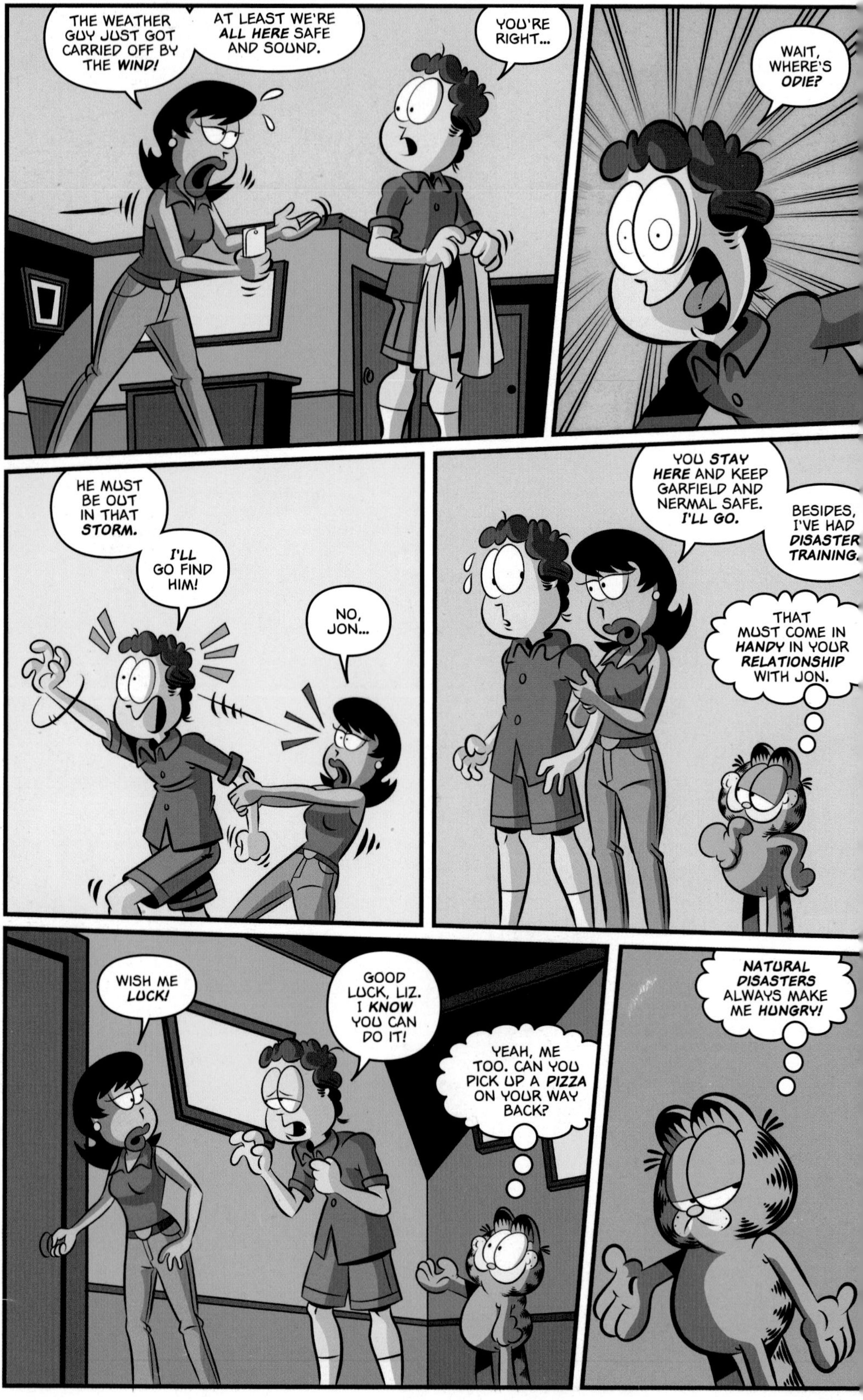
THE WEATHER GUY JUST GOT CARRIED OFF BY THE WIND!
AT LEAST WE'RE ALL HERE SAFE AND SOUND.
YOU'RE RIGHT...
WAIT, WHERE'S ODIE?
HE MUST BE OUT IN THAT STORM.
I'LL GO FIND HIM!
NO, JON...
YOU STAY HERE AND KEEP GARFIELD AND NERMAL SAFE. I'LL GO.
BESIDES, I'VE HAD DISASTER TRAINING.
THAT MUST COME IN HANDY IN YOUR RELATIONSHIP WITH JON.
WISH ME LUCK!
GOOD LUCK, LIZ. I KNOW YOU CAN DO IT!
YEAH, ME TOO. CAN YOU PICK UP A PIZZA ON YOUR WAY BACK?
NATURAL DISASTERS ALWAYS MAKE ME HUNGRY!

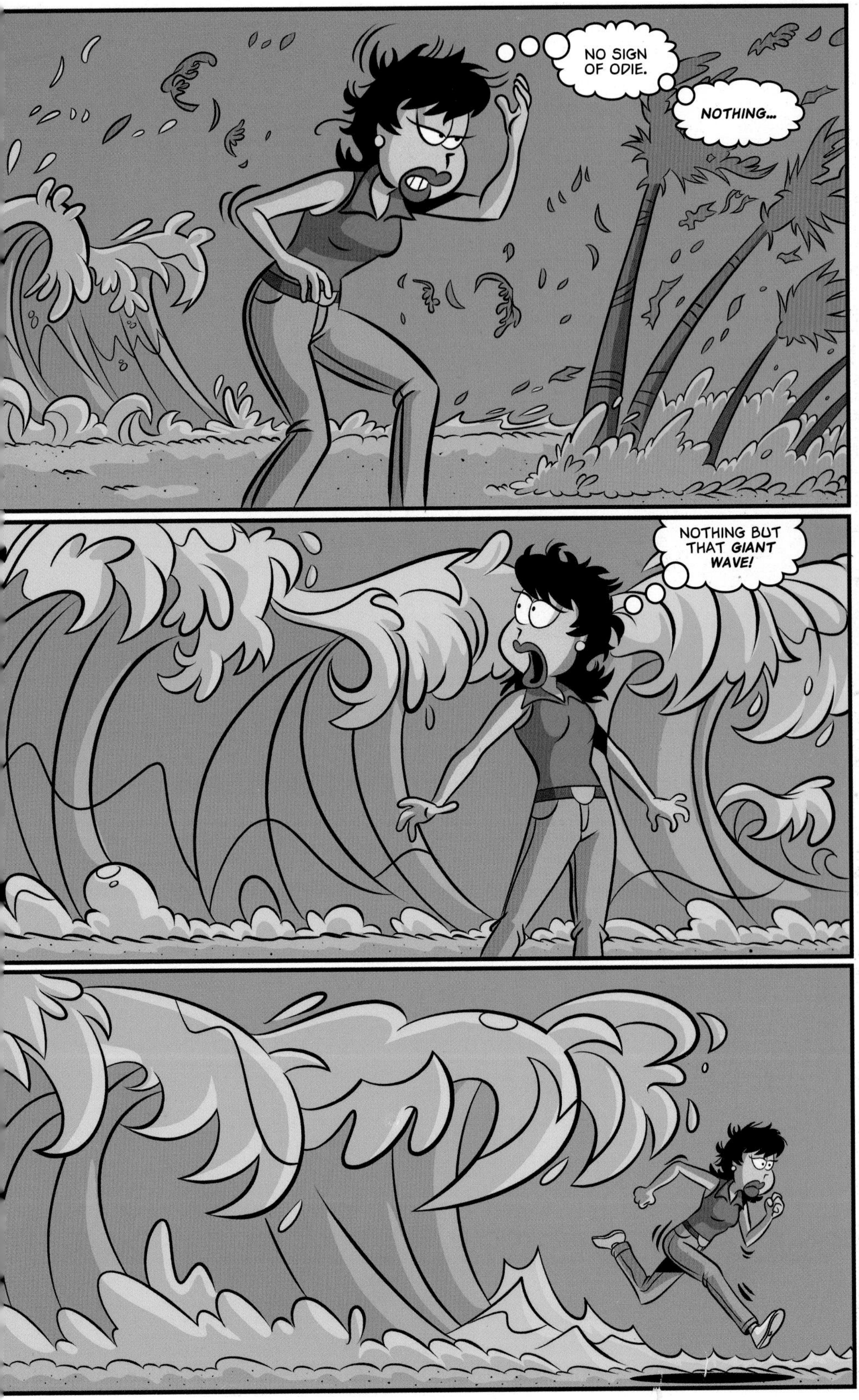
NO SIGN OF ODIE.
NOTHING...
NOTHING BUT THAT GIANT WAVE!

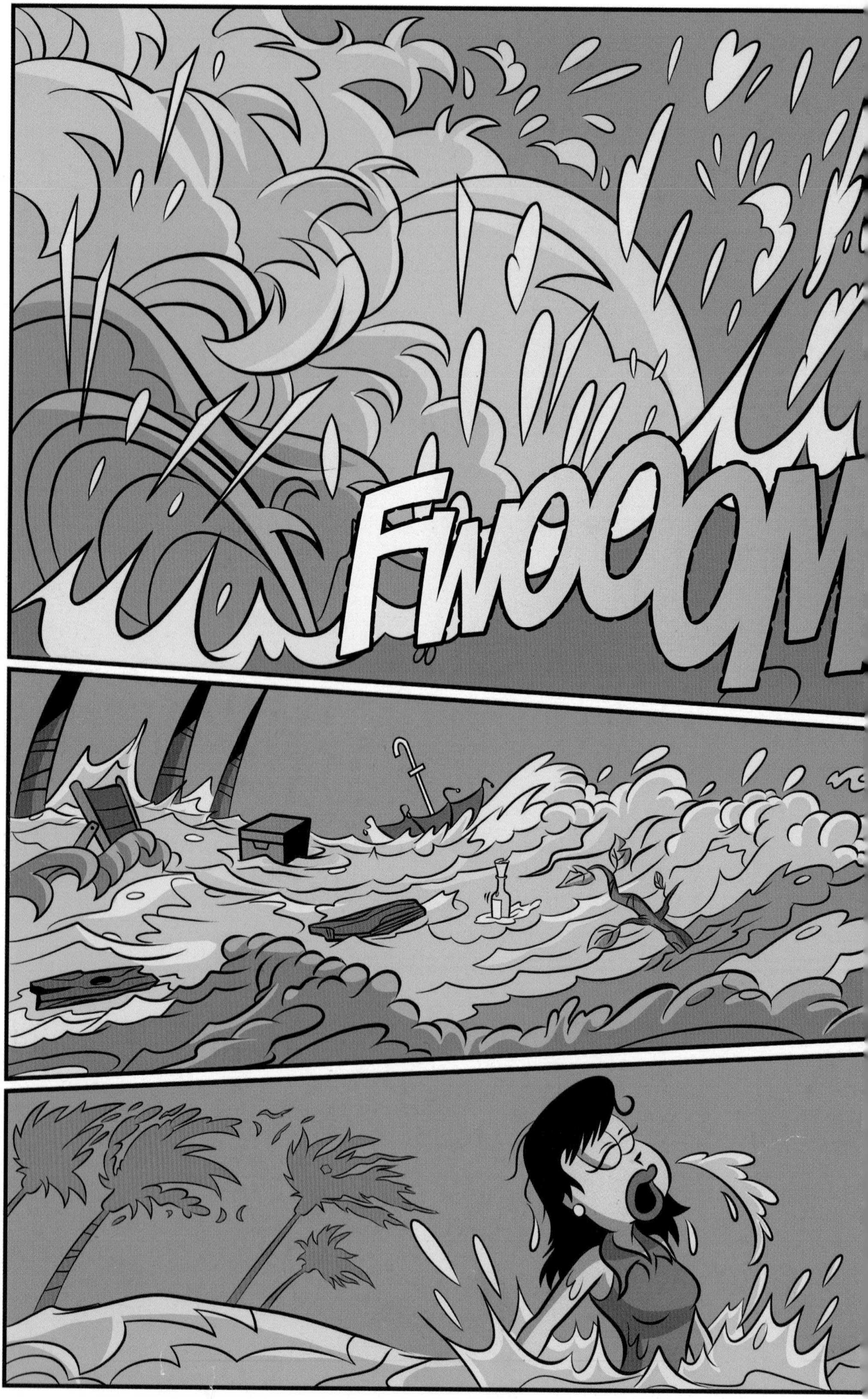
FWOOOM

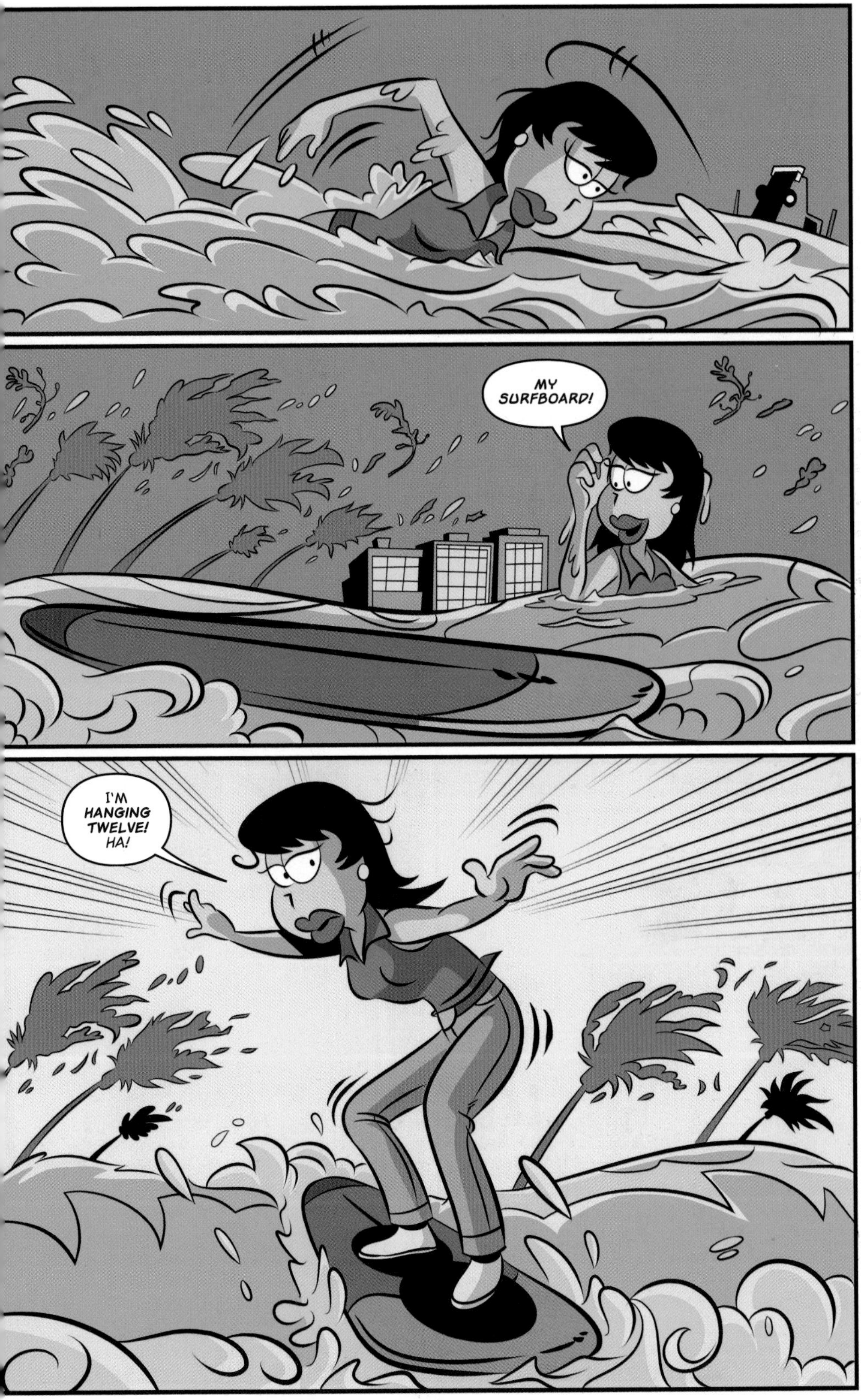
MY SURFBOARD!
I'M HANGING TWELVE! HA!

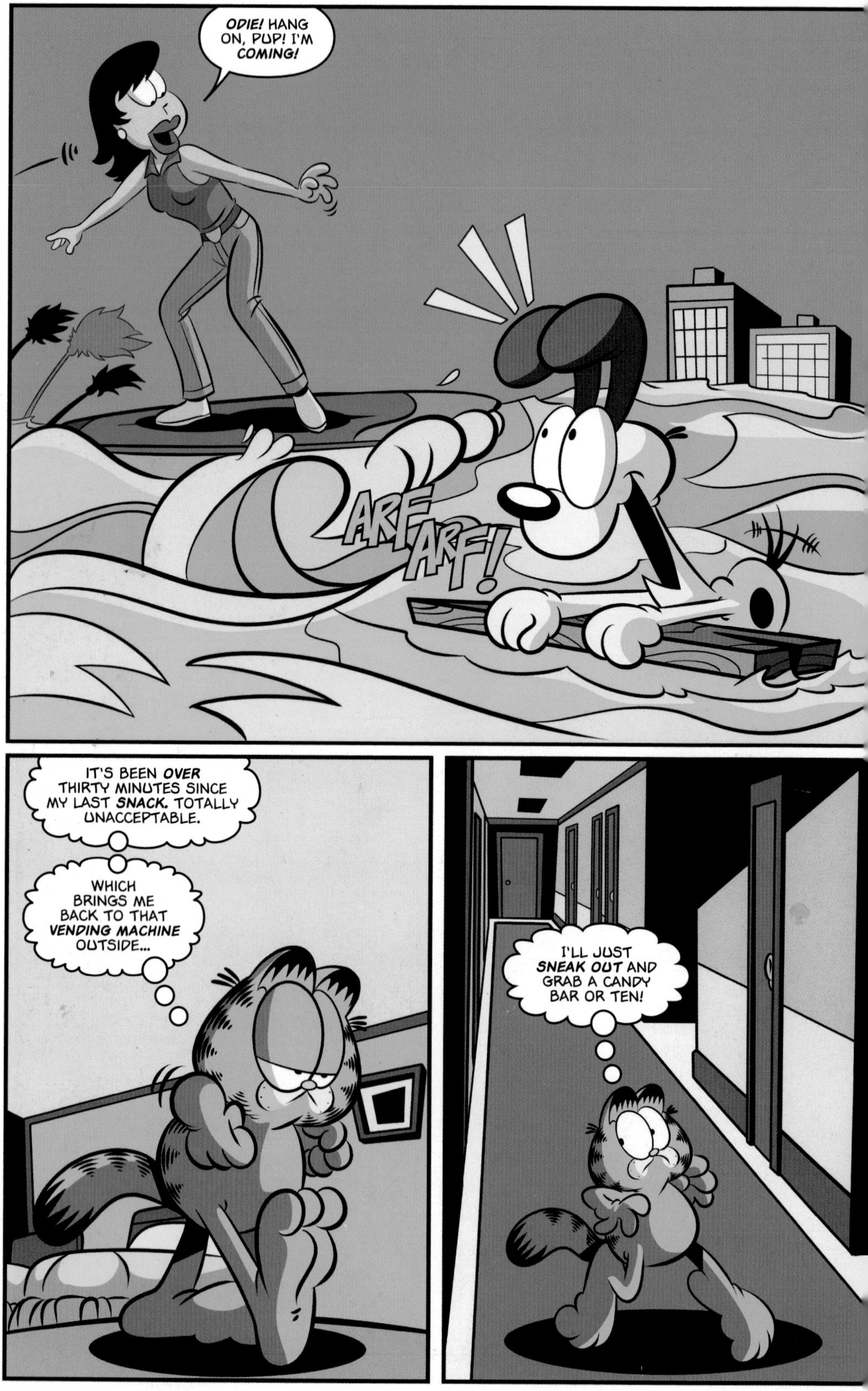
ODIE! HANG ON, PUP! I'M COMING!
ARF ARF!
IT'S BEEN OVER THIRTY MINUTES SINCE MY LAST SNACK. TOTALLY UNACCEPTABLE.
WHICH BRINGS ME BACK TO THAT VENDING MACHINE OUTSIDE...
I'LL JUST SNEAK OUT AND GRAB A CANDY BAR OR TEN!

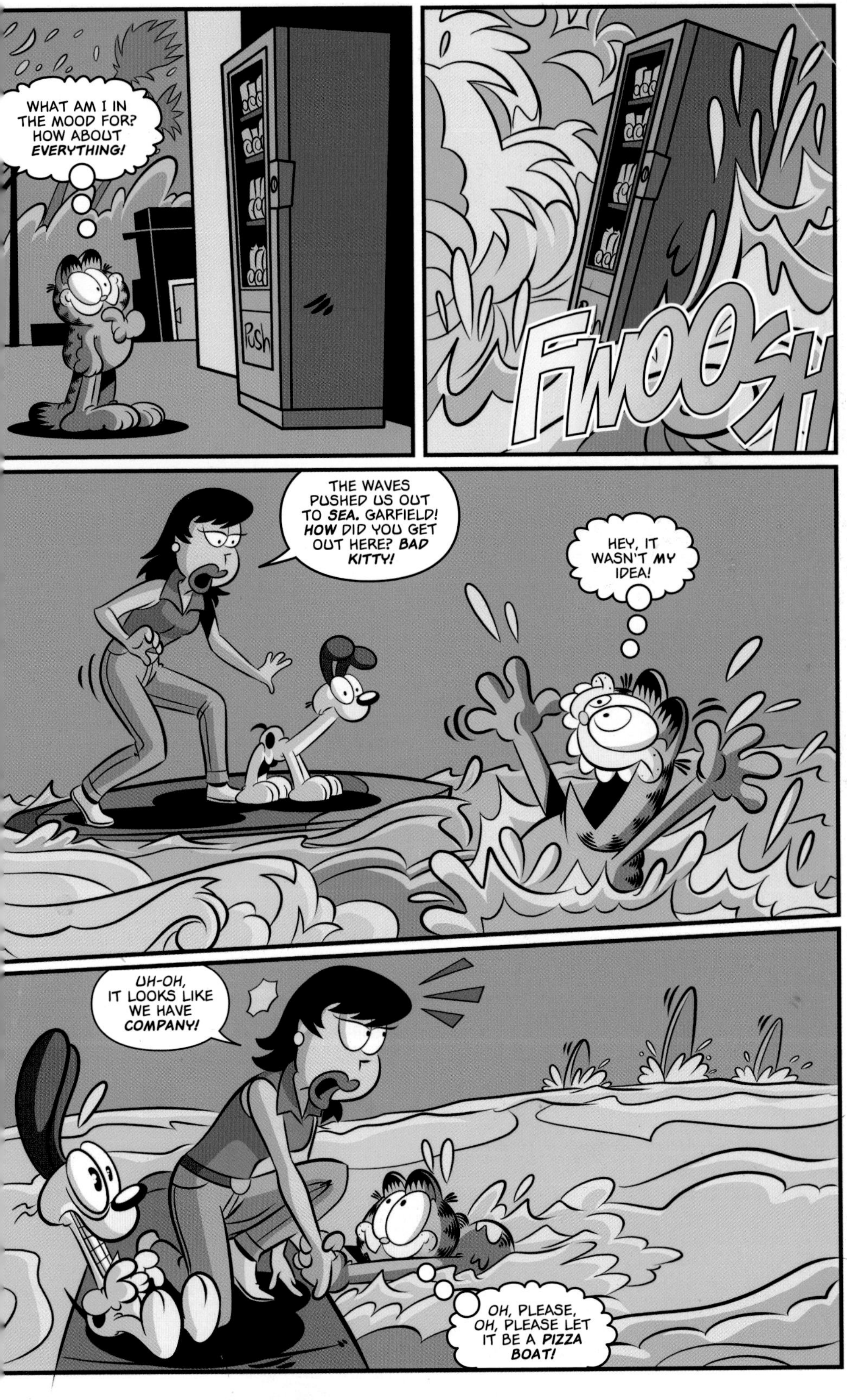
WHAT AM I IN THE MOOD FOR? HOW ABOUT EVERYTHING!
PUSH
FWOOSH
THE WAVES PUSHED US OUT TO SEA. GARFIELD! HOW DID YOU GET OUT HERE? BAD KITTY!
HEY, IT WASN'T MY IDEA!
UH-OH, IT LOOKS LIKE WE HAVE COMPANY!
OH, PLEASE, OH, PLEASE LET IT BE A PIZZA BOAT!

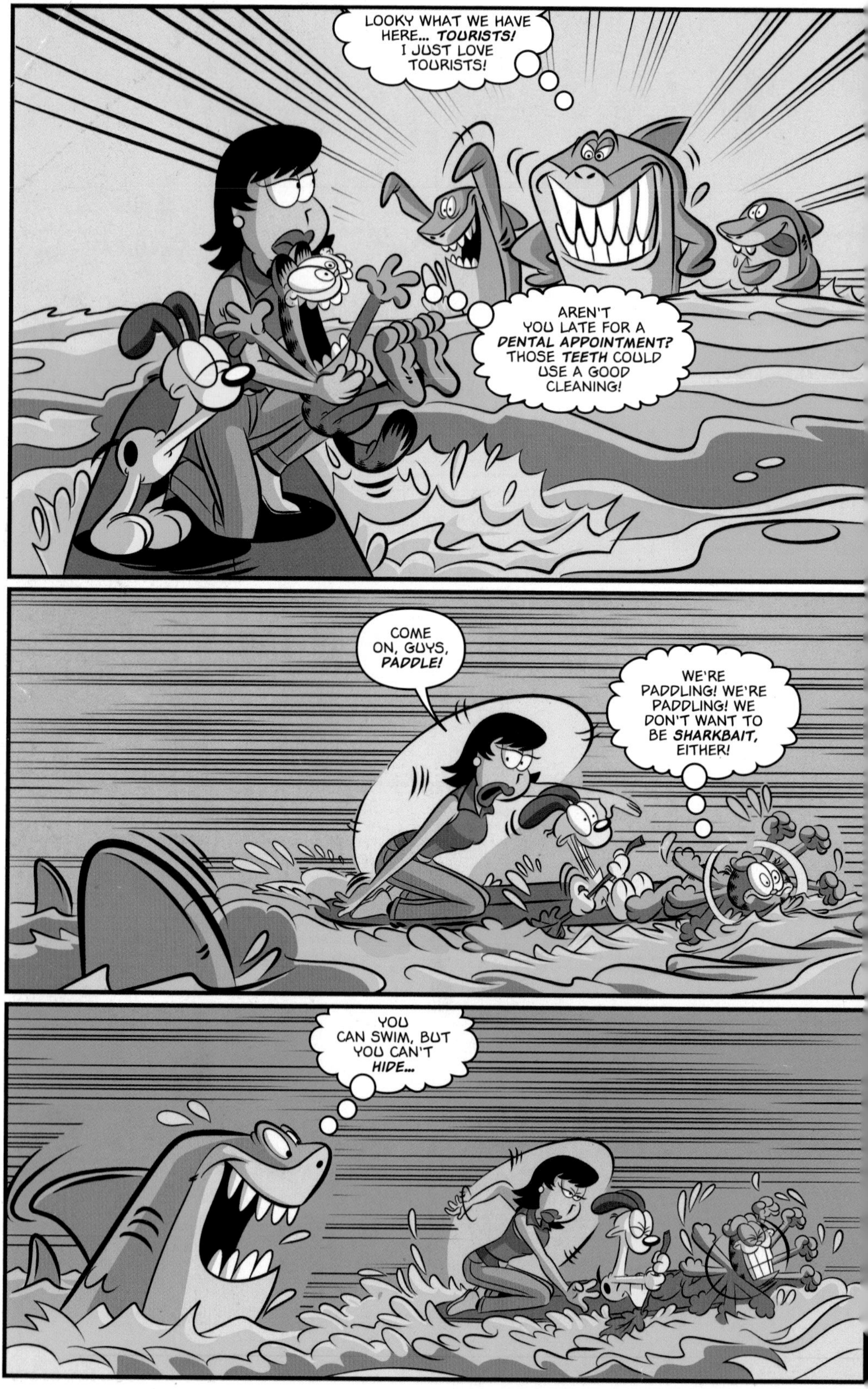
LOOKY WHAT WE HAVE HERE... TOURISTS! I JUST LOVE TOURISTS!
AREN'T YOU LATE FOR A DENTAL APPOINTMENT? THOSE TEETH COULD USE A GOOD CLEANING!
COME ON, GUYS, PADDLE!
WE'RE PADDLING! WE'RE PADDLING! WE DON'T WANT TO BE SHARKBAIT, EITHER!
YOU CAN SWIM, BUT YOU CAN'T HIDE...

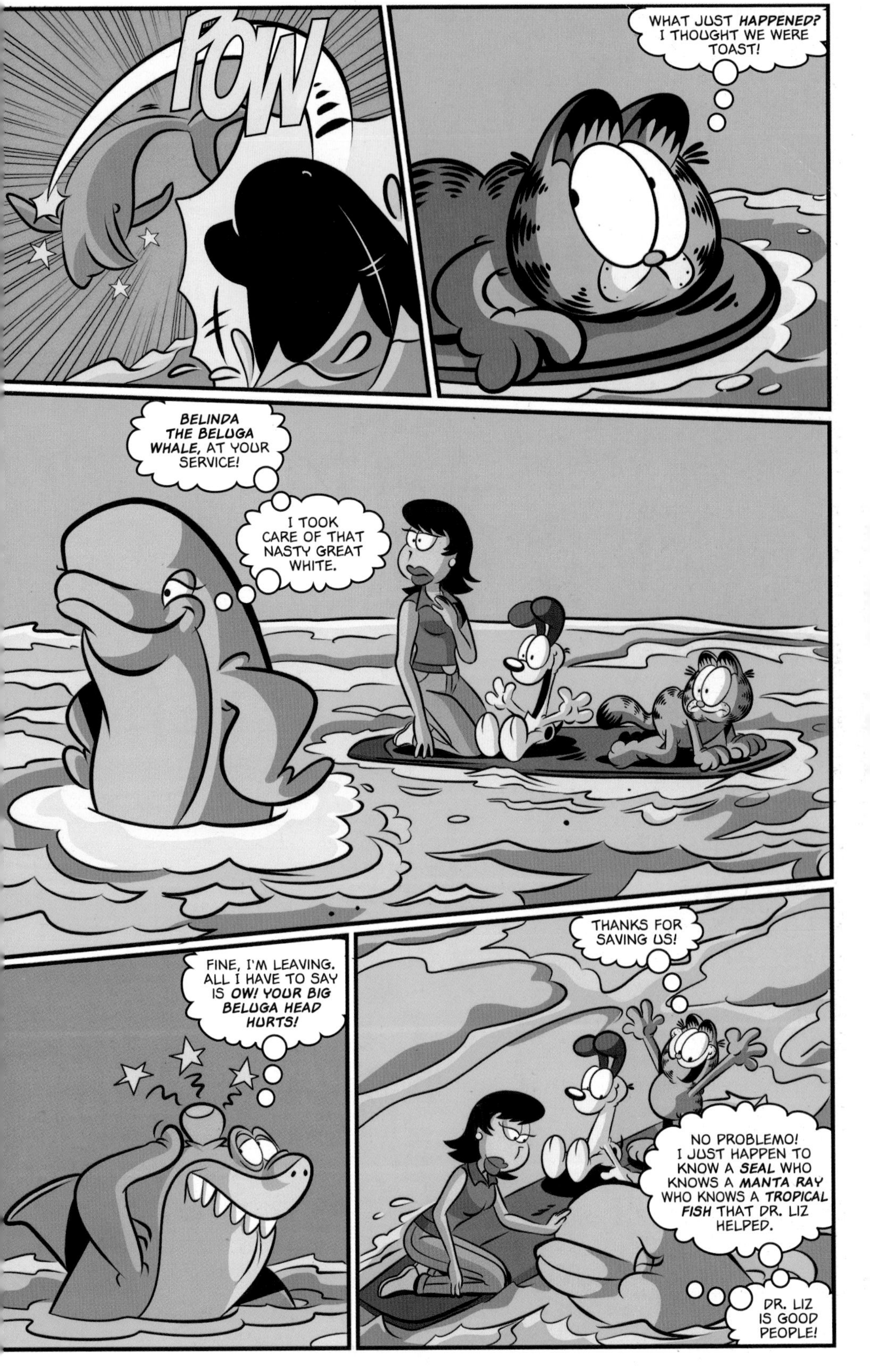
POW
WHAT JUST HAPPENED? I THOUGHT WE WERE TOAST!
BELINDA THE BELUGA WHALE, AT YOUR SERVICE!
I TOOK CARE OF THAT NASTY GREAT WHITE.
FINE, I'M LEAVING. ALL I HAVE TO SAY IS OW! YOUR BIG BELUGA HEAD HURTS!
THANKS FOR SAVING US!
NO PROBLEMO! I JUST HAPPEN TO KNOW A SEAL WHO KNOWS A MANTA RAY WHO KNOWS A TROPICAL FISH THAT DR. LIZ HELPED.
DR. LIZ IS GOOD PEOPLE!

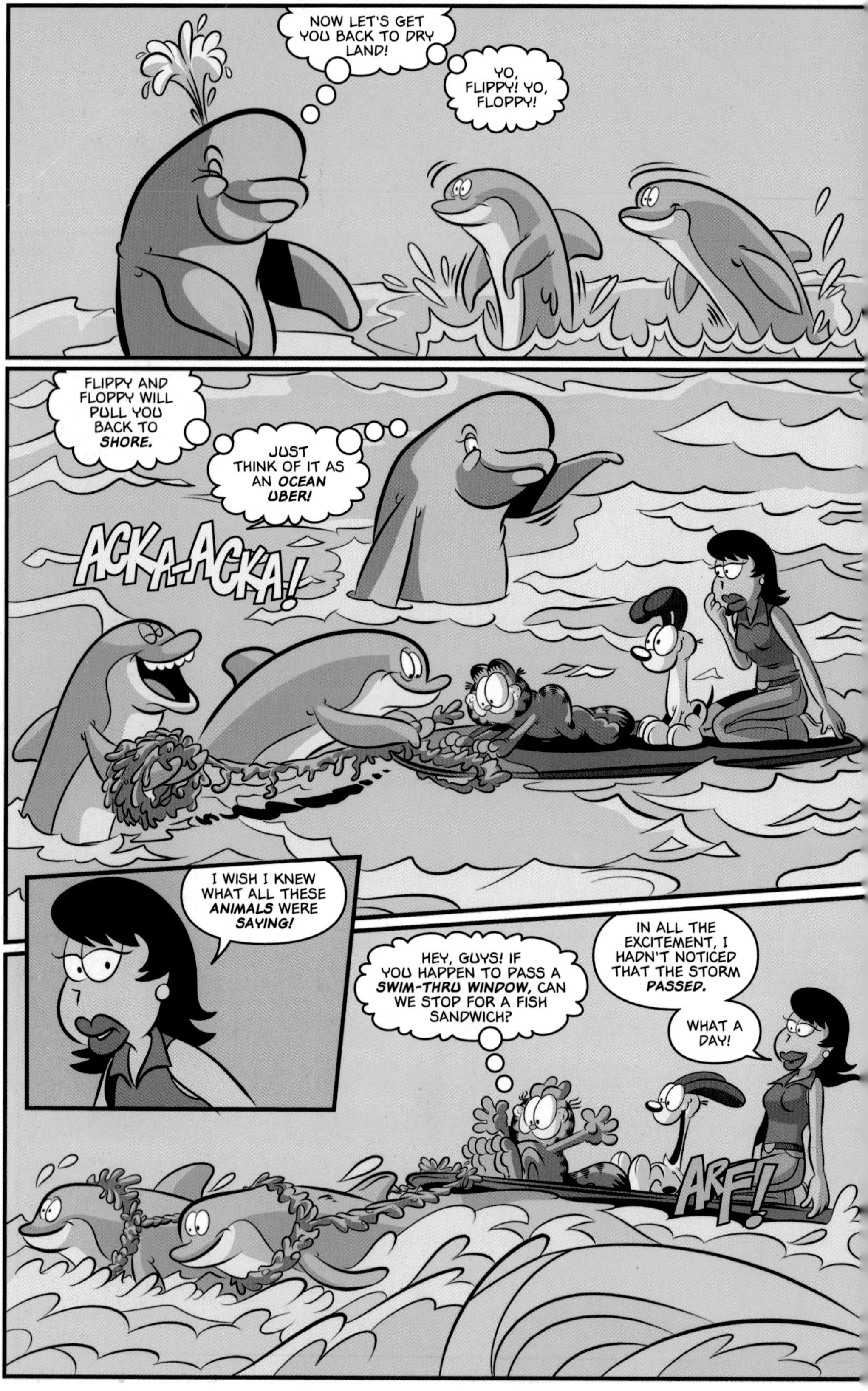

NOW LET'S GET YOU BACK TO DRY LAND!
YO, FLIPPY! YO, FLOPPY!
FLIPPY AND FLOPPY WILL PULL YOU BACK TO SHORE.
JUST THINK OF IT AS AN OCEAN UBER!
ACKA-ACKA!
I WISH I KNEW WHAT ALL THESE ANIMALS WERE SAYING!
HEY, GUYS! IF YOU HAPPEN TO PASS A SWIM-THRU WINDOW, CAN WE STOP FOR A FISH SANDWICH?
IN ALL THE EXCITEMENT, I HADN'T NOTICED THAT THE STORM PASSED.
WHAT A DAY!
ARF!

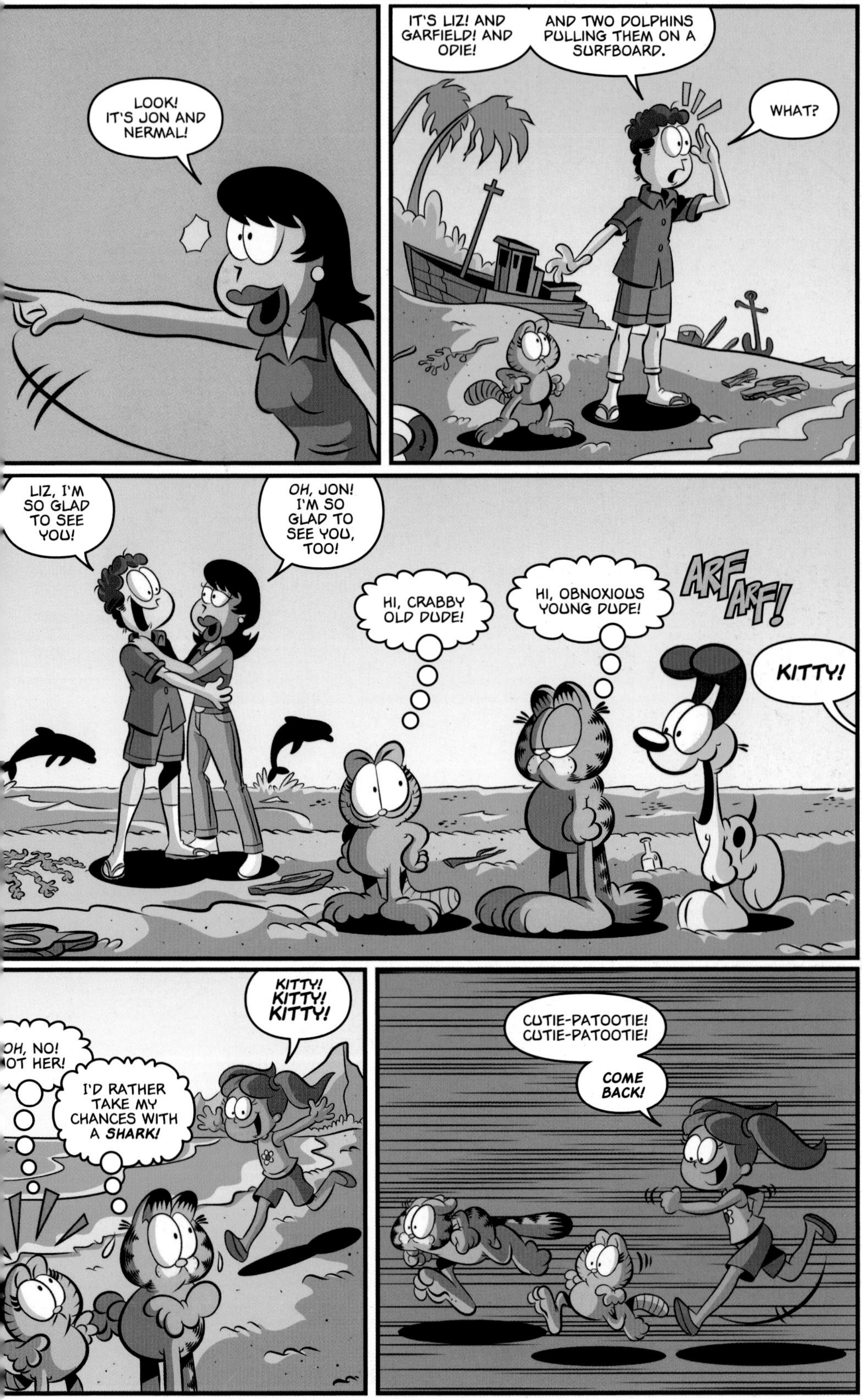
LOOK! IT'S JON AND NERMAL!
IT'S LIZ! AND GARFIELD! AND ODIE!
AND TWO DOLPHINS PULLING THEM ON A SURFBOARD.
WHAT?
LIZ, I'M SO GLAD TO SEE YOU!
OH, JON! I'M SO GLAD TO SEE YOU, TOO!
HI, CRABBY OLD DUDE!
HI, OBNOXIOUS YOUNG DUDE!
ARF ARF!
KITTY!
KITTY! KITTY! KITTY!
OH, NO! NOT HER!
I'D RATHER TAKE MY CHANCES WITH A SHARK!
CUTIE-PATOOTIE! CUTIE-PATOOTIE!
COME BACK!

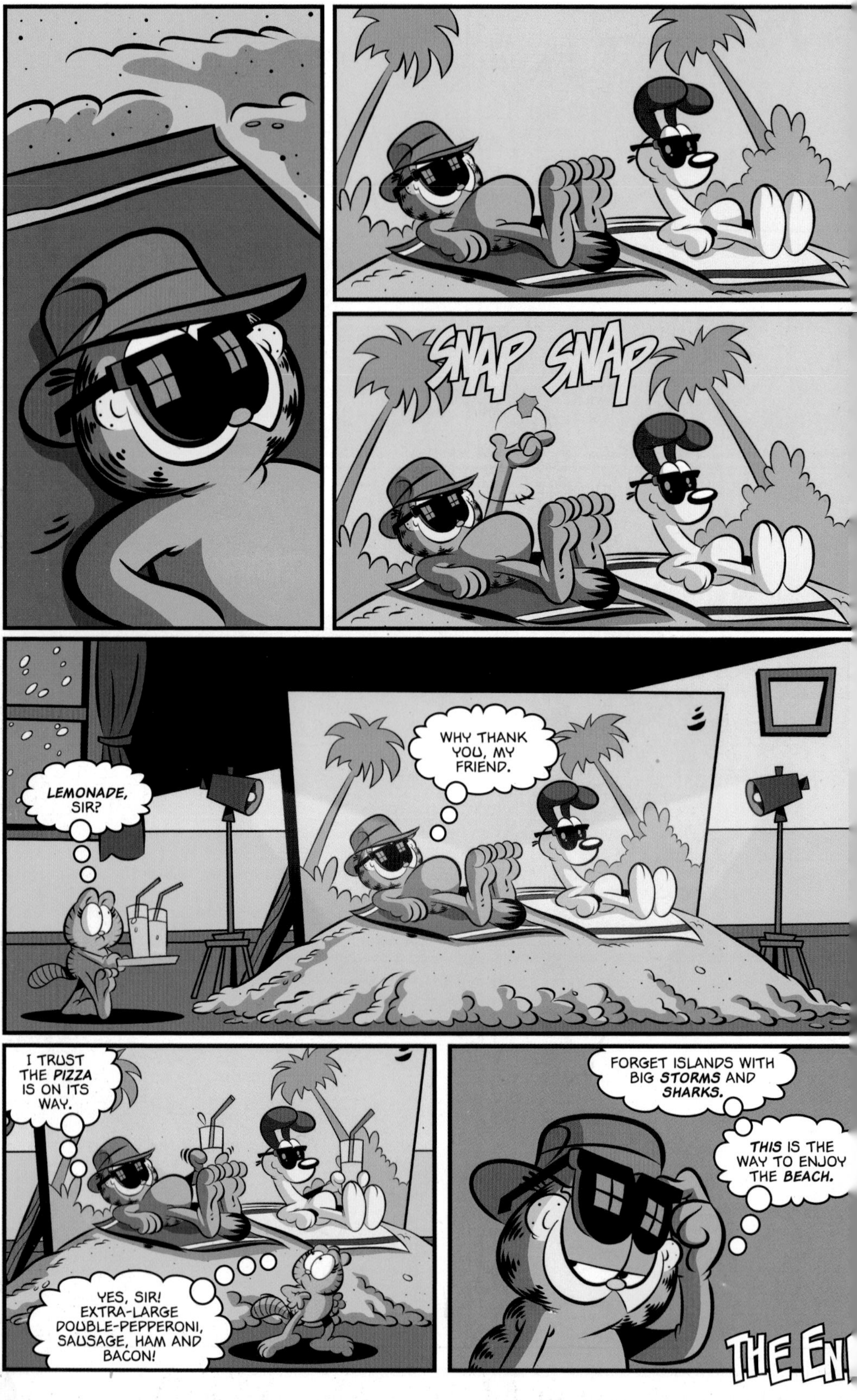
SNAP SNAP
LEMONADE, SIR?
WHY THANK YOU, MY FRIEND.
I TRUST THE PIZZA IS ON ITS WAY.
YES, SIR! EXTRA-LARGE DOUBLE-PEPPERONI, SAUSAGE, HAM AND BACON!
FORGET ISLANDS WITH BIG STORMS AND SHARKS.
THIS IS THE WAY TO ENJOY THE BEACH.

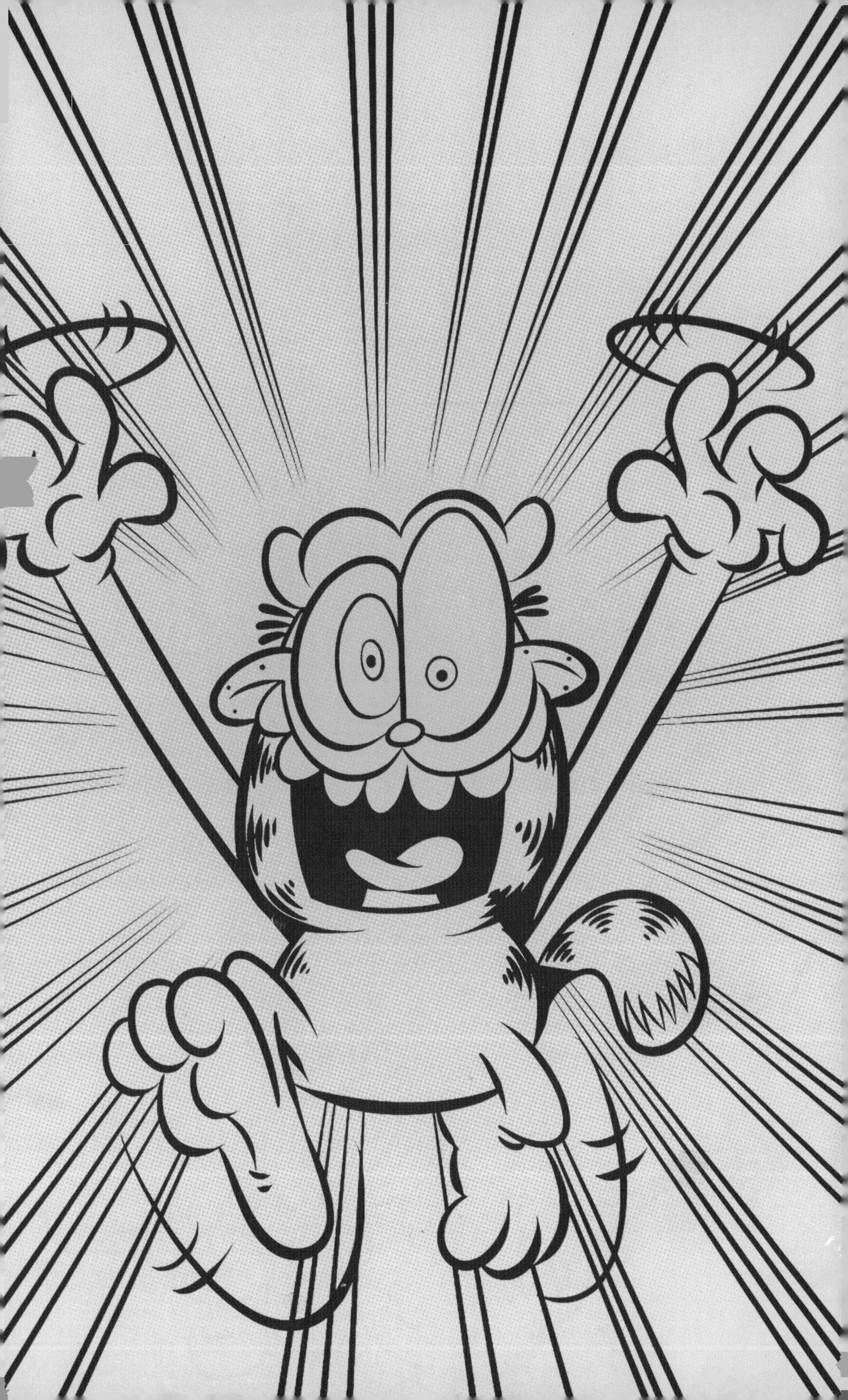

"LOUIE'S LASAGNA CLUB"

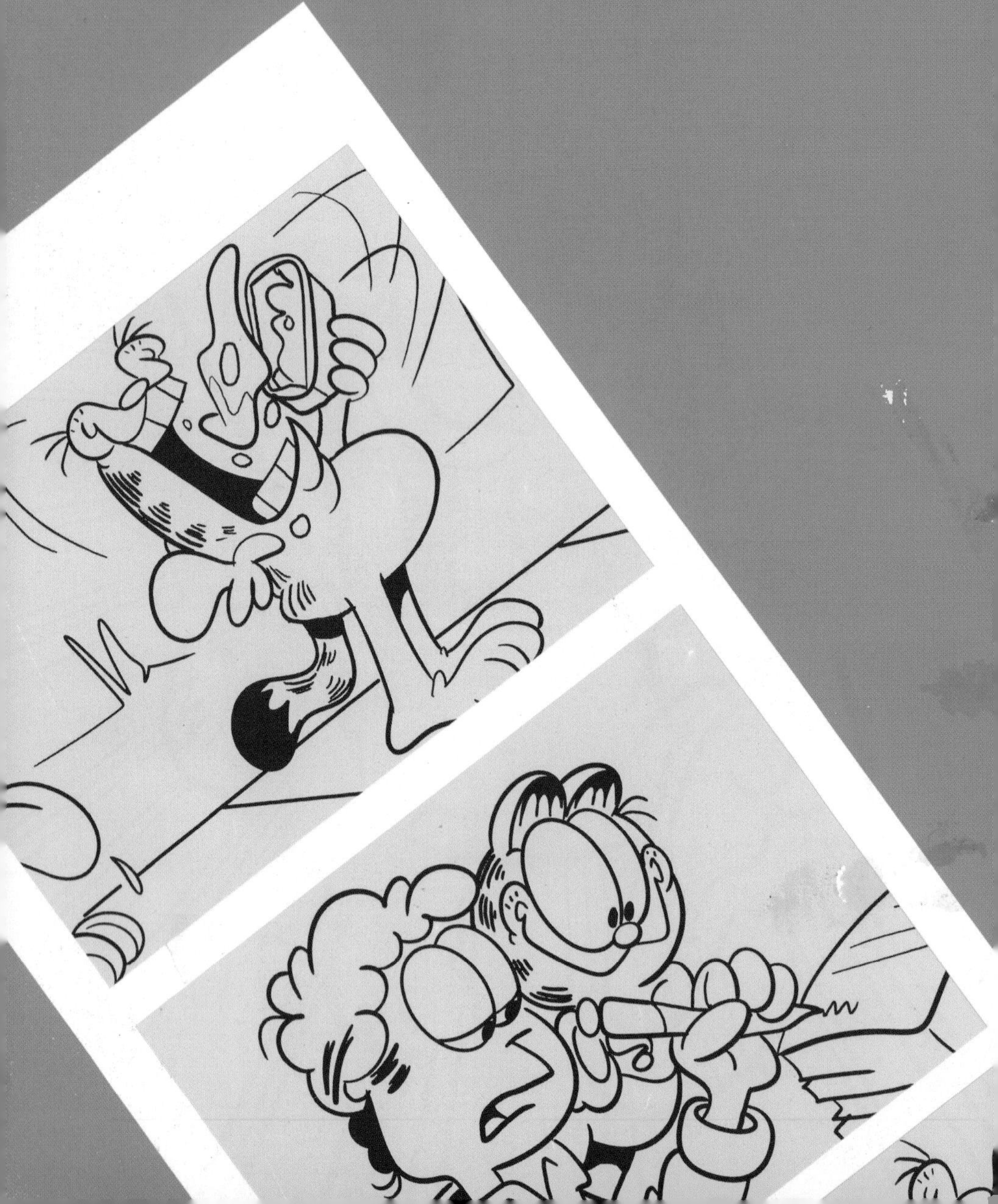

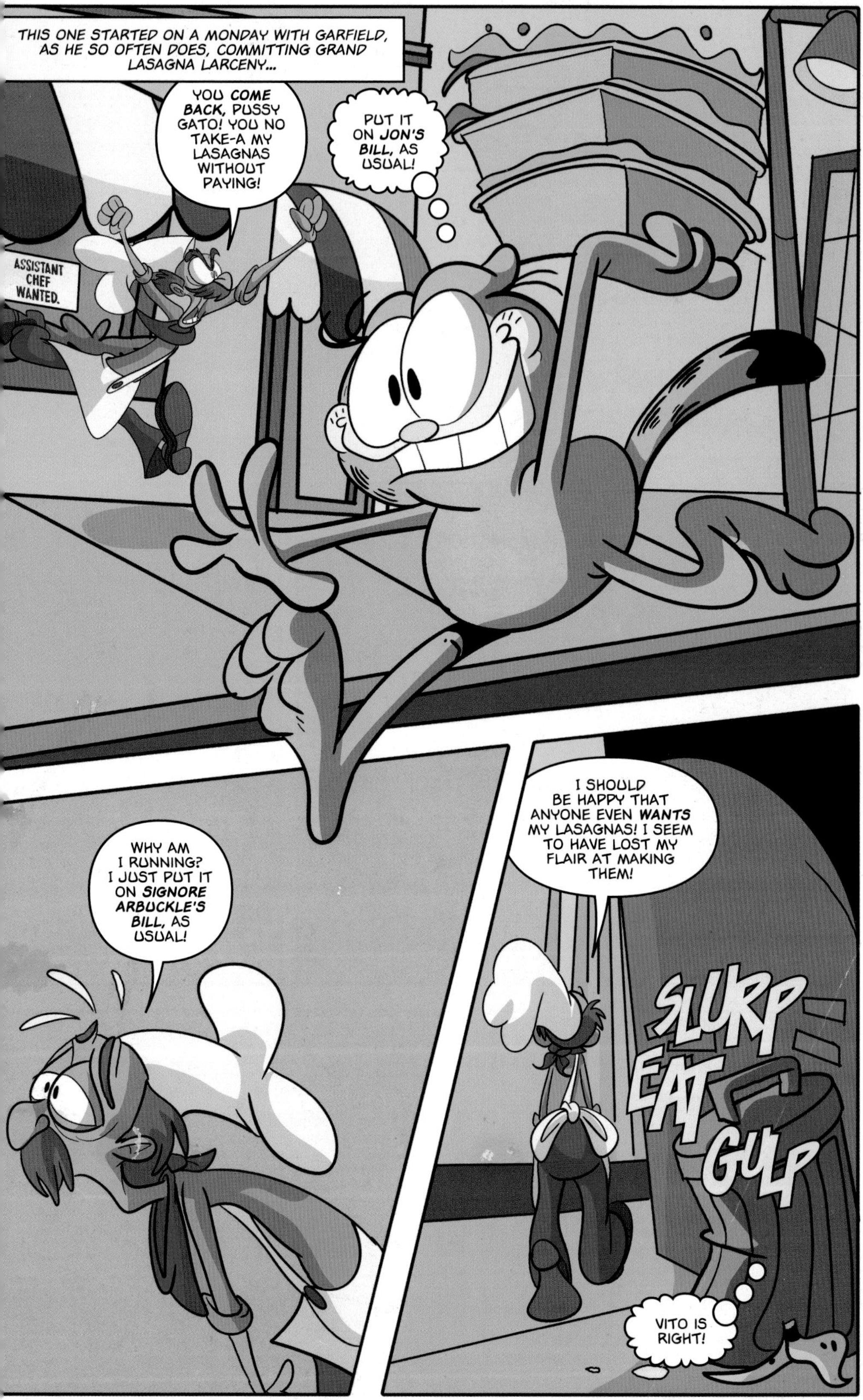
THIS ONE STARTED ON A MONDAY WITH GARFIELD, AS HE SO OFTEN DOES, COMMITTING GRAND LASAGNA LARCENY...
YOU COME BACK, PUSSY GATO! YOU NO TAKE-A MY LASAGNAS WITHOUT PAYING!
PUT IT ON JON'S BILL, AS USUAL!
ASSISTANT CHEF WANTED.
WHY AM I RUNNING? I JUST PUT IT ON SIGNORE ARBUCKLE'S BILL, AS USUAL!
I SHOULD BE HAPPY THAT ANYONE EVEN WANTS MY LASAGNAS! I SEEM TO HAVE LOST MY FLAIR AT MAKING THEM!
SLURP
EAT
GULP
VITO IS RIGHT!

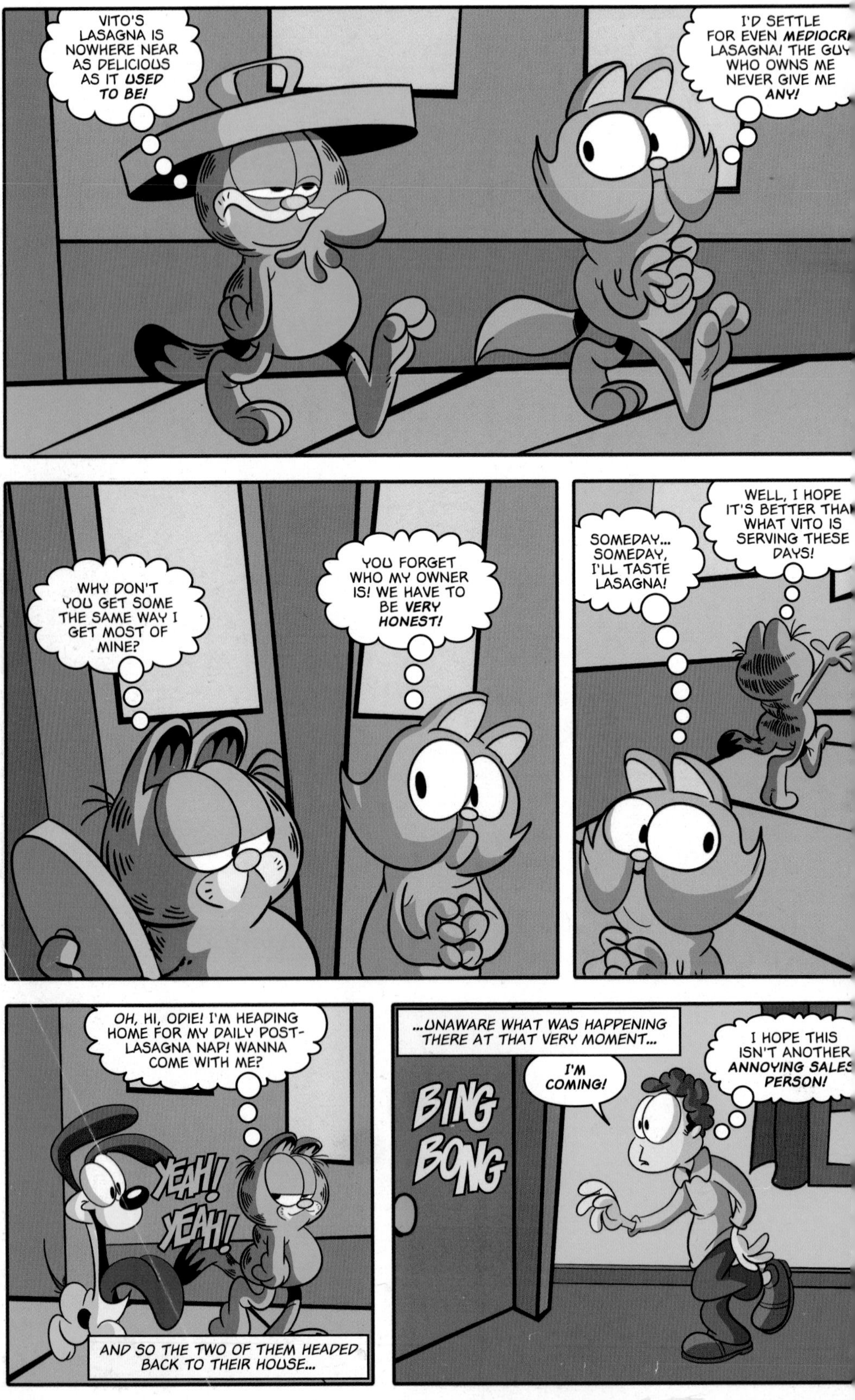
VITO'S LASAGNA IS NOWHERE NEAR AS DELICIOUS AS IT *USED TO BE!*
I'D SETTLE FOR EVEN *MEDIOCR* LASAGNA! THE GUY WHO OWNS ME NEVER GIVE ME *ANY!*
WHY DON'T YOU GET SOME THE SAME WAY I GET MOST OF MINE?
YOU FORGET WHO MY OWNER IS! WE HAVE TO BE *VERY HONEST!*
SOMEDAY... SOMEDAY, I'LL TASTE LASAGNA!
WELL, I HOPE IT'S BETTER THA WHAT VITO IS SERVING THESE DAYS!
OH, HI, ODIE! I'M HEADING HOME FOR MY DAILY POST-LASAGNA NAP! WANNA COME WITH ME?
YEAH! YEAH!
AND SO THE TWO OF THEM HEADED BACK TO THEIR HOUSE...
...UNAWARE WHAT WAS HAPPENING THERE AT THAT VERY MOMENT...
BING BONG
I'M COMING!
I HOPE THIS ISN'T ANOTHER *ANNOYING SALES PERSON!*

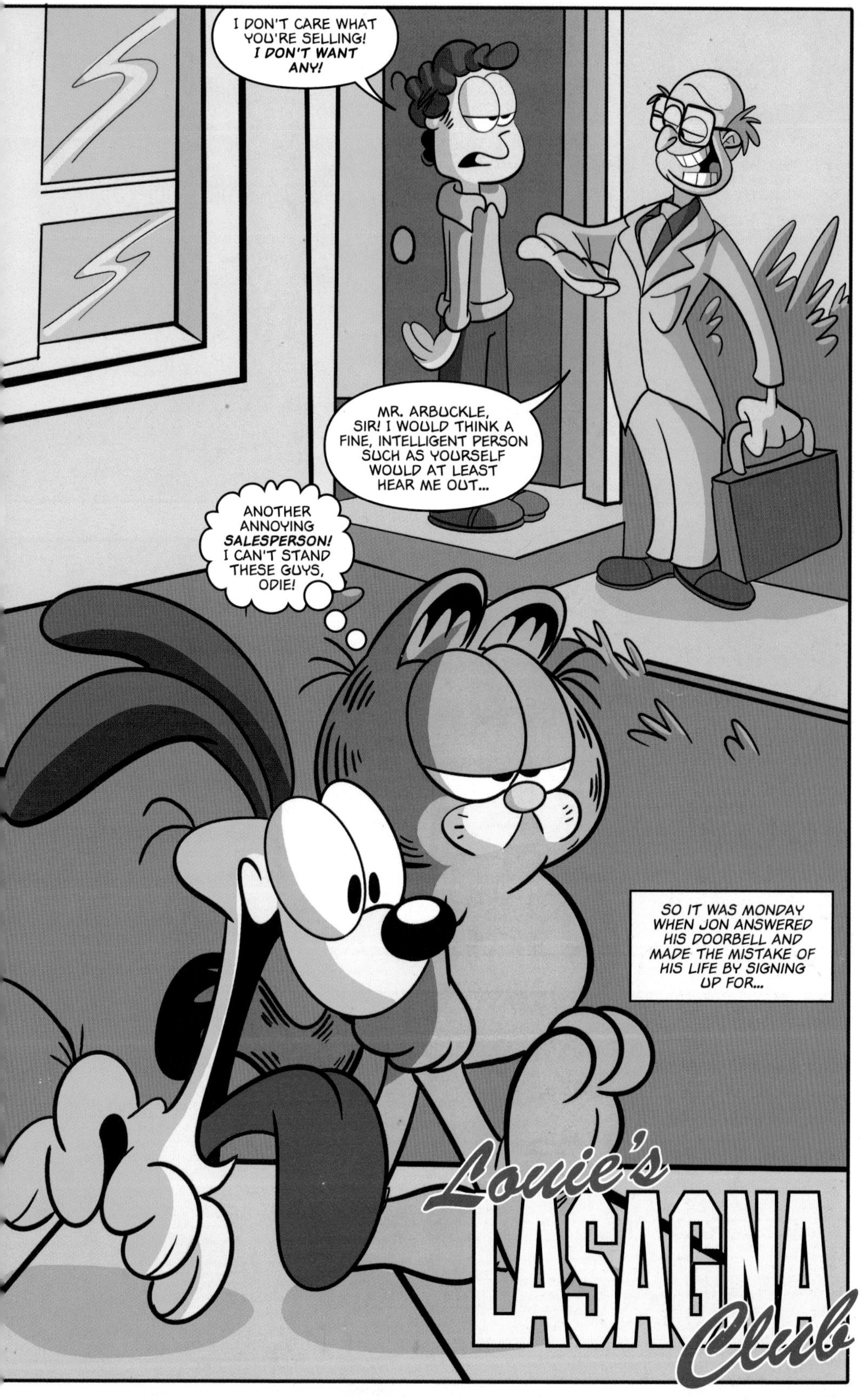
I DON'T CARE WHAT YOU'RE SELLING! I DON'T WANT ANY!
MR. ARBUCKLE, SIR! I WOULD THINK A FINE, INTELLIGENT PERSON SUCH AS YOURSELF WOULD AT LEAST HEAR ME OUT...
ANOTHER ANNOYING SALESPERSON! I CAN'T STAND THESE GUYS, ODIE!
SO IT WAS MONDAY WHEN JON ANSWERED HIS DOORBELL AND MADE THE MISTAKE OF HIS LIFE BY SIGNING UP FOR...
Louie's LASAGNA Club

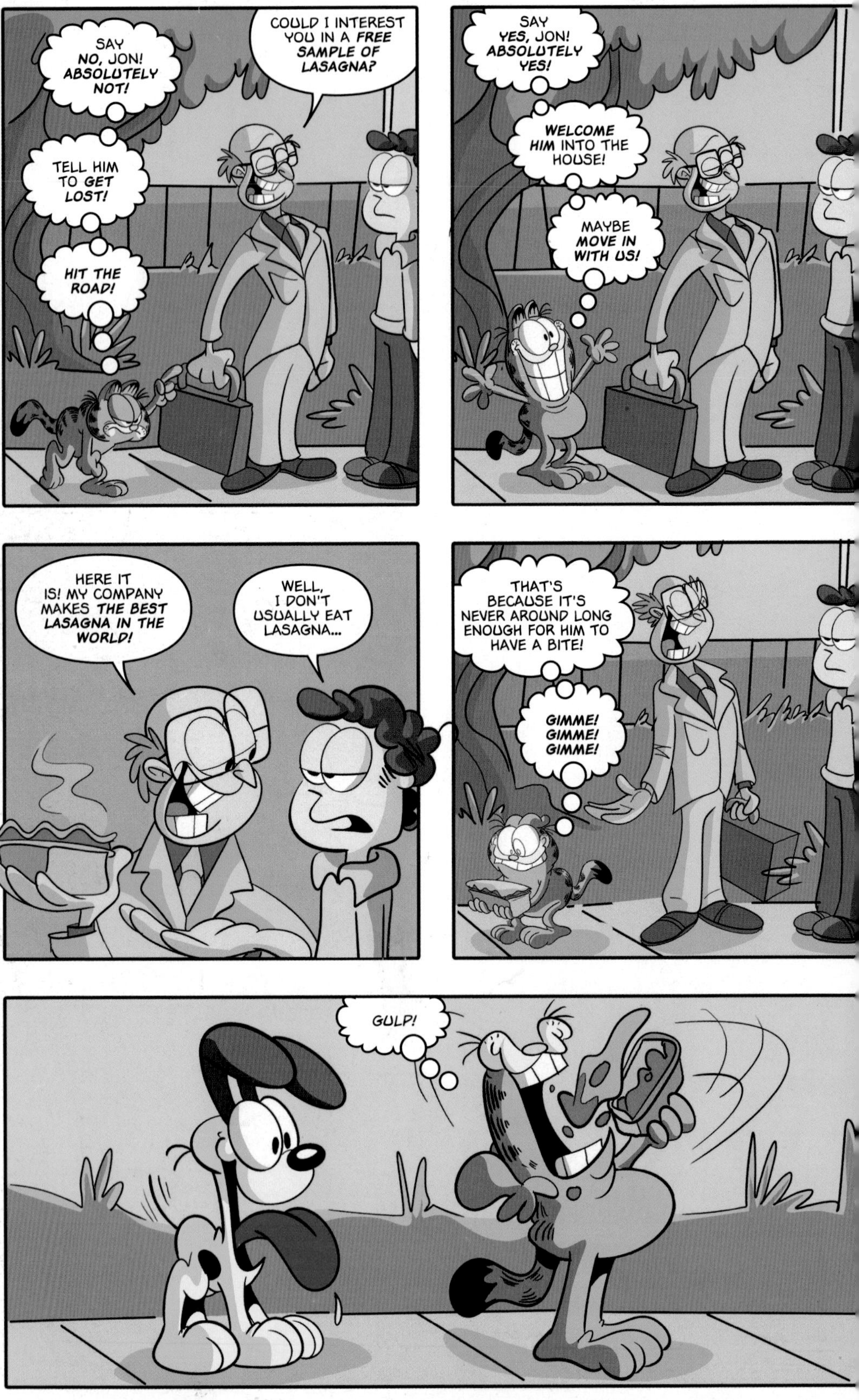
SAY NO, JON! ABSOLUTELY NOT!
TELL HIM TO GET LOST!
HIT THE ROAD!
COULD I INTEREST YOU IN A FREE SAMPLE OF LASAGNA?
SAY YES, JON! ABSOLUTELY YES!
WELCOME HIM INTO THE HOUSE!
MAYBE MOVE IN WITH US!
HERE IT IS! MY COMPANY MAKES THE BEST LASAGNA IN THE WORLD!
WELL, I DON'T USUALLY EAT LASAGNA...
THAT'S BECAUSE IT'S NEVER AROUND LONG ENOUGH FOR HIM TO HAVE A BITE!
GIMME! GIMME! GIMME!
GULP!

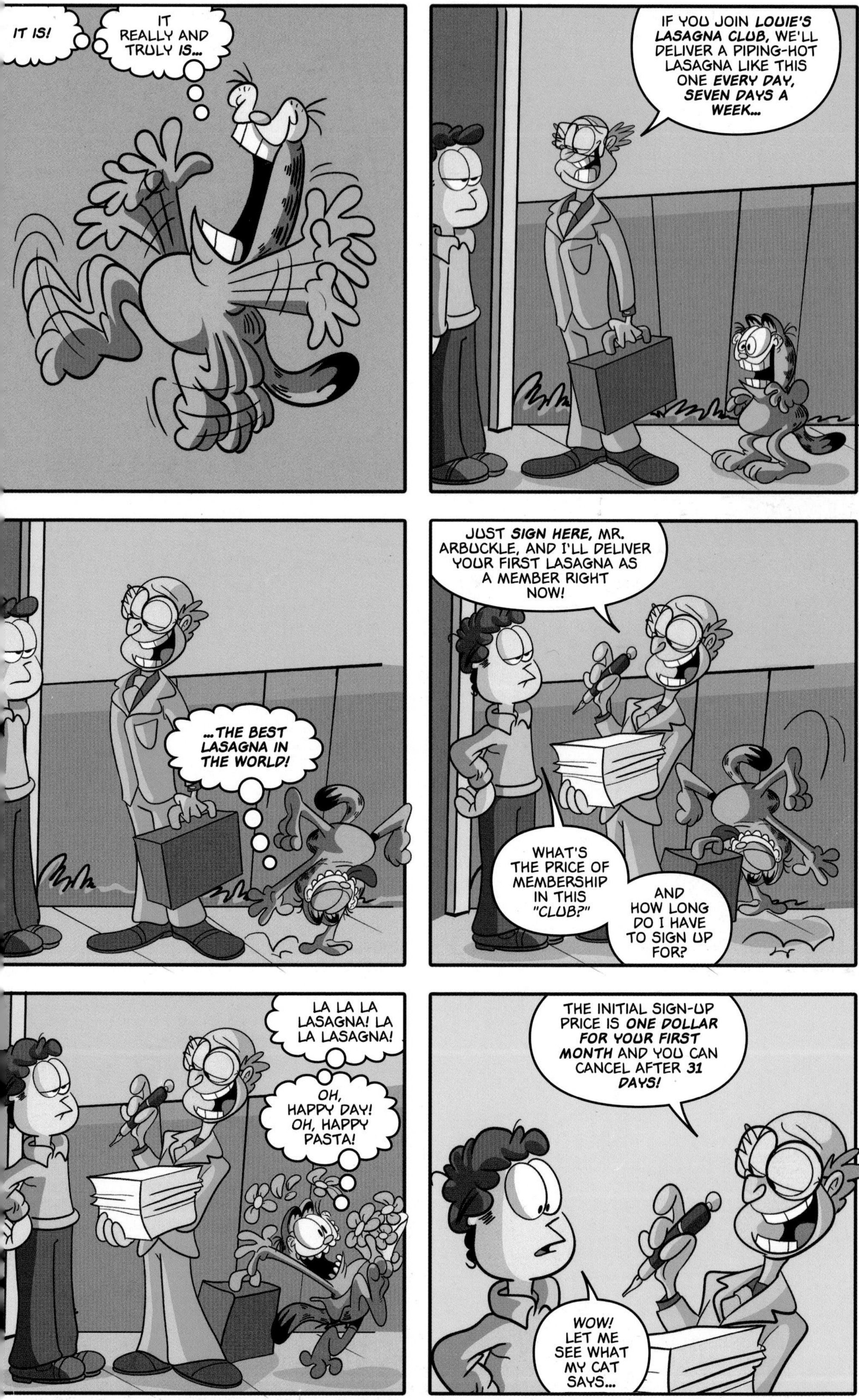
IT IS!
IT REALLY AND TRULY IS...
IF YOU JOIN LOUIE'S LASAGNA CLUB, WE'LL DELIVER A PIPING-HOT LASAGNA LIKE THIS ONE EVERY DAY, SEVEN DAYS A WEEK...
...THE BEST LASAGNA IN THE WORLD!
JUST SIGN HERE, MR. ARBUCKLE, AND I'LL DELIVER YOUR FIRST LASAGNA AS A MEMBER RIGHT NOW!
WHAT'S THE PRICE OF MEMBERSHIP IN THIS "CLUB?"
AND HOW LONG DO I HAVE TO SIGN UP FOR?
LA LA LA LASAGNA! LA LA LASAGNA!
OH, HAPPY DAY! OH, HAPPY PASTA!
THE INITIAL SIGN-UP PRICE IS ONE DOLLAR FOR YOUR FIRST MONTH AND YOU CAN CANCEL AFTER 31 DAYS!
WOW! LET ME SEE WHAT MY CAT SAYS...

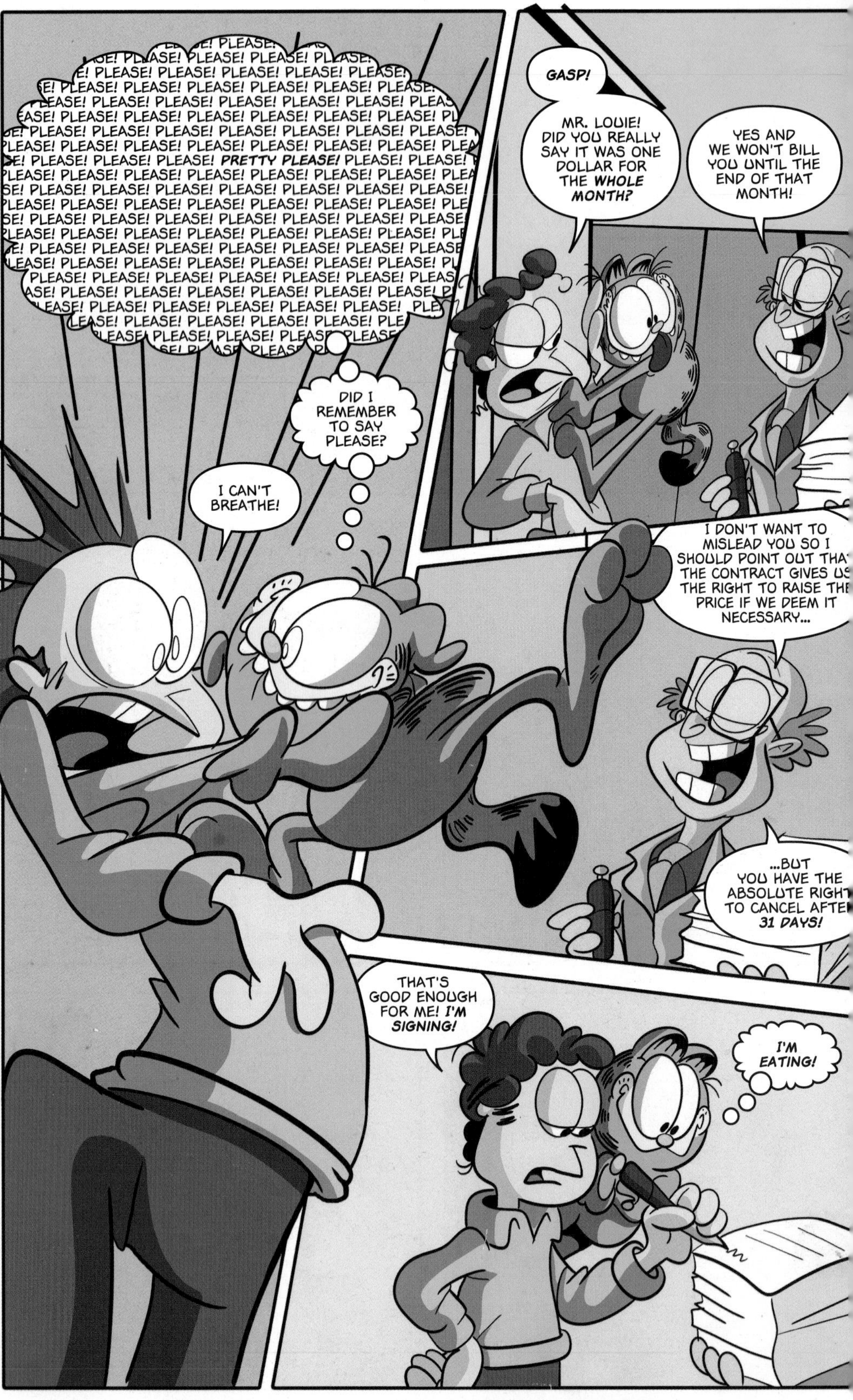

PLEASE! PLEASE! PLEASE! PLEASE! PLEASE! PLEASE! PLEASE! PLEASE!
PLEASE! PLEASE! PLEASE! PLEASE! PRETTY PLEASE! PLEASE! PLEASE!
PLEASE! PLEASE! PLEASE! PLEASE! PLEASE! PLEASE! PLEASE! PLEASE!
I CAN'T BREATHE!
DID I REMEMBER TO SAY PLEASE?
GASP!
MR. LOUIE! DID YOU REALLY SAY IT WAS ONE DOLLAR FOR THE WHOLE MONTH?
YES AND WE WON'T BILL YOU UNTIL THE END OF THAT MONTH!
I DON'T WANT TO MISLEAD YOU SO I SHOULD POINT OUT THAT THE CONTRACT GIVES US THE RIGHT TO RAISE THE PRICE IF WE DEEM IT NECESSARY...
...BUT YOU HAVE THE ABSOLUTE RIGHT TO CANCEL AFTER 31 DAYS!
THAT'S GOOD ENOUGH FOR ME! I'M SIGNING!
I'M EATING!

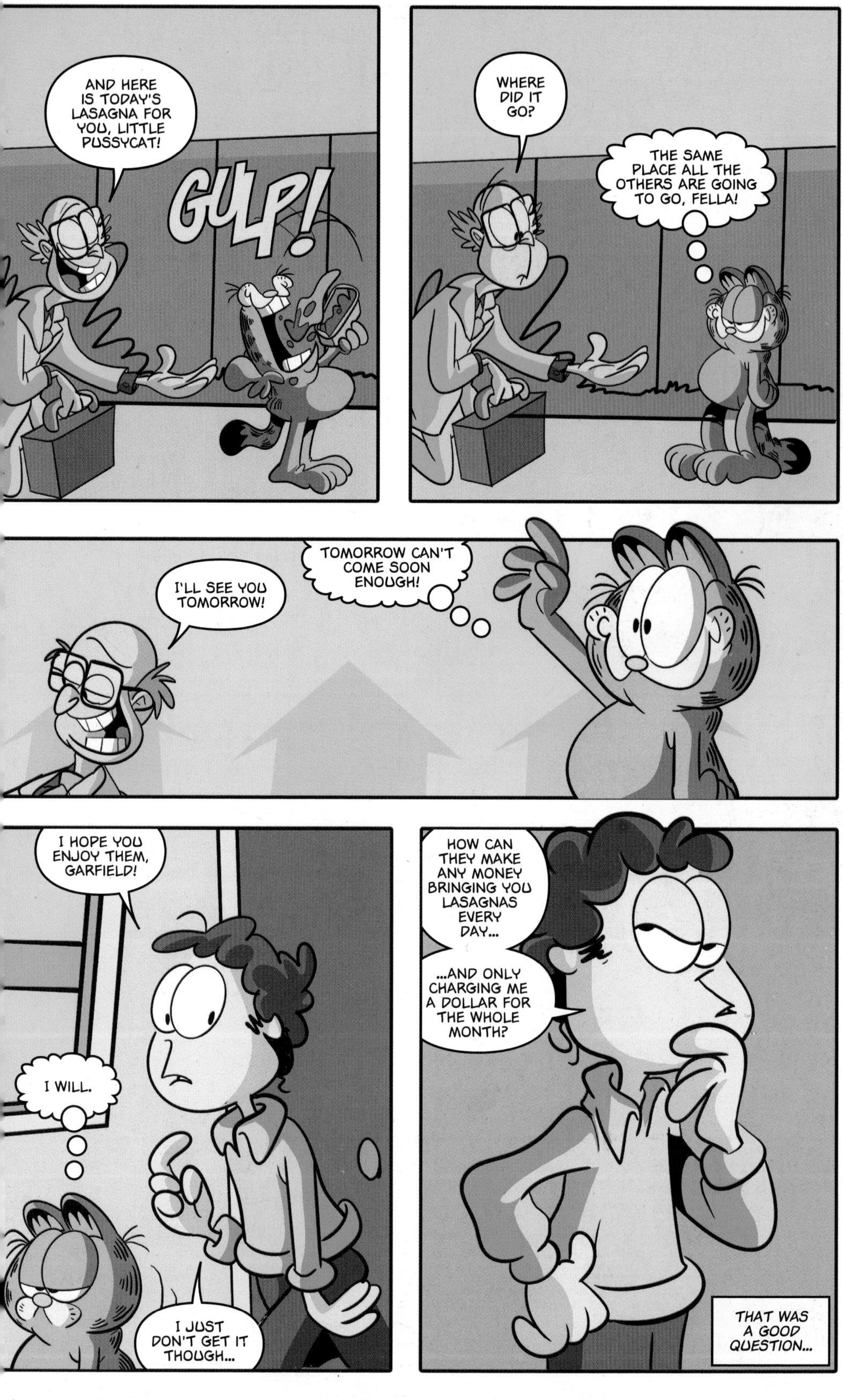
AND HERE IS TODAY'S LASAGNA FOR YOU, LITTLE PUSSYCAT!
GULP!
WHERE DID IT GO?
THE SAME PLACE ALL THE OTHERS ARE GOING TO GO, FELLA!
I'LL SEE YOU TOMORROW!
TOMORROW CAN'T COME SOON ENOUGH!
I HOPE YOU ENJOY THEM, GARFIELD!
I WILL.
I JUST DON'T GET IT THOUGH...
HOW CAN THEY MAKE ANY MONEY BRINGING YOU LASAGNAS EVERY DAY...
...AND ONLY CHARGING ME A DOLLAR FOR THE WHOLE MONTH?
THAT WAS A GOOD QUESTION...

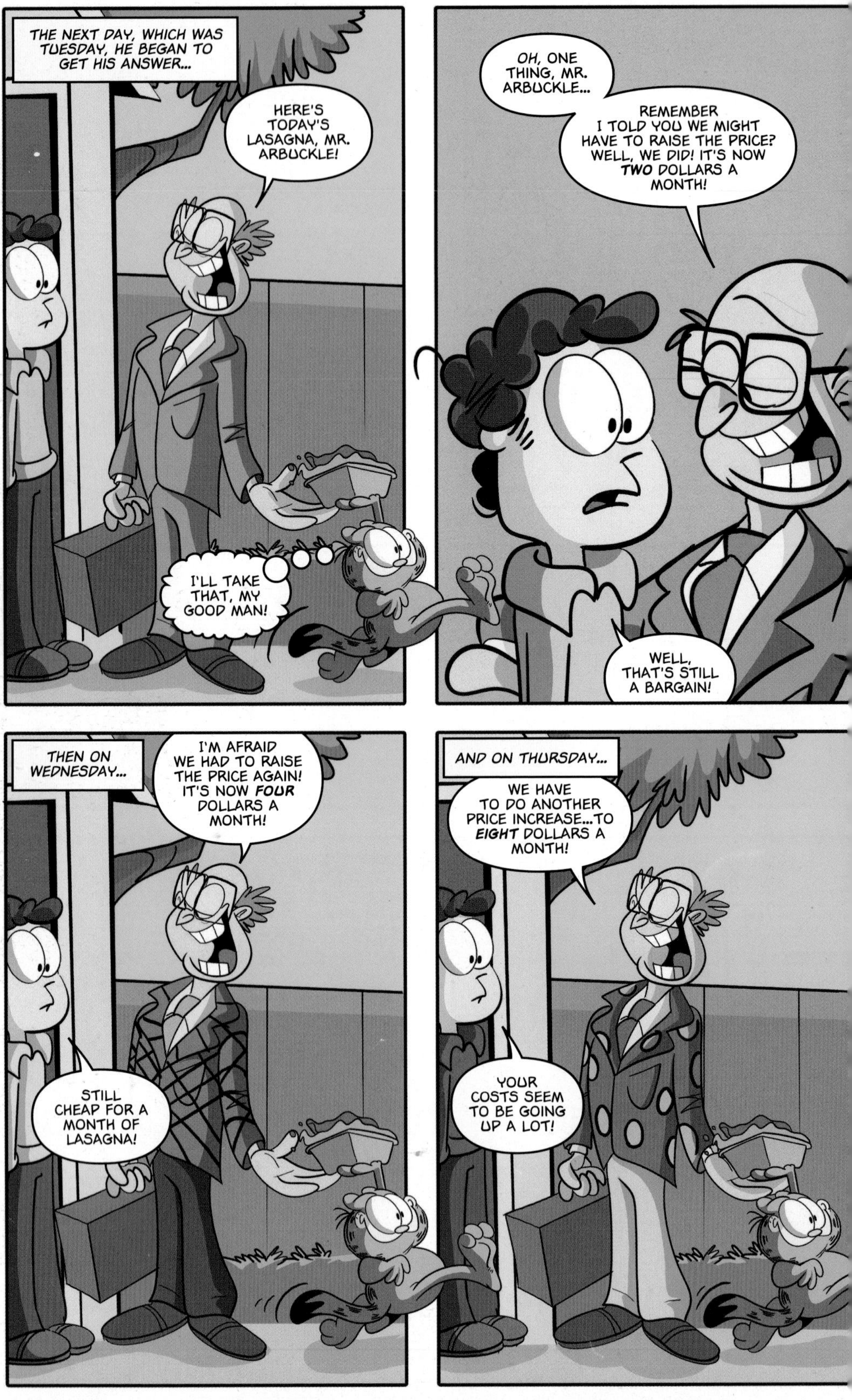
THE NEXT DAY, WHICH WAS TUESDAY, HE BEGAN TO GET HIS ANSWER...
HERE'S TODAY'S LASAGNA, MR. ARBUCKLE!
I'LL TAKE THAT, MY GOOD MAN!
OH, ONE THING, MR. ARBUCKLE...
REMEMBER I TOLD YOU WE MIGHT HAVE TO RAISE THE PRICE? WELL, WE DID! IT'S NOW **TWO** DOLLARS A MONTH!
WELL, THAT'S STILL A BARGAIN!
THEN ON WEDNESDAY...
I'M AFRAID WE HAD TO RAISE THE PRICE AGAIN! IT'S NOW **FOUR** DOLLARS A MONTH!
STILL CHEAP FOR A MONTH OF LASAGNA!
AND ON THURSDAY...
WE HAVE TO DO ANOTHER PRICE INCREASE...TO **EIGHT** DOLLARS A MONTH!
YOUR COSTS SEEM TO BE GOING UP A LOT!

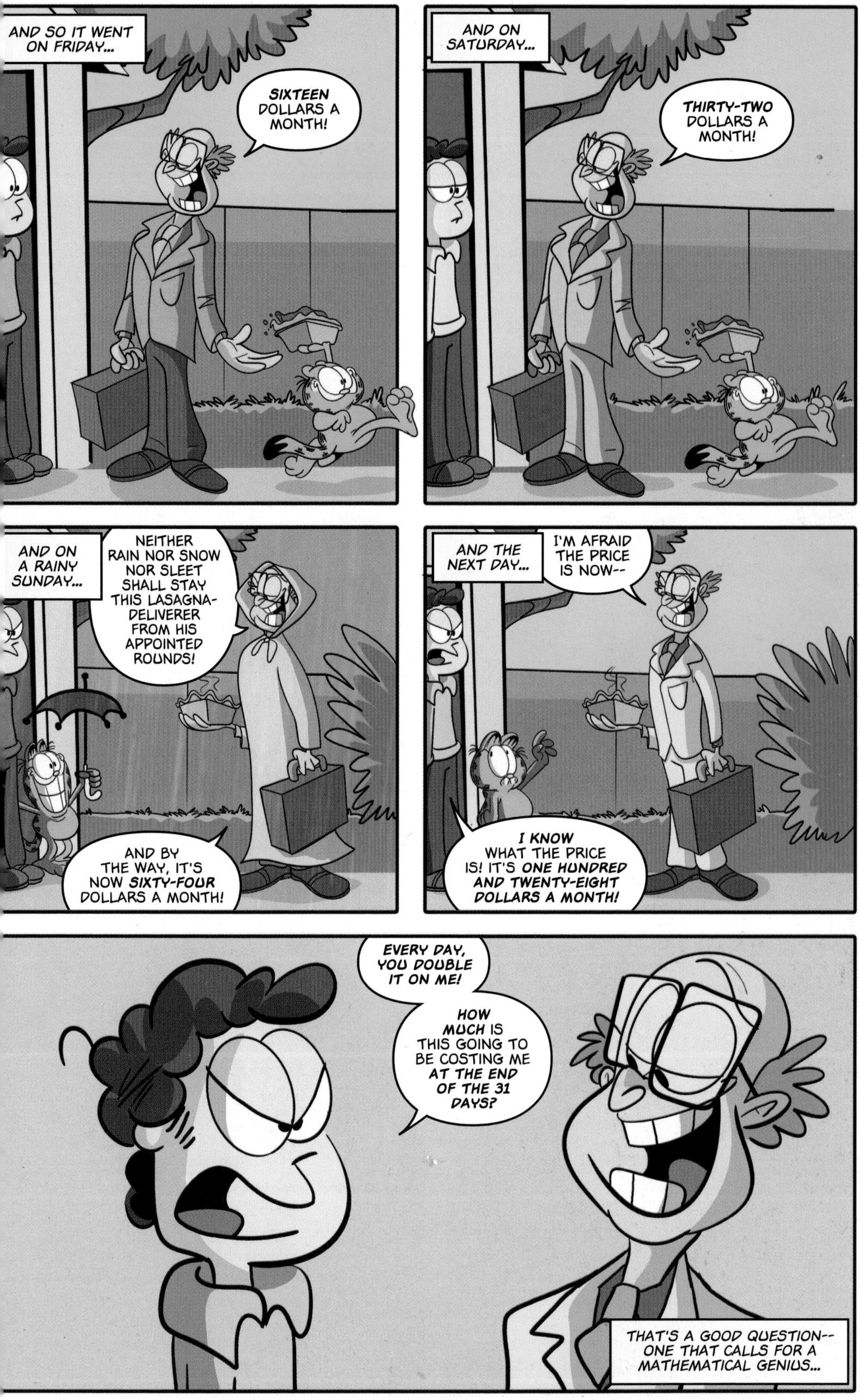
AND SO IT WENT ON FRIDAY...
SIXTEEN DOLLARS A MONTH!
AND ON SATURDAY...
THIRTY-TWO DOLLARS A MONTH!
AND ON A RAINY SUNDAY...
NEITHER RAIN NOR SNOW NOR SLEET SHALL STAY THIS LASAGNA-DELIVERER FROM HIS APPOINTED ROUNDS!
AND BY THE WAY, IT'S NOW SIXTY-FOUR DOLLARS A MONTH!
AND THE NEXT DAY...
I'M AFRAID THE PRICE IS NOW--
I KNOW WHAT THE PRICE IS! IT'S ONE HUNDRED AND TWENTY-EIGHT DOLLARS A MONTH!
EVERY DAY, YOU DOUBLE IT ON ME!
HOW MUCH IS THIS GOING TO BE COSTING ME AT THE END OF THE 31 DAYS?
THAT'S A GOOD QUESTION-- ONE THAT CALLS FOR A MATHEMATICAL GENIUS...

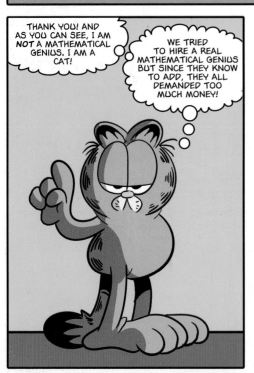

We interrupt this comic book to bring you an educational message from a mathematical genius...
THANK YOU! AND AS YOU CAN SEE, I AM NOT A MATHEMATICAL GENIUS. I AM A CAT!
WE TRIED TO HIRE A REAL MATHEMATICAL GENIUS BUT SINCE THEY KNOW TO ADD, THEY ALL DEMANDED TOO MUCH MONEY!
AND DON'T LET THE WORD "EDUCATIONAL" SCARE YOU OFF TO SOME OTHER COMIC BOOK!
LATER ON, WE'LL HAVE SOMEONE GET HIT WITH A PIE TO MAKE UP FOR IT!
NOW THEN...
AS YOU KNOW IF YOU'RE SMARTER THAN THE FOLKS WHO WRITE AND DRAW THE COMIC, TWO TIMES TWO EQUALS FOUR!
2 X 2 = 4
IF YOU DOUBLE FOUR, IT'S A LARGER INCREASE BECAUSE FOUR IS A HIGHER NUMBER THAN TWO!
2 X 2 = 4
2 X 4 = 8

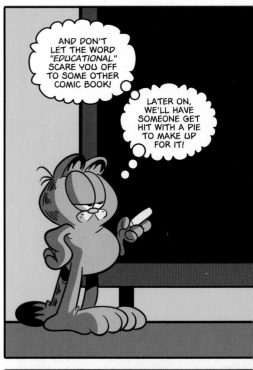

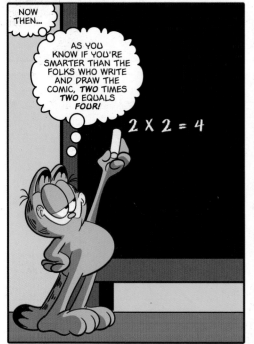

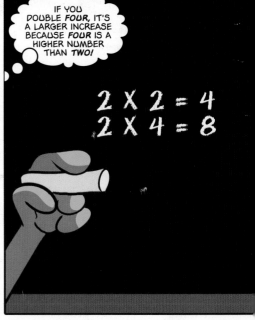

EACH INCREASE GETS
ARGER AND LARGER
BECAUSE THE NUMBER YOU'RE DOUBLING GETS LARGER...
2 X 4 = 8
2 X 8 = 16
2 X 16 = 32
2 X 32 = 64
2 X 64 = 128
SEE? WE'RE ALREADY OVER ONE HUNDRED...
...AND IN THREE MORE STEPS, WE'RE OVER ONE THOUSAND...
2 X 4 = 8
2 X 8 = 16
2 X 16 = 32
2 X 32 = 64
2 X 64 = 128
2 X 128 = 256
2 X 256 = 512
2 X 512 = 1024
2 X 8 = 16
2 X 16 = 32
2 X 32 = 64
2 X 64 = 128
2 X 128 = 256
2 X 256 = 512
2 X 512 = 1024
2 X 1024 = 2048
ONE MORE
TEP AND WE'RE
OVER TWO THOUSAND...
I'M JUST ABOUT OUT OF CHALK BUT YOU CAN TRY THIS YOURSELF AT HOME...
GET OUT A CALCULATOR OR USE THE ONE ON YOUR SMARTPHONE!
2 X 8 = 16
2 X 16 = 32
2 X 32 = 64
2 X 64 = 128
2 X 128 = 256
2 X 256 = 512
2 X 512 = 1024
2 X 1024 = 2048
START BY DOING 2 X 2 AND THEN KEEP HITTING THE EQUAL SIGN (=) AND SEE HOW FAST THE NUMBERS JUMP UP...
2 X 524,288 = 1,048,576
BY THE 21ST STEP, YOU'LL BE OVER A MILLION DOLLARS AND IT DOESN'T STOP THERE!
WE NOW RETURN YOU TO YOUR REGULARLY SCHEDULED COMIC BOOK IN PROGRESS...

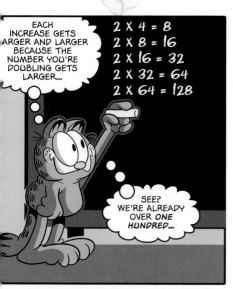

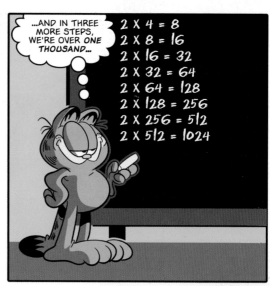

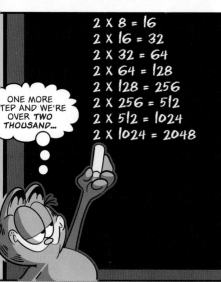

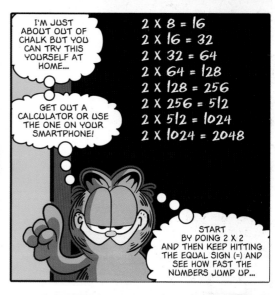

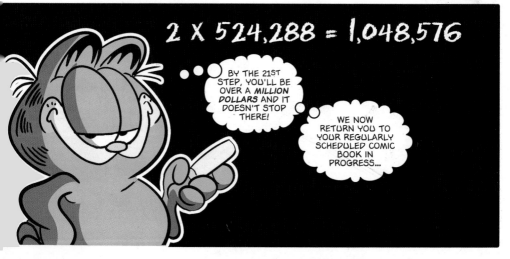

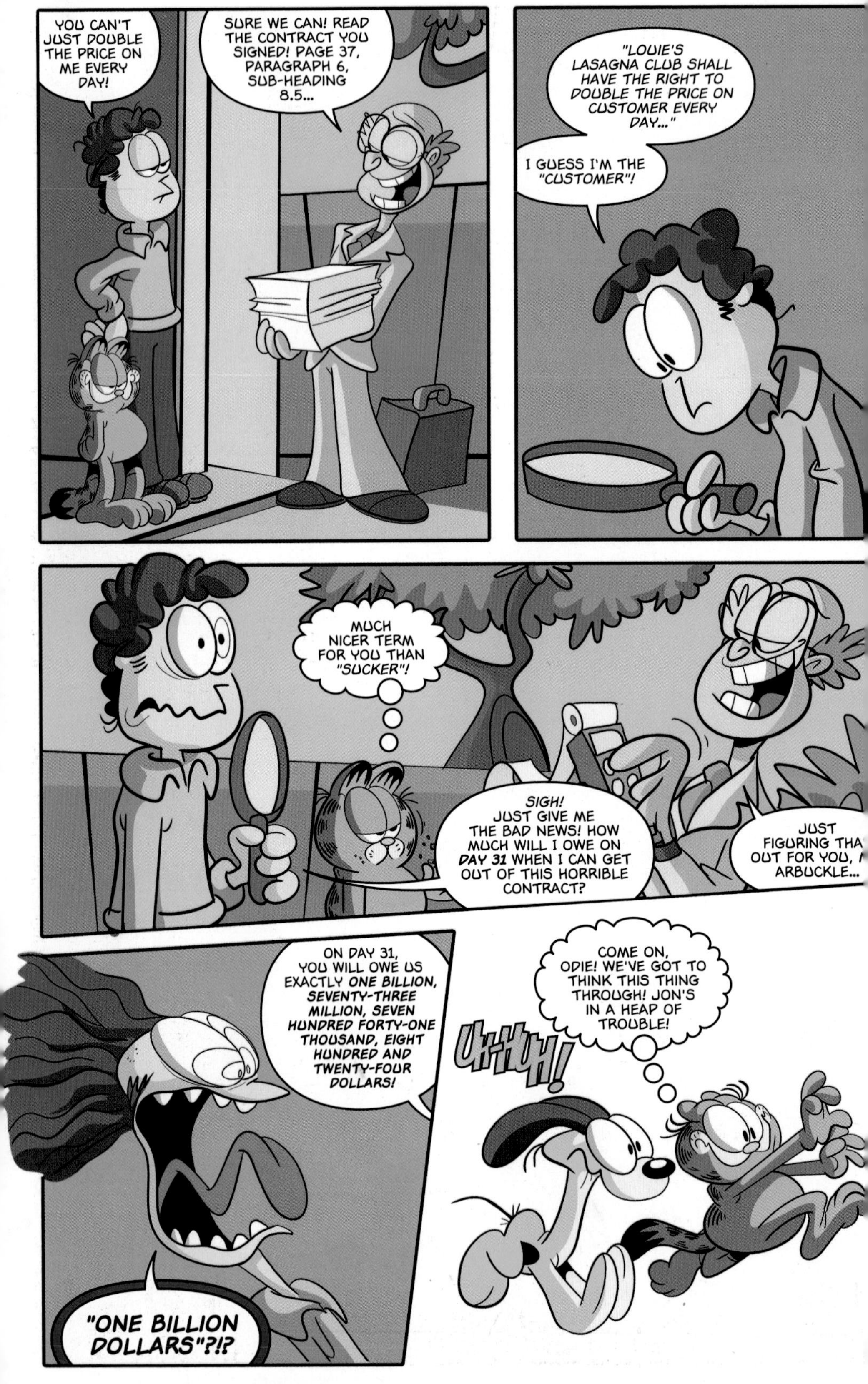
YOU CAN'T JUST DOUBLE THE PRICE ON ME EVERY DAY!
SURE WE CAN! READ THE CONTRACT YOU SIGNED! PAGE 37, PARAGRAPH 6, SUB-HEADING 8.5...
"LOUIE'S LASAGNA CLUB SHALL HAVE THE RIGHT TO DOUBLE THE PRICE ON CUSTOMER EVERY DAY..."
I GUESS I'M THE "CUSTOMER"!
MUCH NICER TERM FOR YOU THAN "SUCKER"!
SIGH! JUST GIVE ME THE BAD NEWS! HOW MUCH WILL I OWE ON DAY 31 WHEN I CAN GET OUT OF THIS HORRIBLE CONTRACT?
JUST FIGURING THA OUT FOR YOU, ARBUCKLE...
ON DAY 31, YOU WILL OWE US EXACTLY ONE BILLION, SEVENTY-THREE MILLION, SEVEN HUNDRED FORTY-ONE THOUSAND, EIGHT HUNDRED AND TWENTY-FOUR DOLLARS!
"ONE BILLION DOLLARS"?!?
COME ON, ODIE! WE'VE GOT TO THINK THIS THING THROUGH! JON'S IN A HEAP OF TROUBLE!
UH-HUH!

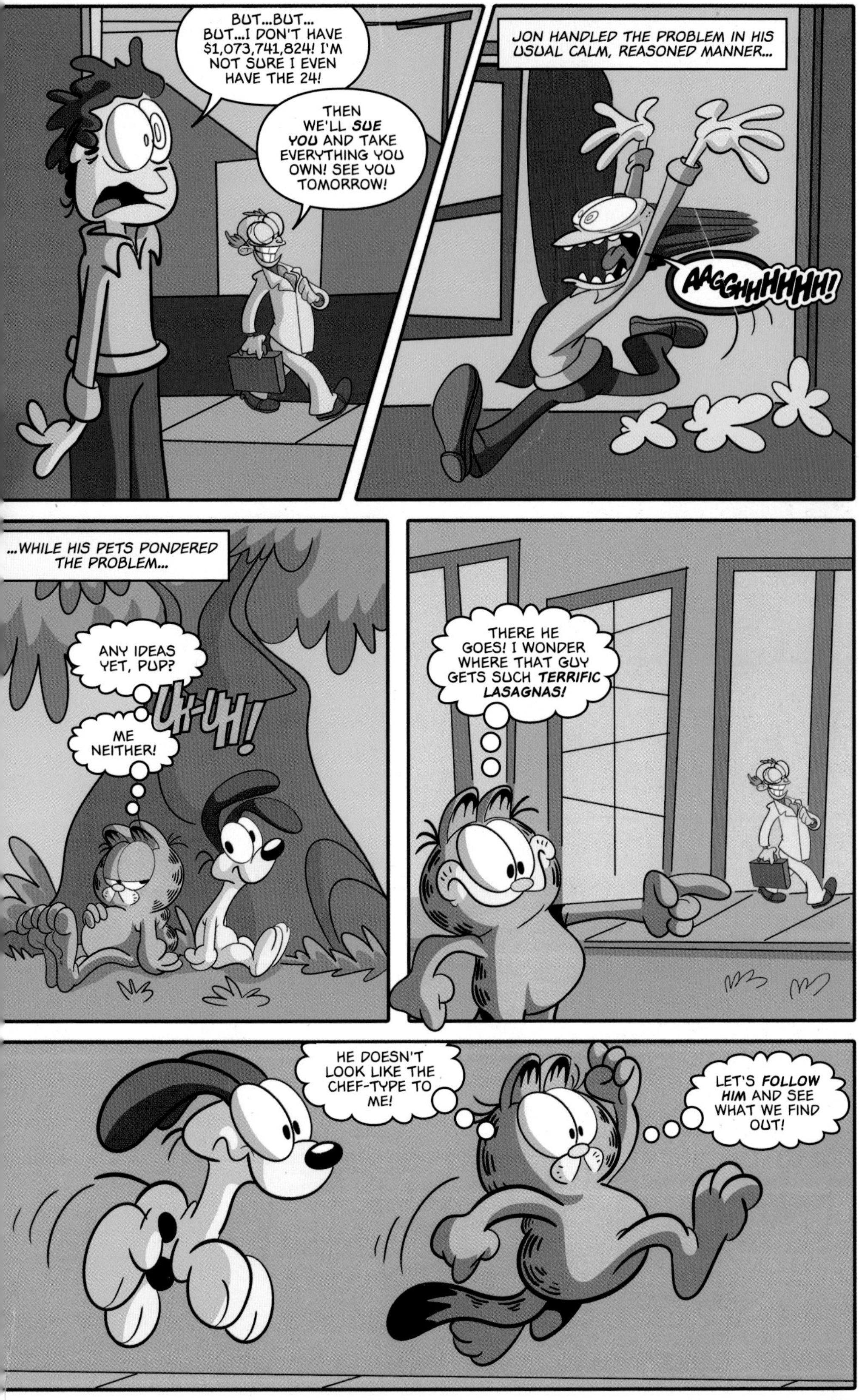
BUT...BUT... BUT...I DON'T HAVE $1,073,741,824! I'M NOT SURE I EVEN HAVE THE 24!
THEN WE'LL SUE YOU AND TAKE EVERYTHING YOU OWN! SEE YOU TOMORROW!
JON HANDLED THE PROBLEM IN HIS USUAL CALM, REASONED MANNER...
AAGGHHHHHH!
...WHILE HIS PETS PONDERED THE PROBLEM...
ANY IDEAS YET, PUP?
UH-UH!
ME NEITHER!
THERE HE GOES! I WONDER WHERE THAT GUY GETS SUCH TERRIFIC LASAGNAS!
HE DOESN'T LOOK LIKE THE CHEF-TYPE TO ME!
LET'S FOLLOW HIM AND SEE WHAT WE FIND OUT!

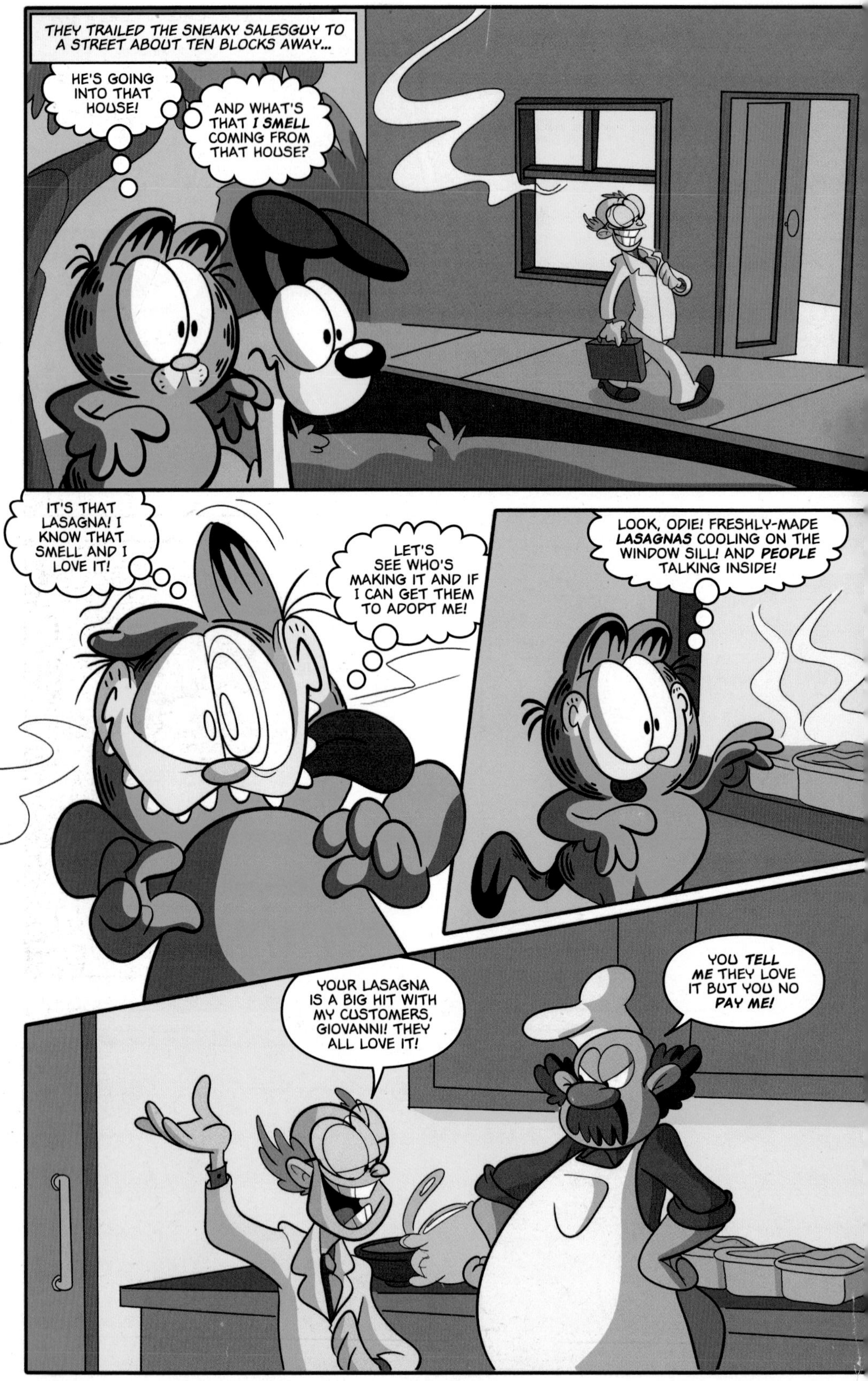
THEY TRAILED THE SNEAKY SALESGUY TO A STREET ABOUT TEN BLOCKS AWAY...
HE'S GOING INTO THAT HOUSE!
AND WHAT'S THAT I SMELL COMING FROM THAT HOUSE?
IT'S THAT LASAGNA! I KNOW THAT SMELL AND I LOVE IT!
LET'S SEE WHO'S MAKING IT AND IF I CAN GET THEM TO ADOPT ME!
LOOK, ODIE! FRESHLY-MADE LASAGNAS COOLING ON THE WINDOW SILL! AND PEOPLE TALKING INSIDE!
YOUR LASAGNA IS A BIG HIT WITH MY CUSTOMERS, GIOVANNI! THEY ALL LOVE IT!
YOU TELL ME THEY LOVE IT BUT YOU NO PAY ME!

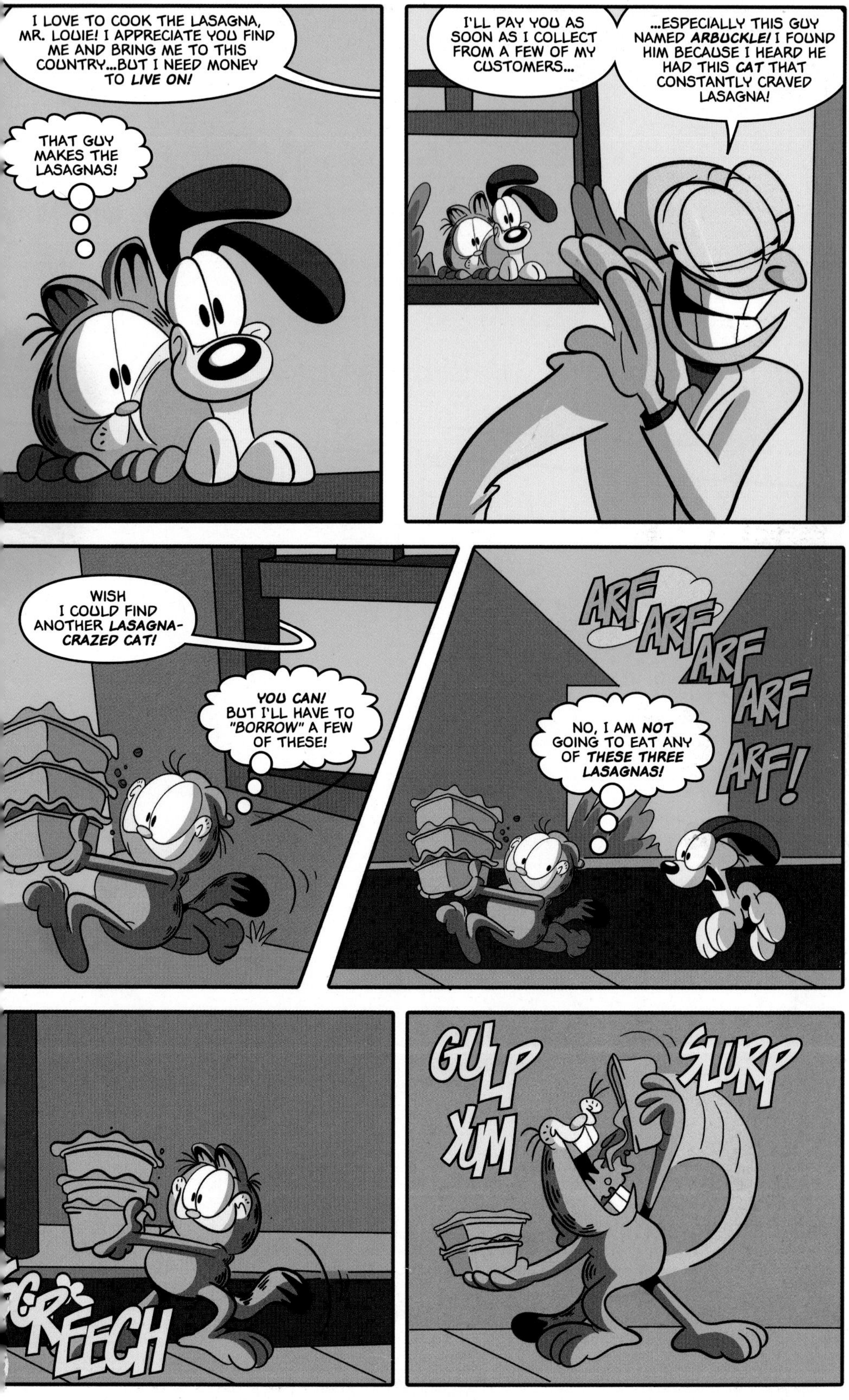
I LOVE TO COOK THE LASAGNA, MR. LOUIE! I APPRECIATE YOU FIND ME AND BRING ME TO THIS COUNTRY...BUT I NEED MONEY TO *LIVE ON!*
THAT GUY MAKES THE LASAGNAS!
I'LL PAY YOU AS SOON AS I COLLECT FROM A FEW OF MY CUSTOMERS...
...ESPECIALLY THIS GUY NAMED *ARBUCKLE!* I FOUND HIM BECAUSE I HEARD HE HAD THIS *CAT* THAT CONSTANTLY CRAVED LASAGNA!
WISH I COULD FIND ANOTHER *LASAGNA-CRAZED CAT!*
YOU CAN! BUT I'LL HAVE TO *"BORROW"* A FEW OF THESE!
ARF ARF ARF ARF ARF!
NO, I AM *NOT* GOING TO EAT ANY OF *THESE THREE LASAGNAS!*
SCREECH
GULP
SLURP
YUM

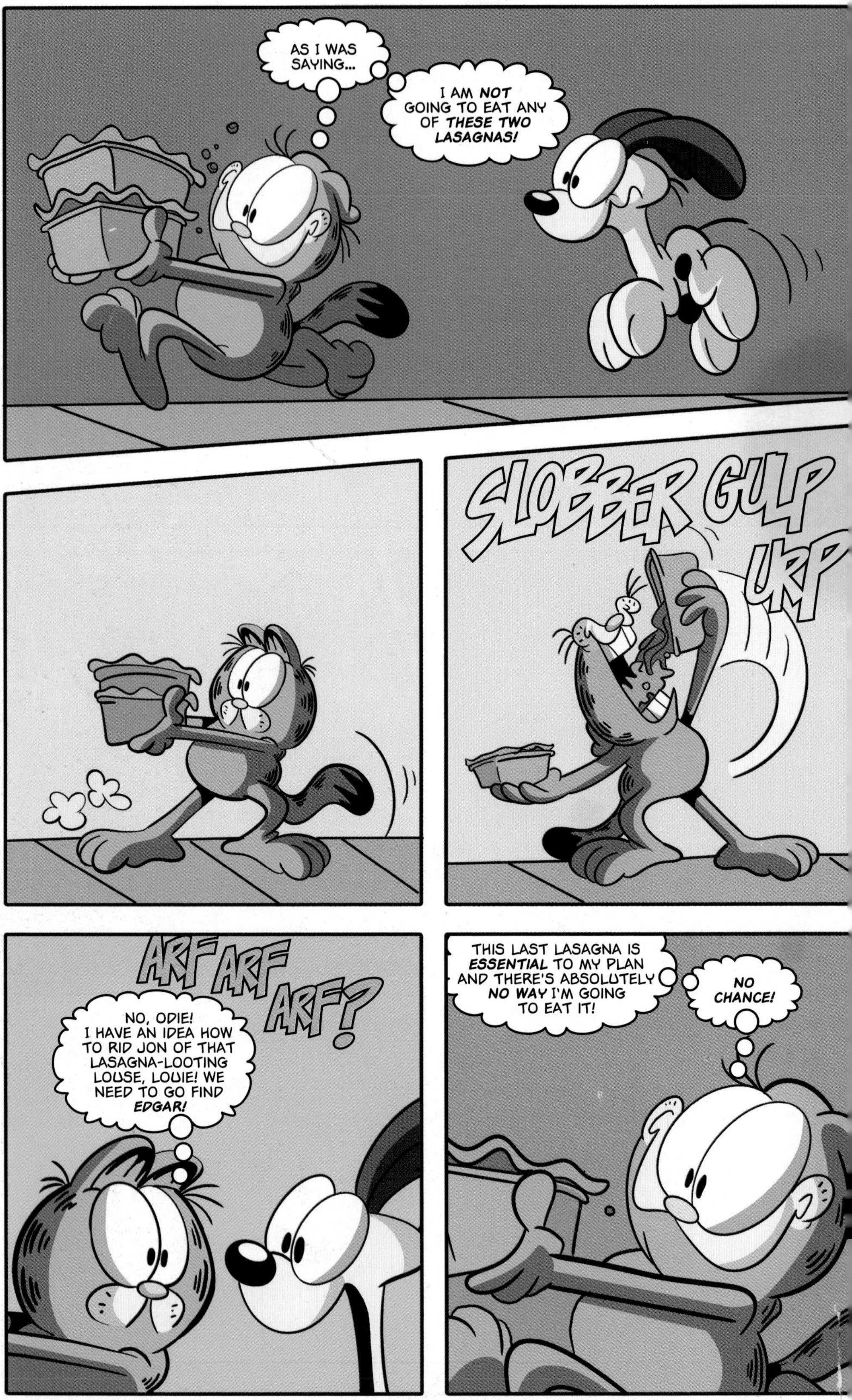
AS I WAS SAYING...
I AM NOT GOING TO EAT ANY OF THESE TWO LASAGNAS!
SLOBBER GULP
URP
ARF ARF ARF?
NO, ODIE! I HAVE AN IDEA HOW TO RID JON OF THAT LASAGNA-LOOTING LOUSE, LOUIE! WE NEED TO GO FIND EDGAR!
THIS LAST LASAGNA IS ESSENTIAL TO MY PLAN AND THERE'S ABSOLUTELY NO WAY I'M GOING TO EAT IT!
NO CHANCE!

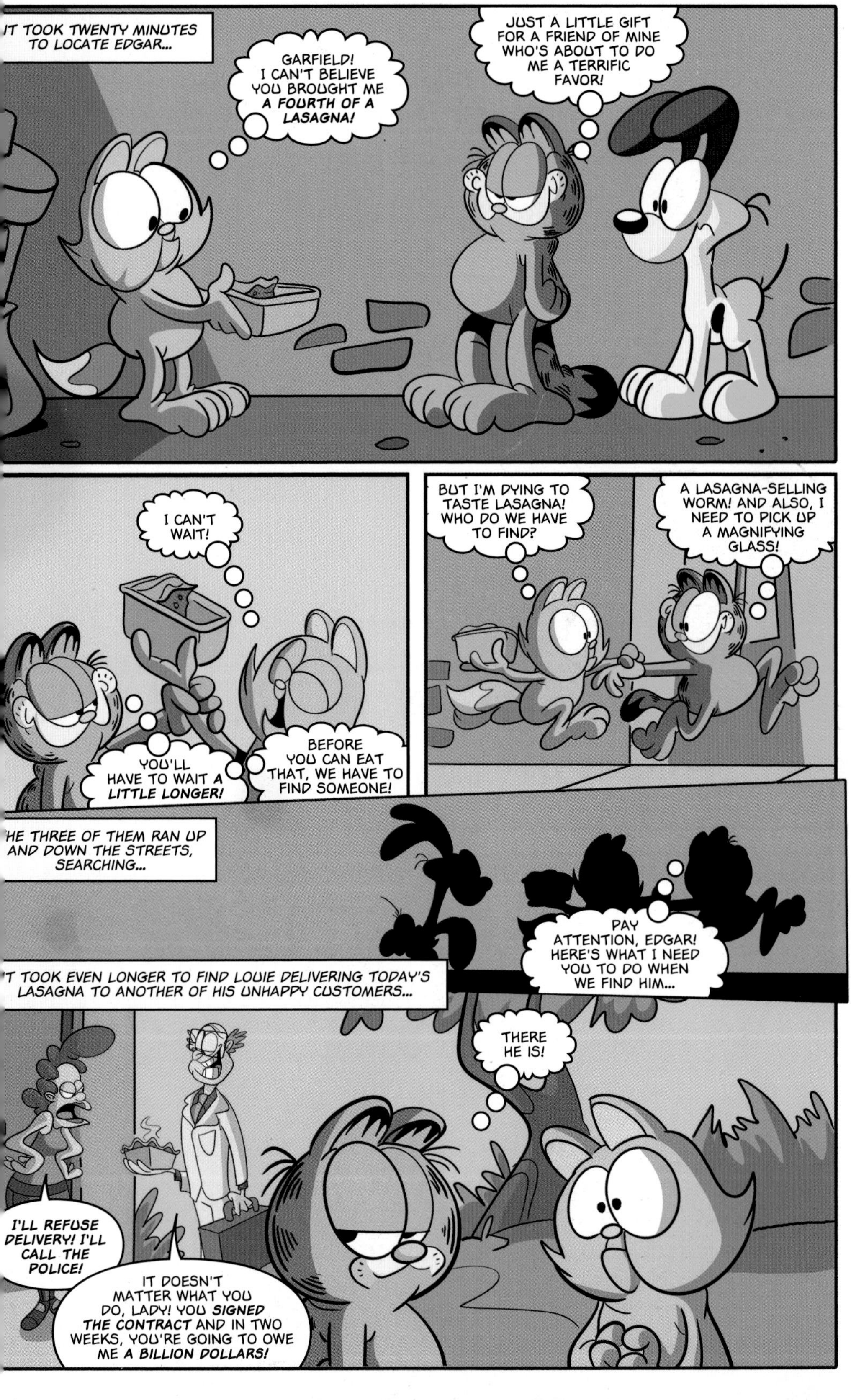

IT TOOK TWENTY MINUTES TO LOCATE EDGAR...
GARFIELD! I CAN'T BELIEVE YOU BROUGHT ME A FOURTH OF A LASAGNA!
JUST A LITTLE GIFT FOR A FRIEND OF MINE WHO'S ABOUT TO DO ME A TERRIFIC FAVOR!
I CAN'T WAIT!
YOU'LL HAVE TO WAIT A LITTLE LONGER!
BEFORE YOU CAN EAT THAT, WE HAVE TO FIND SOMEONE!
BUT I'M DYING TO TASTE LASAGNA! WHO DO WE HAVE TO FIND?
A LASAGNA-SELLING WORM! AND ALSO, I NEED TO PICK UP A MAGNIFYING GLASS!
HE THREE OF THEM RAN UP AND DOWN THE STREETS, SEARCHING...
PAY ATTENTION, EDGAR! HERE'S WHAT I NEED YOU TO DO WHEN WE FIND HIM...
T TOOK EVEN LONGER TO FIND LOUIE DELIVERING TODAY'S LASAGNA TO ANOTHER OF HIS UNHAPPY CUSTOMERS...
THERE HE IS!
I'LL REFUSE DELIVERY! I'LL CALL THE POLICE!
IT DOESN'T MATTER WHAT YOU DO, LADY! YOU SIGNED THE CONTRACT AND IN TWO WEEKS, YOU'RE GOING TO OWE ME A BILLION DOLLARS!

I'LL BE BACK TOMORROW WITH *TOMORROW'S* LASAGNA!

I HATE YOU!

HERE HE COMES! NOW DO WHAT I TOLD YOU TO DO!

GOT IT!

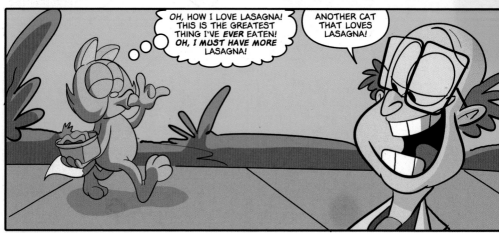

OH, HOW I LOVE LASAGNA! THIS IS THE GREATEST THING I'VE EVER EATEN! OH, I MUST HAVE MORE LASAGNA!

ANOTHER CAT THAT LOVES LASAGNA!

HEY, CAT! WOULD YOU LIKE TO HAVE A *HOT* LASAGNA EVERY DAY?

THEN TAKE ME TO YOUR OWNER!

ANOTHER CUSTOMER WHO'S GOING TO WIND UP OWING ME EVERYTHING THEY HAVE!

PERFECT--!

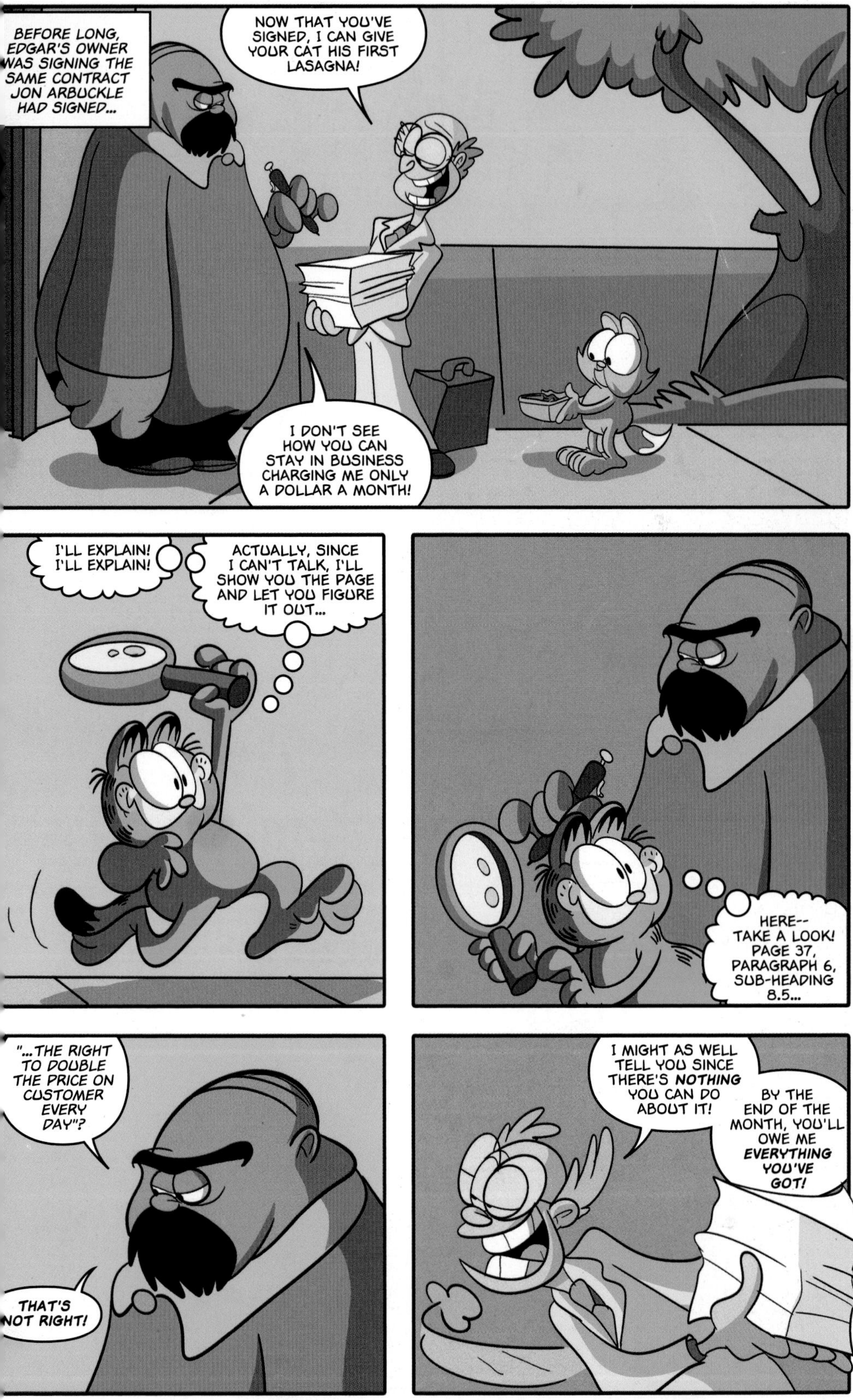
BEFORE LONG, EDGAR'S OWNER WAS SIGNING THE SAME CONTRACT JON ARBUCKLE HAD SIGNED...
NOW THAT YOU'VE SIGNED, I CAN GIVE YOUR CAT HIS FIRST LASAGNA!
I DON'T SEE HOW YOU CAN STAY IN BUSINESS CHARGING ME ONLY A DOLLAR A MONTH!
I'LL EXPLAIN! I'LL EXPLAIN!
ACTUALLY, SINCE I CAN'T TALK, I'LL SHOW YOU THE PAGE AND LET YOU FIGURE IT OUT...
HERE-- TAKE A LOOK! PAGE 37, PARAGRAPH 6, SUB-HEADING 8.5...
"...THE RIGHT TO DOUBLE THE PRICE ON CUSTOMER EVERY DAY"?
THAT'S NOT RIGHT!
I MIGHT AS WELL TELL YOU SINCE THERE'S NOTHING YOU CAN DO ABOUT IT!
BY THE END OF THE MONTH, YOU'LL OWE ME EVERYTHING YOU'VE GOT!

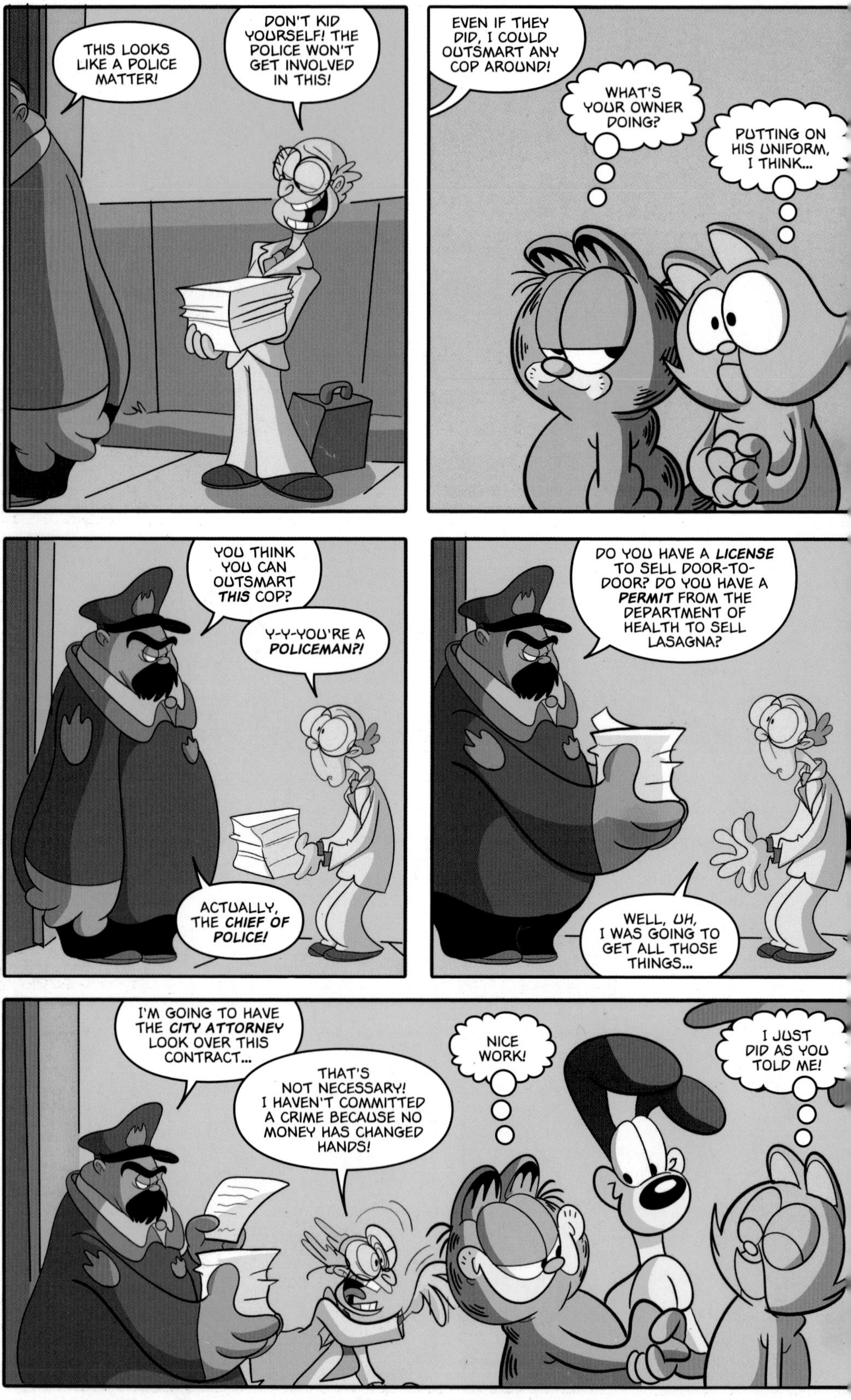
THIS LOOKS LIKE A POLICE MATTER!
DON'T KID YOURSELF! THE POLICE WON'T GET INVOLVED IN THIS!
EVEN IF THEY DID, I COULD OUTSMART ANY COP AROUND!
WHAT'S YOUR OWNER DOING?
PUTTING ON HIS UNIFORM, I THINK...
YOU THINK YOU CAN OUTSMART *THIS* COP?
Y-Y-YOU'RE A *POLICEMAN?!*
ACTUALLY, THE *CHIEF OF POLICE!*
DO YOU HAVE A *LICENSE* TO SELL DOOR-TO-DOOR? DO YOU HAVE A *PERMIT* FROM THE DEPARTMENT OF HEALTH TO SELL LASAGNA?
WELL, UH, I WAS GOING TO GET ALL THOSE THINGS...
I'M GOING TO HAVE THE *CITY ATTORNEY* LOOK OVER THIS CONTRACT...
THAT'S NOT NECESSARY! I HAVEN'T COMMITTED A CRIME BECAUSE NO MONEY HAS CHANGED HANDS!
NICE WORK!
I JUST DID AS YOU TOLD ME!

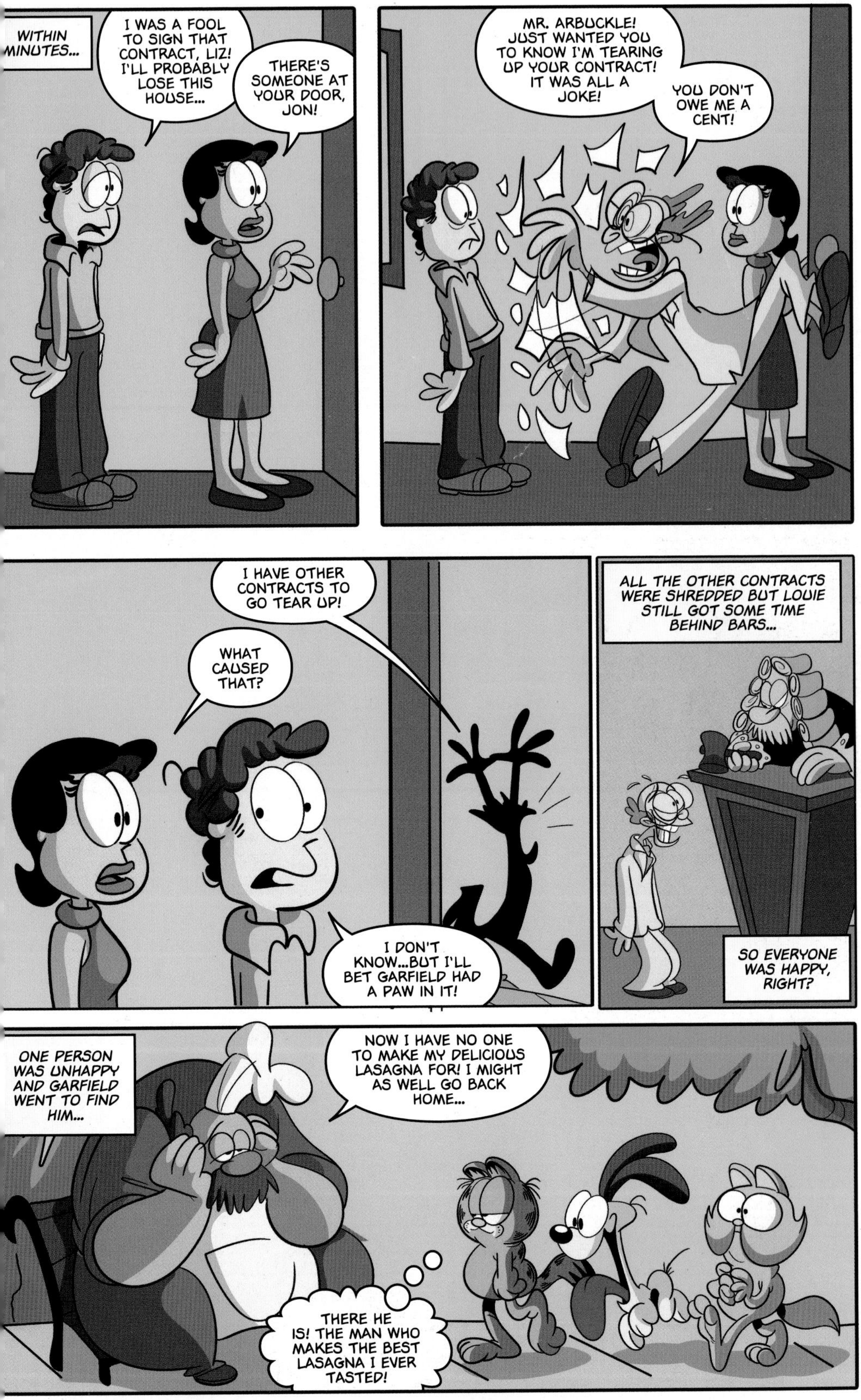
WITHIN MINUTES...
I WAS A FOOL TO SIGN THAT CONTRACT, LIZ! I'LL PROBABLY LOSE THIS HOUSE...
THERE'S SOMEONE AT YOUR DOOR, JON!
MR. ARBUCKLE! JUST WANTED YOU TO KNOW I'M TEARING UP YOUR CONTRACT! IT WAS ALL A JOKE!
YOU DON'T OWE ME A CENT!
I HAVE OTHER CONTRACTS TO GO TEAR UP!
WHAT CAUSED THAT?
I DON'T KNOW...BUT I'LL BET GARFIELD HAD A PAW IN IT!
ALL THE OTHER CONTRACTS WERE SHREDDED BUT LOUIE STILL GOT SOME TIME BEHIND BARS...
SO EVERYONE WAS HAPPY, RIGHT?
ONE PERSON WAS UNHAPPY AND GARFIELD WENT TO FIND HIM...
NOW I HAVE NO ONE TO MAKE MY DELICIOUS LASAGNA FOR! I MIGHT AS WELL GO BACK HOME...
THERE HE IS! THE MAN WHO MAKES THE BEST LASAGNA I EVER TASTED!

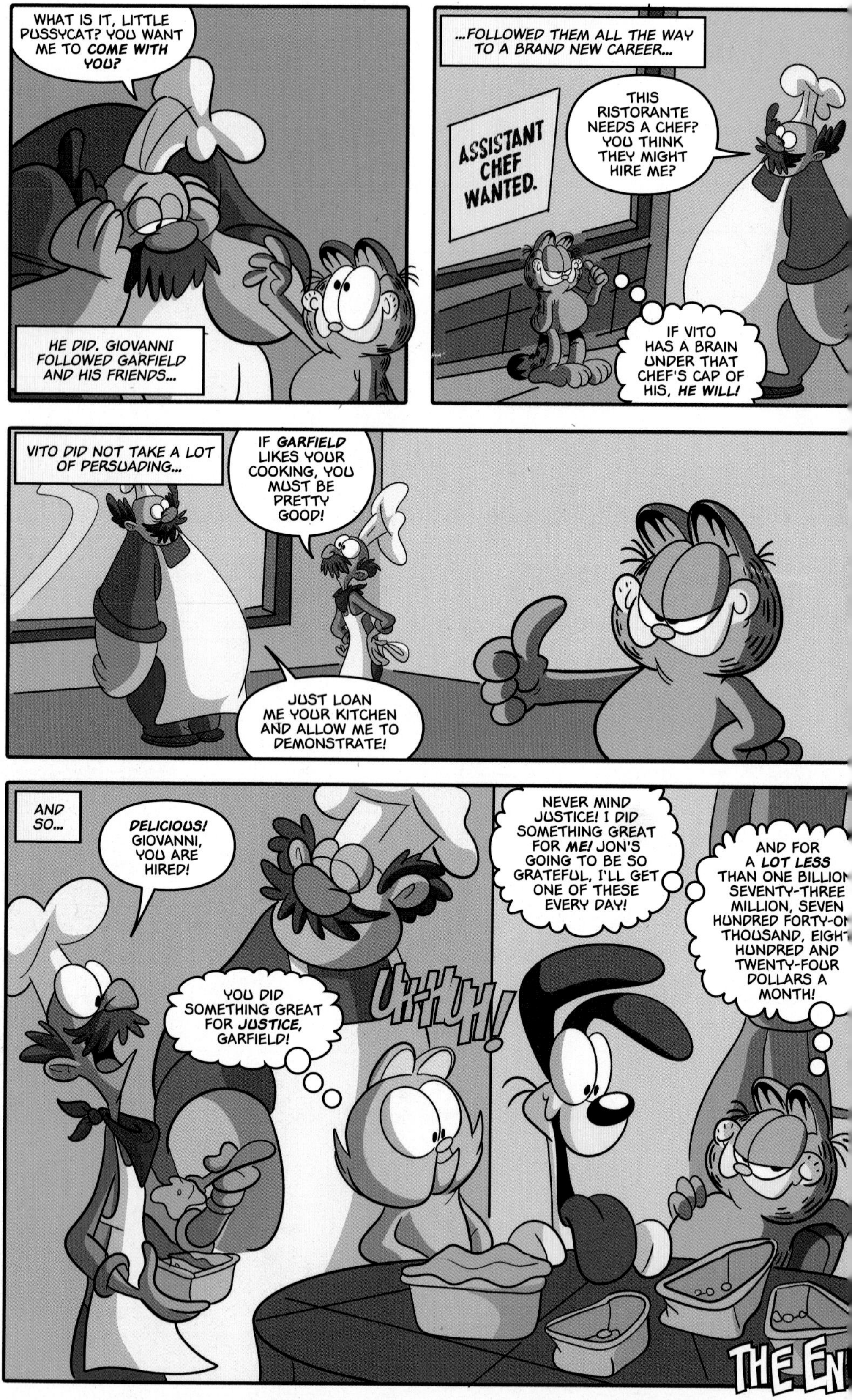
WHAT IS IT, LITTLE PUSSYCAT? YOU WANT ME TO COME WITH YOU?
HE DID. GIOVANNI FOLLOWED GARFIELD AND HIS FRIENDS...
...FOLLOWED THEM ALL THE WAY TO A BRAND NEW CAREER...
ASSISTANT CHEF WANTED.
THIS RISTORANTE NEEDS A CHEF? YOU THINK THEY MIGHT HIRE ME?
IF VITO HAS A BRAIN UNDER THAT CHEF'S CAP OF HIS, HE WILL!
VITO DID NOT TAKE A LOT OF PERSUADING...
IF GARFIELD LIKES YOUR COOKING, YOU MUST BE PRETTY GOOD!
JUST LOAN ME YOUR KITCHEN AND ALLOW ME TO DEMONSTRATE!
AND SO...
DELICIOUS! GIOVANNI, YOU ARE HIRED!
YOU DID SOMETHING GREAT FOR JUSTICE, GARFIELD!
UH-HUH!
NEVER MIND JUSTICE! I DID SOMETHING GREAT FOR ME! JON'S GOING TO BE SO GRATEFUL, I'LL GET ONE OF THESE EVERY DAY!
AND FOR A LOT LESS THAN ONE BILLION SEVENTY-THREE MILLION, SEVEN HUNDRED FORTY-ONE THOUSAND, EIGHT HUNDRED AND TWENTY-FOUR DOLLARS A MONTH!
THE END

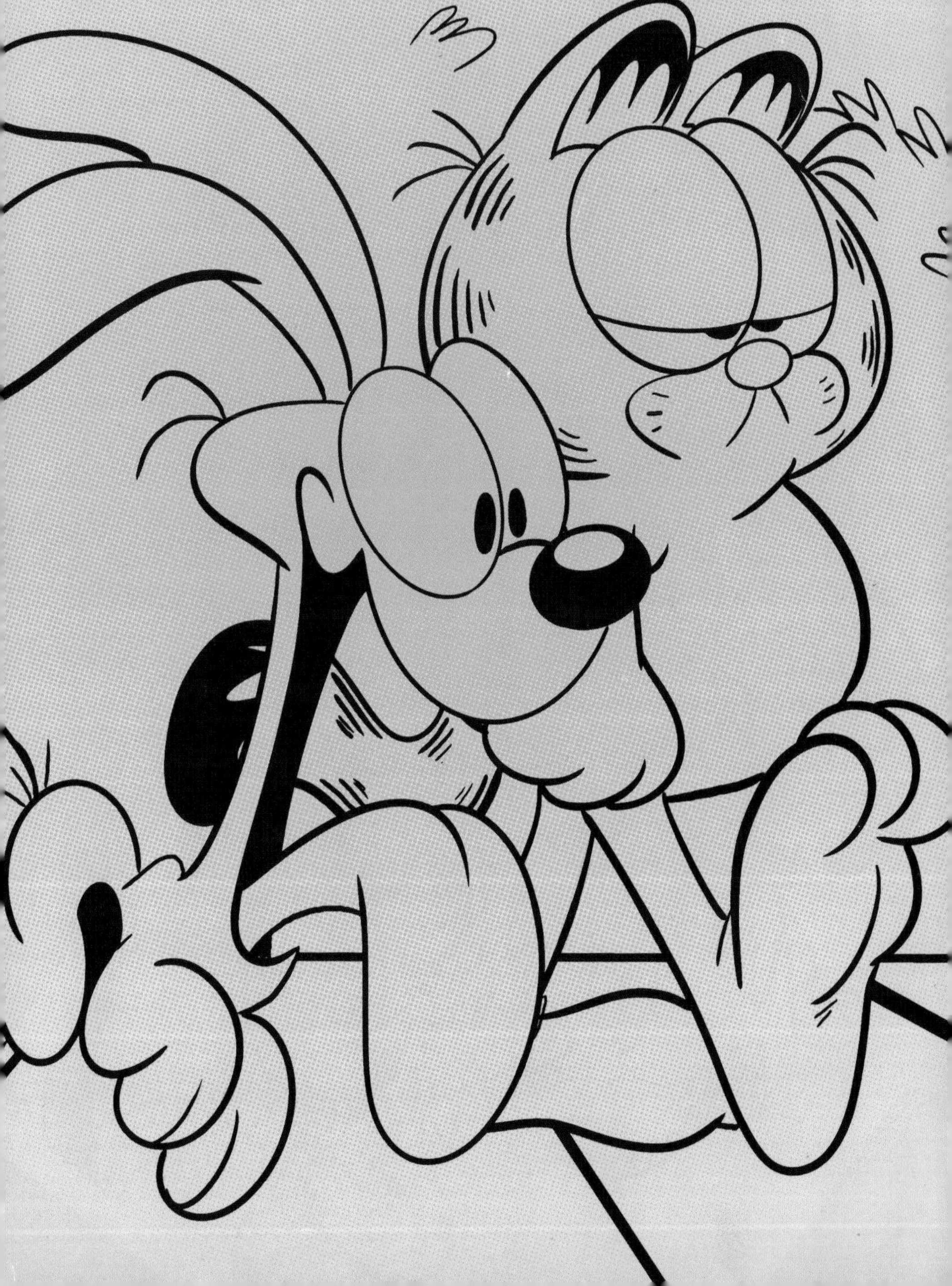

"GARFIELD THE BARBARIAN"

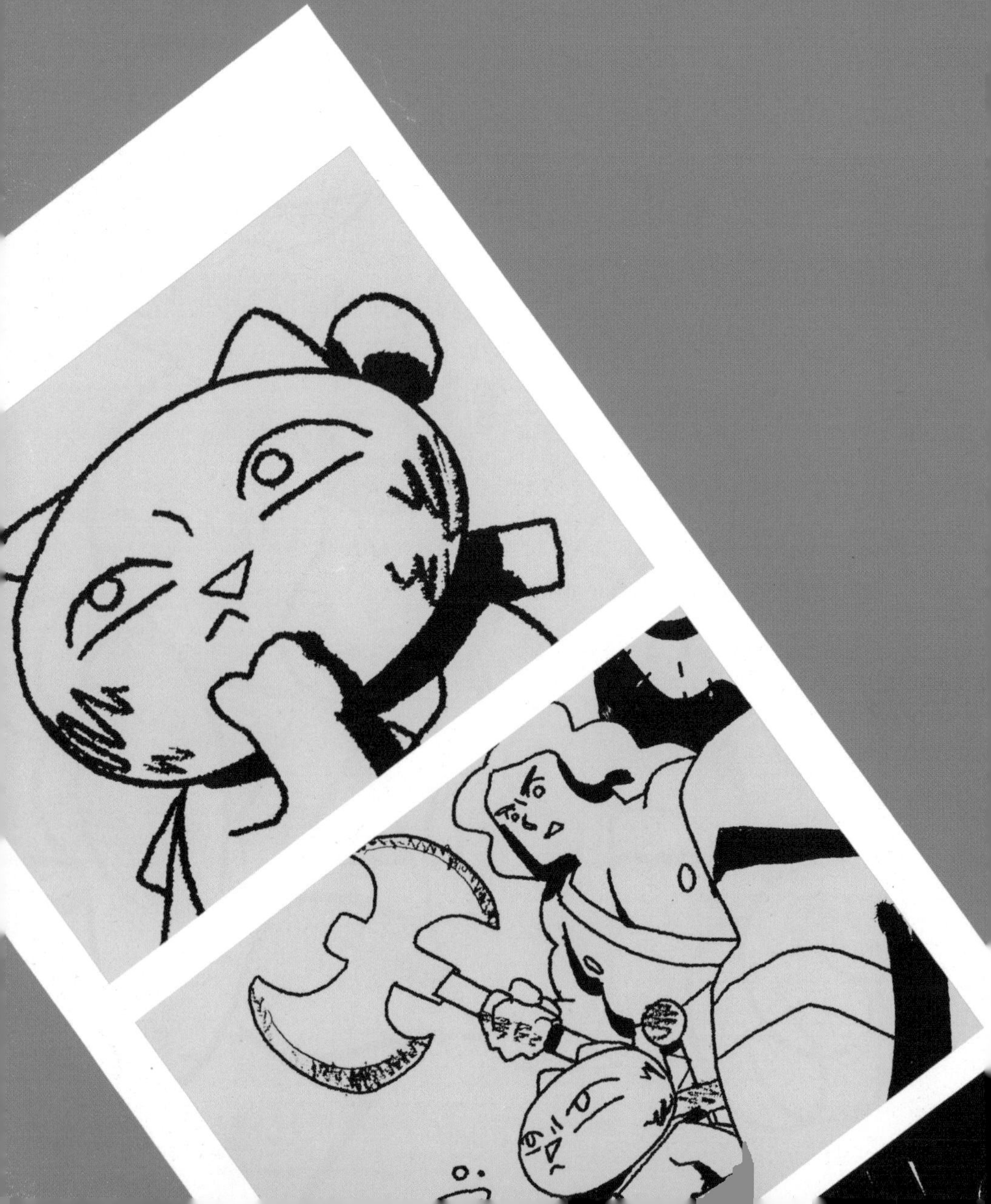

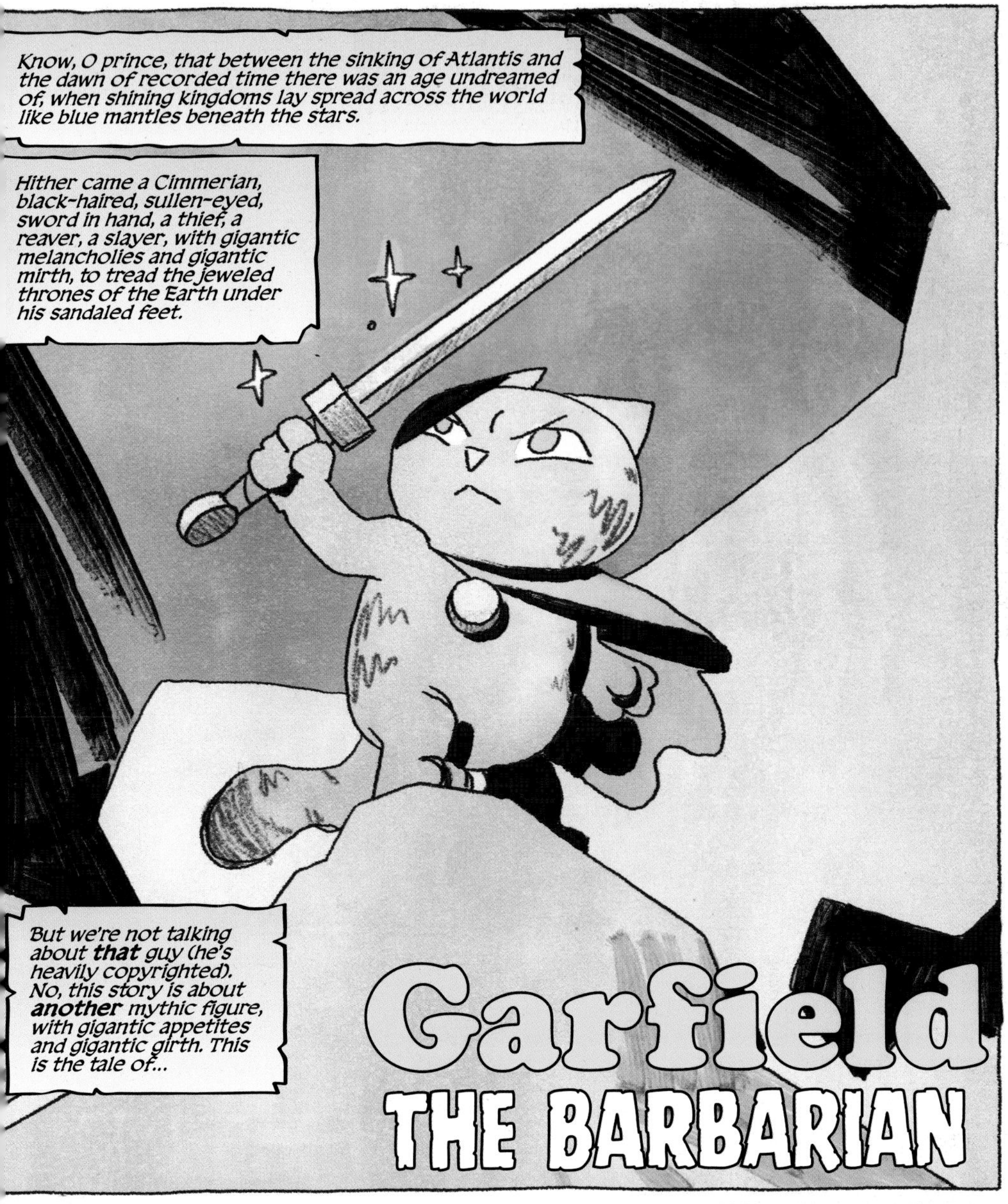
Know, O prince, that between the sinking of Atlantis and the dawn of recorded time there was an age undreamed of, when shining kingdoms lay spread across the world like blue mantles beneath the stars.
Hither came a Cimmerian, black-haired, sullen-eyed, sword in hand, a thief, a reaver, a slayer, with gigantic melancholies and gigantic mirth, to tread the jeweled thrones of the Earth under his sandaled feet.
But we're not talking about **that** guy (he's heavily copyrighted). No, this story is about **another** mythic figure, with gigantic appetites and gigantic girth. This is the tale of...
Garfield
THE BARBARIAN

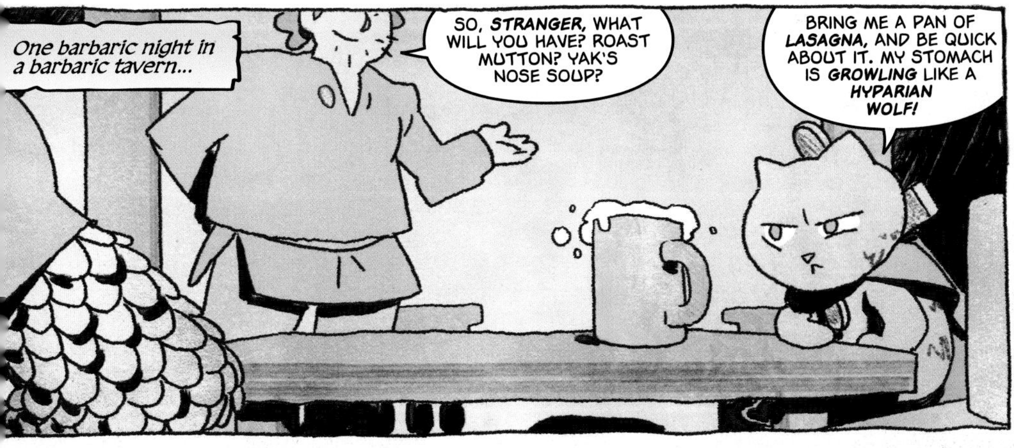
One barbaric night in a barbaric tavern...
SO, **STRANGER**, WHAT WILL YOU HAVE? ROAST MUTTON? YAK'S NOSE SOUP?
BRING ME A PAN OF **LASAGNA**, AND BE QUICK ABOUT IT. MY STOMACH IS **GROWLING** LIKE A **HYPARIAN WOLF!**

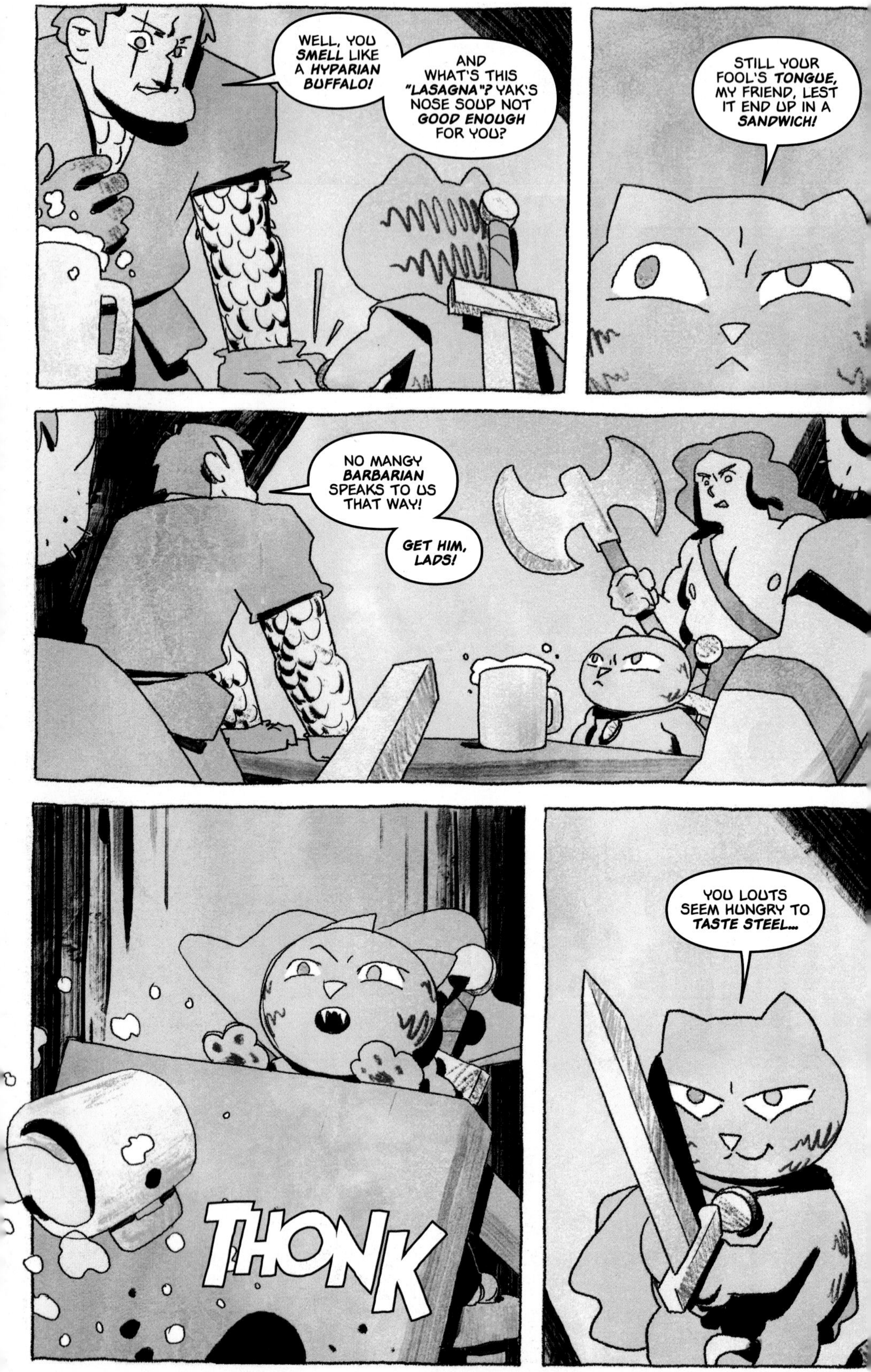
WELL, YOU SMELL LIKE A HYPARIAN BUFFALO!
AND WHAT'S THIS "LASAGNA"? YAK'S NOSE SOUP NOT GOOD ENOUGH FOR YOU?
STILL YOUR FOOL'S TONGUE, MY FRIEND, LEST IT END UP IN A SANDWICH!
NO MANGY BARBARIAN SPEAKS TO US THAT WAY!
GET HIM, LADS!
THONK
YOU LOUTS SEEM HUNGRY TO TASTE STEEL...

WAIT!

WHOSE HAND *STILLS* MY BLADE?!

YOU WIELD THAT SWORD WELL, MY BARBARIAN FRIEND. A PITY TO *STAIN* IT WITH THE *BLOOD* OF *FOOLS.*

YOUR SWORD COULD BE PUT TO MUCH *BETTER*--AND MORE *PROFITABLE*-- USE.

ALL RIGHT, YOU HAVE MY *ATTENTION.* WHAT'S THIS *PROFIT* YOU SPEAK OF?

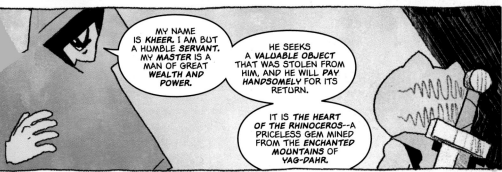

MY NAME IS *KHEER.* I AM BUT A HUMBLE *SERVANT.* MY *MASTER* IS A MAN OF GREAT *WEALTH* AND *POWER.*

HE SEEKS A *VALUABLE* OBJECT THAT WAS STOLEN FROM HIM, AND HE WILL PAY *HANDSOMELY* FOR ITS RETURN.

IT IS *THE HEART OF THE RHINOCEROS*--A PRICELESS GEM MINED FROM THE *ENCHANTED MOUNTAINS* OF YAG-DAHR.

PRICELESS? SO HOW MUCH DO I GET TO *STEAL BACK* THIS SHINY HUNK OF *ROCK?*

THREE HUNDRED PIECES OF SILVER--AND *TWENTY PANS* OF THE PASTA CONCOCTION YOU CALL LASAGNA!

MAKE IT TWENTY-FIVE PANS AND WE HAVE A *DEAL.* I THINK I'LL WORK UP AN *APPETITE* ON THIS QUEST.

HERE IS A *MAP* TO WHERE THE HEART OF THE RHINOCEROS IS BEING HELD.

YOU WILL TRAVEL OVER THE MOUNTAINS OF YAG-DAHR, HOME OF THE *SNOW SERPENTS,* THROUGH THE VALLEY OF THE *FLYING HARPIES,* TO THE *TOWER OF MELBA,* WHERE THE GEM IS *GUARDED* BY A FEROCIOUS CREATURE KNOWN AS *GAK.*

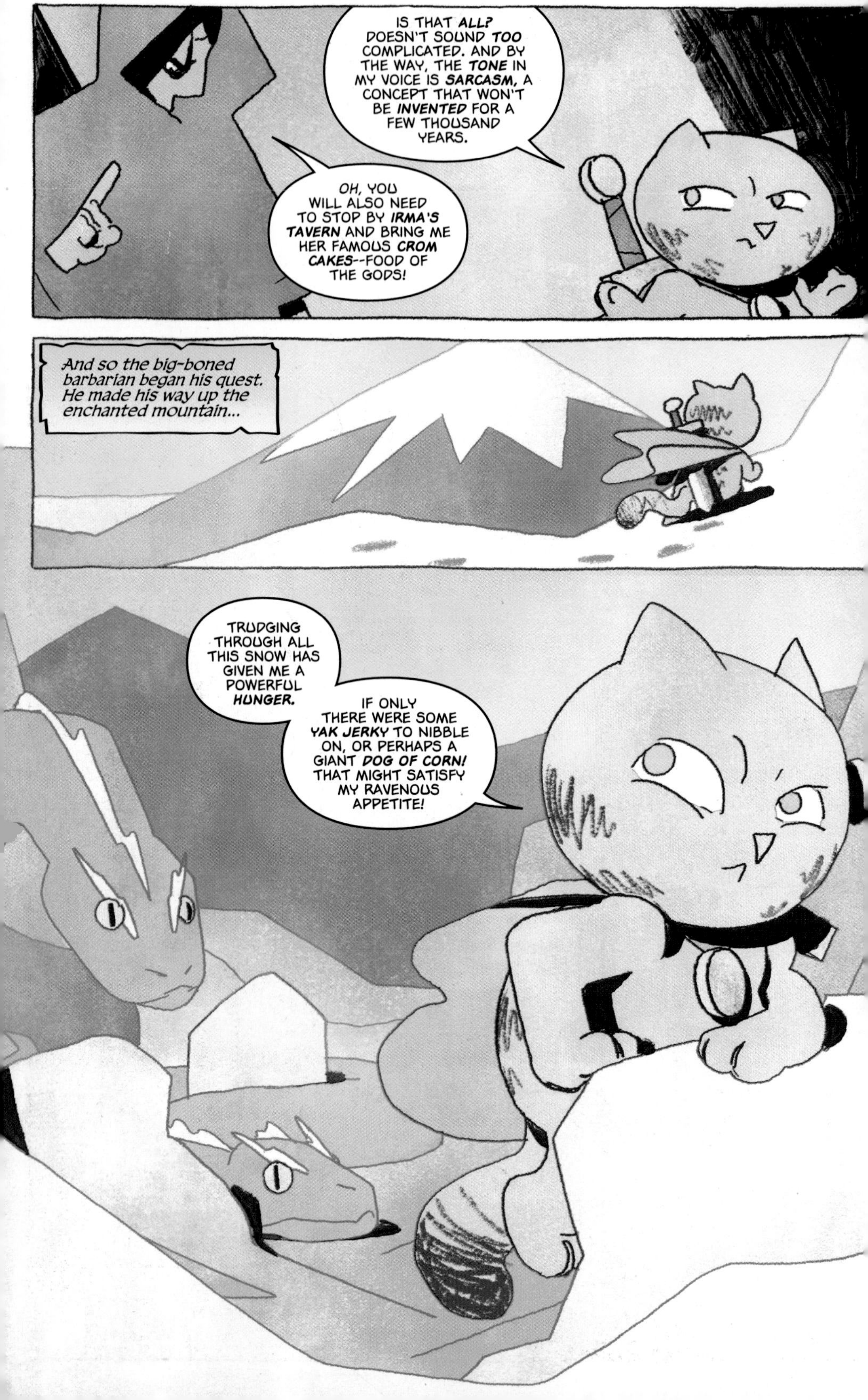
IS THAT ALL? DOESN'T SOUND TOO COMPLICATED. AND BY THE WAY, THE TONE IN MY VOICE IS SARCASM, A CONCEPT THAT WON'T BE INVENTED FOR A FEW THOUSAND YEARS.
OH, YOU WILL ALSO NEED TO STOP BY IRMA'S TAVERN AND BRING ME HER FAMOUS CROM CAKES--FOOD OF THE GODS!
And so the big-boned barbarian began his quest. He made his way up the enchanted mountain...
TRUDGING THROUGH ALL THIS SNOW HAS GIVEN ME A POWERFUL HUNGER.
IF ONLY THERE WERE SOME YAK JERKY TO NIBBLE ON, OR PERHAPS A GIANT DOG OF CORN! THAT MIGHT SATISFY MY RAVENOUS APPETITE!

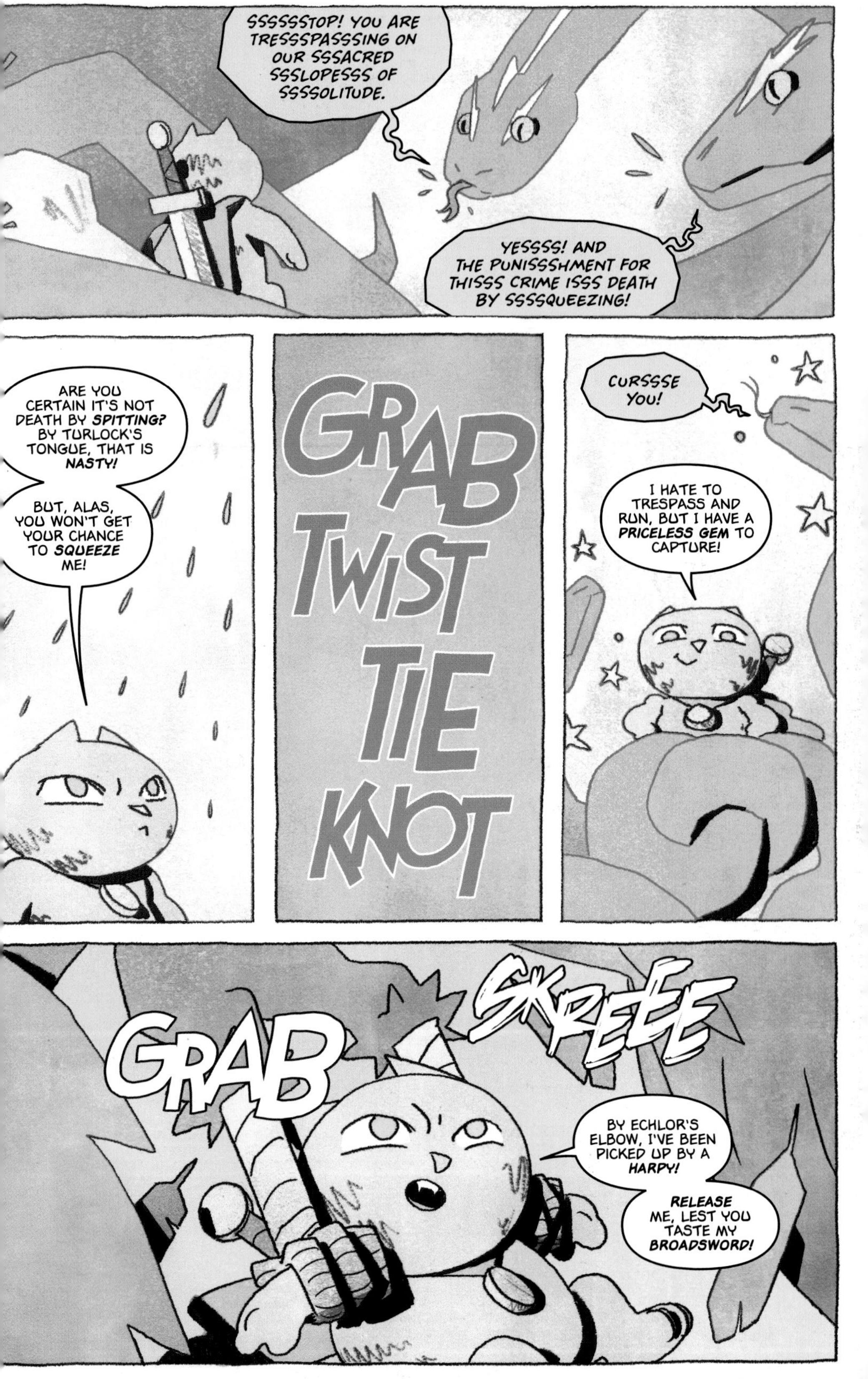
SSSSSSTOP! YOU ARE TRESSSPASSSING ON OUR SSSACRED SSSLOPESSS OF SSSSOLITUDE.
YESSSS! AND THE PUNISSSHMENT FOR THISSS CRIME ISSS DEATH BY SSSSQUEEZING!
ARE YOU CERTAIN IT'S NOT DEATH BY SPITTING? BY TURLOCK'S TONGUE, THAT IS NASTY!
BUT, ALAS, YOU WON'T GET YOUR CHANCE TO SQUEEZE ME!
GRAB TWIST TIE KNOT
CURSSSE YOU!
I HATE TO TRESPASS AND RUN, BUT I HAVE A PRICELESS GEM TO CAPTURE!
GRAB
SKREEE
BY ECHLOR'S ELBOW, I'VE BEEN PICKED UP BY A HARPY!
RELEASE ME, LEST YOU TASTE MY BROADSWORD!

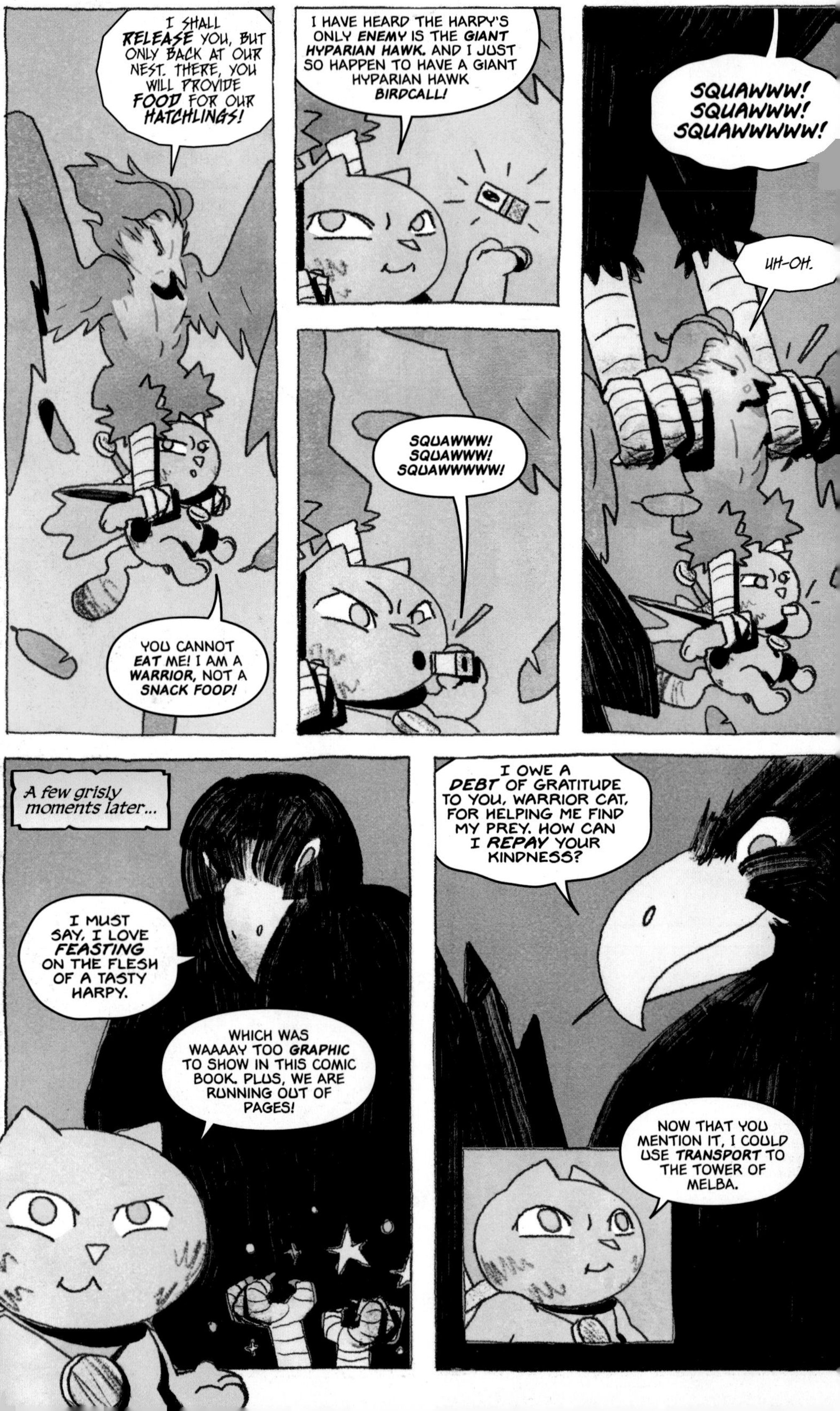

I SHALL RELEASE YOU, BUT ONLY BACK AT OUR NEST. THERE, YOU WILL PROVIDE FOOD FOR OUR HATCHLINGS!
YOU CANNOT EAT ME! I AM A WARRIOR, NOT A SNACK FOOD!
I HAVE HEARD THE HARPY'S ONLY ENEMY IS THE GIANT HYPARIAN HAWK. AND I JUST SO HAPPEN TO HAVE A GIANT HYPARIAN HAWK BIRDCALL!
SQUAWWW! SQUAWWW! SQUAWWWWW!
SQUAWWW! SQUAWWW! SQUAWWWWW!
UH-OH.
A few grisly moments later...
I MUST SAY, I LOVE FEASTING ON THE FLESH OF A TASTY HARPY.
WHICH WAS WAAAAY TOO GRAPHIC TO SHOW IN THIS COMIC BOOK. PLUS, WE ARE RUNNING OUT OF PAGES!
I OWE A DEBT OF GRATITUDE TO YOU, WARRIOR CAT, FOR HELPING ME FIND MY PREY. HOW CAN I REPAY YOUR KINDNESS?
NOW THAT YOU MENTION IT, I COULD USE TRANSPORT TO THE TOWER OF MELBA.

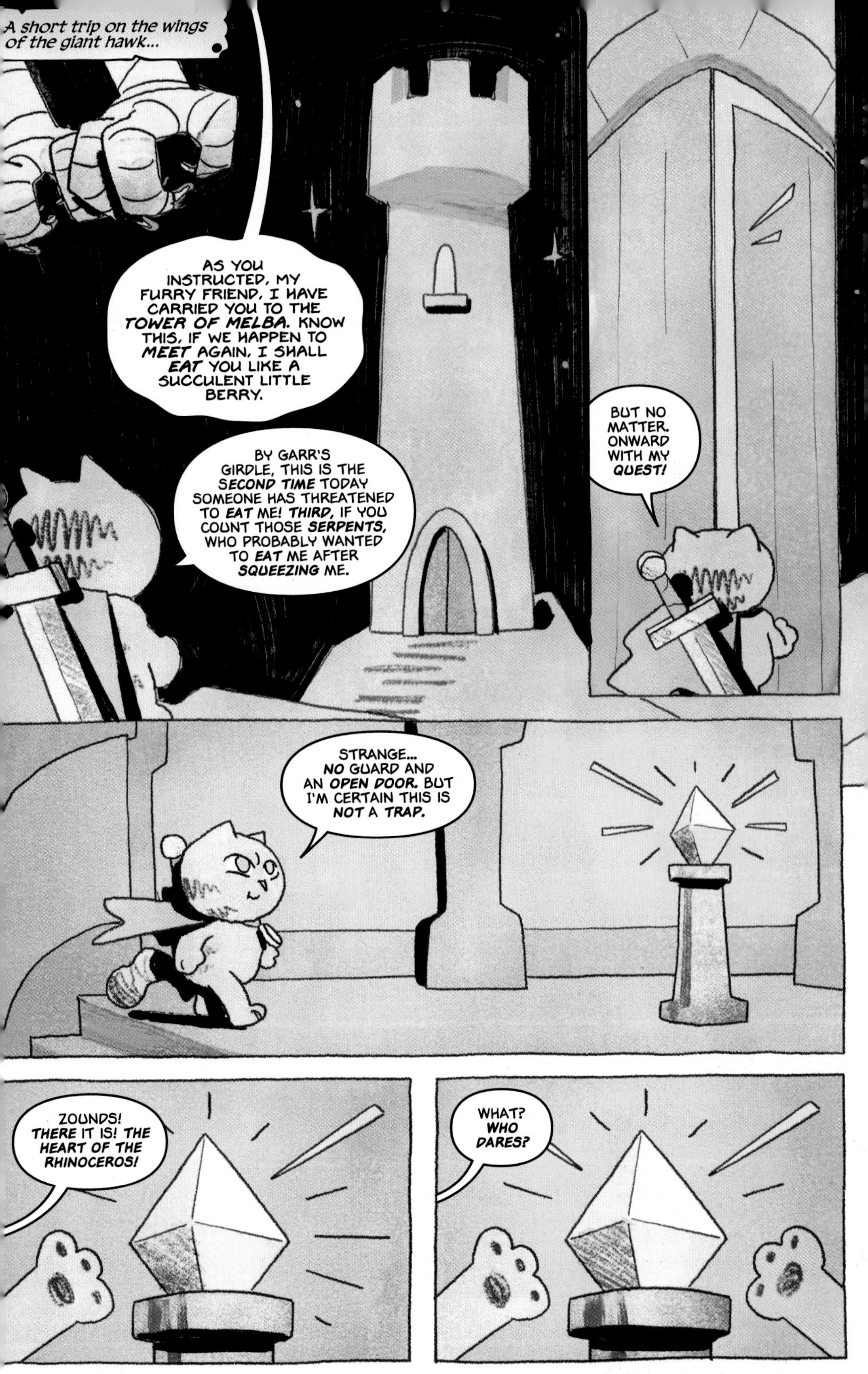
A short trip on the wings of the giant hawk...
AS YOU INSTRUCTED, MY FURRY FRIEND, I HAVE CARRIED YOU TO THE *TOWER OF MELBA*. KNOW THIS, IF WE HAPPEN TO *MEET* AGAIN, I SHALL *EAT* YOU LIKE A SUCCULENT LITTLE BERRY.
BY GARR'S GIRDLE, THIS IS THE *SECOND TIME* TODAY SOMEONE HAS THREATENED TO *EAT* ME! *THIRD*, IF YOU COUNT THOSE *SERPENTS*, WHO PROBABLY WANTED TO *EAT* ME AFTER *SQUEEZING* ME.
BUT NO MATTER. ONWARD WITH MY *QUEST!*
STRANGE... *NO* GUARD AND AN *OPEN DOOR*. BUT I'M CERTAIN THIS IS *NOT* A *TRAP*.
ZOUNDS! *THERE* IT IS! *THE HEART OF THE RHINOCEROS!*
WHAT? *WHO DARES?*

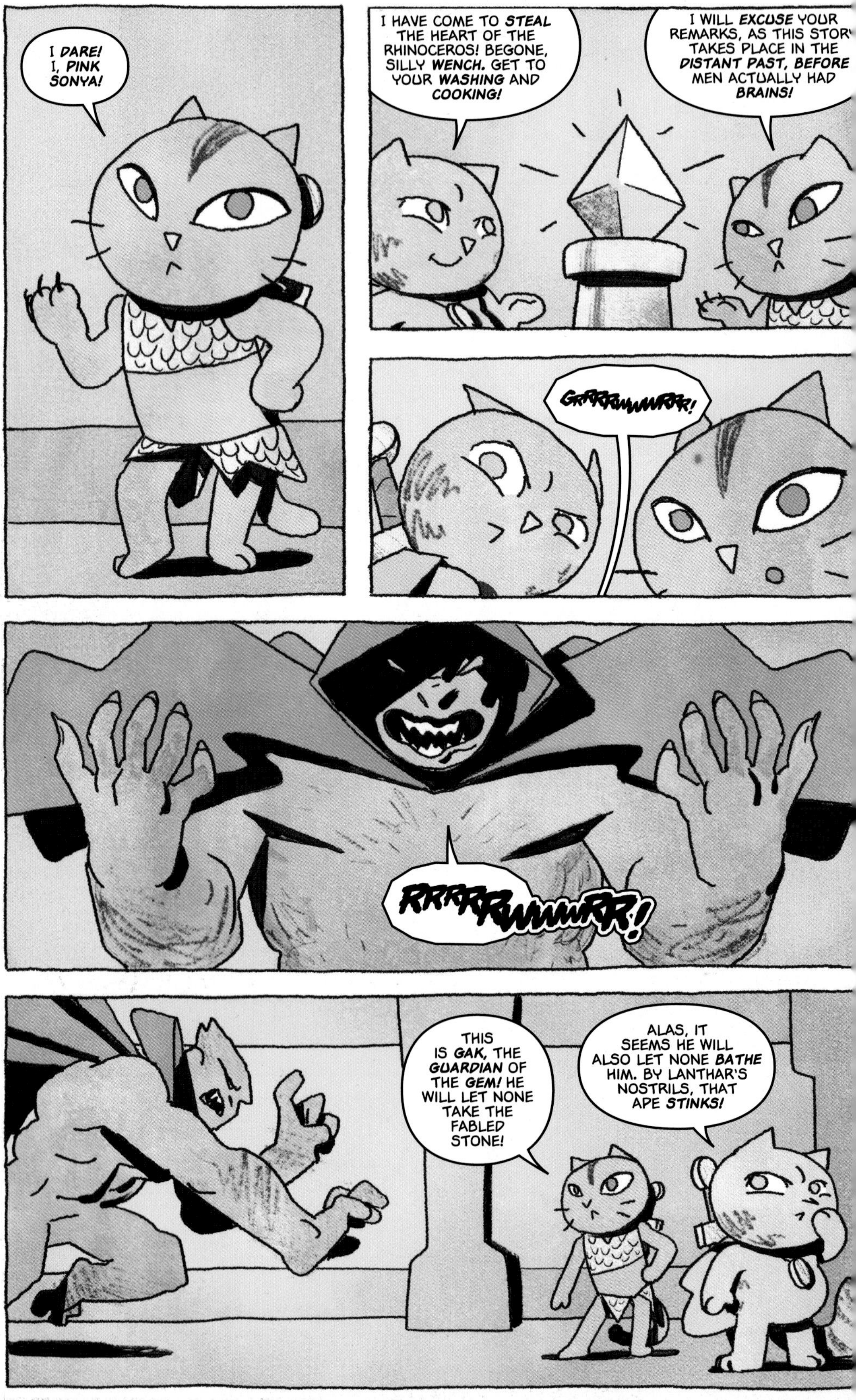
I DARE! I, PINK SONYA!
I HAVE COME TO STEAL THE HEART OF THE RHINOCEROS! BEGONE, SILLY WENCH. GET TO YOUR WASHING AND COOKING!
I WILL EXCUSE YOUR REMARKS, AS THIS STORY TAKES PLACE IN THE DISTANT PAST, BEFORE MEN ACTUALLY HAD BRAINS!
GRRRRWWWRRR!
RRRRRWWWWRR!
THIS IS GAK, THE GUARDIAN OF THE GEM! HE WILL LET NONE TAKE THE FABLED STONE!
ALAS, IT SEEMS HE WILL ALSO LET NONE BATHE HIM. BY LANTHAR'S NOSTRILS, THAT APE STINKS!

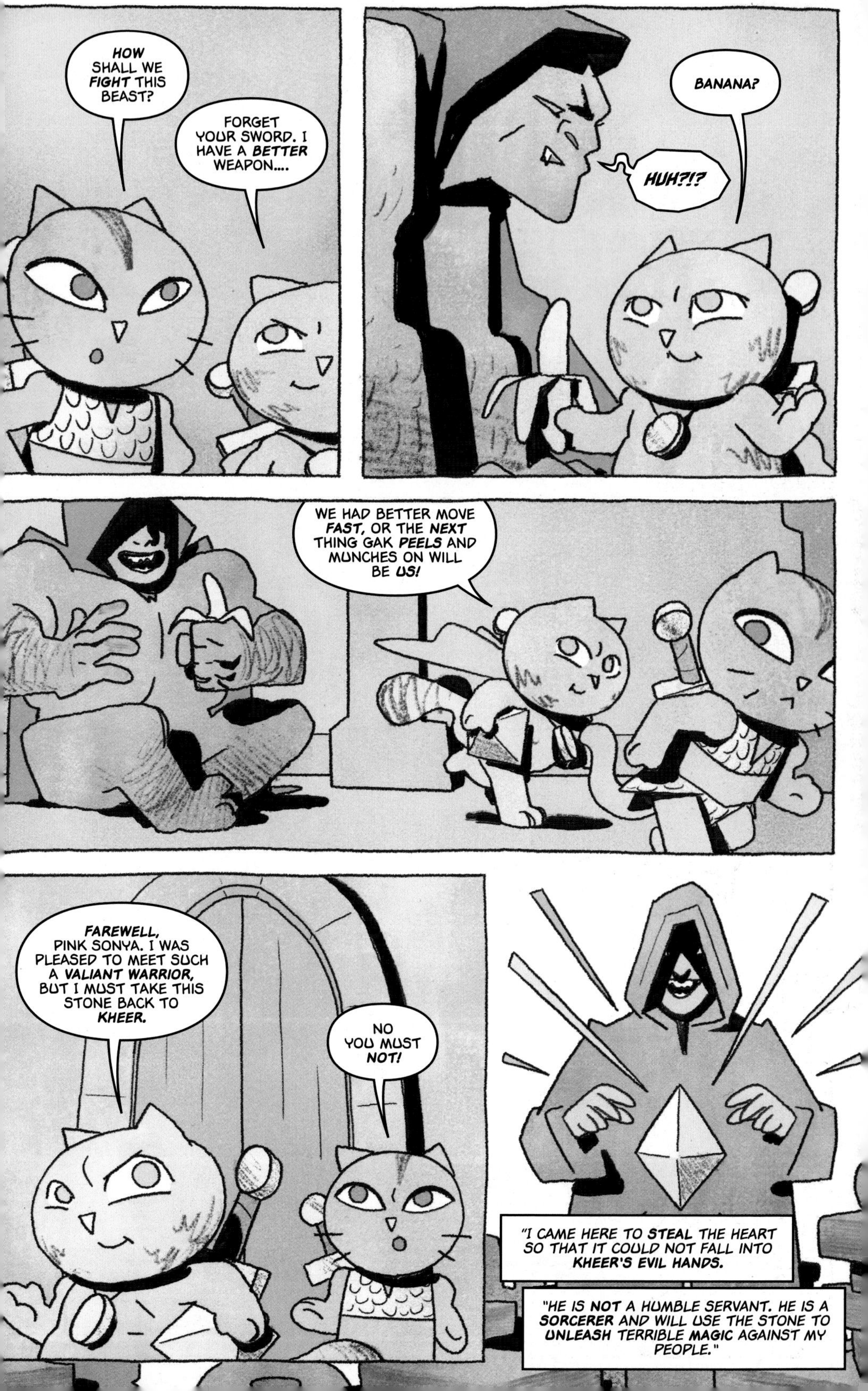
HOW SHALL WE FIGHT THIS BEAST?
FORGET YOUR SWORD. I HAVE A BETTER WEAPON....
BANANA?
HUH?!?
WE HAD BETTER MOVE FAST, OR THE NEXT THING GAK PEELS AND MUNCHES ON WILL BE US!
FAREWELL, PINK SONYA. I WAS PLEASED TO MEET SUCH A VALIANT WARRIOR, BUT I MUST TAKE THIS STONE BACK TO KHEER.
NO YOU MUST NOT!
"I CAME HERE TO STEAL THE HEART SO THAT IT COULD NOT FALL INTO KHEER'S EVIL HANDS.
"HE IS NOT A HUMBLE SERVANT. HE IS A SORCERER AND WILL USE THE STONE TO UNLEASH TERRIBLE MAGIC AGAINST MY PEOPLE."

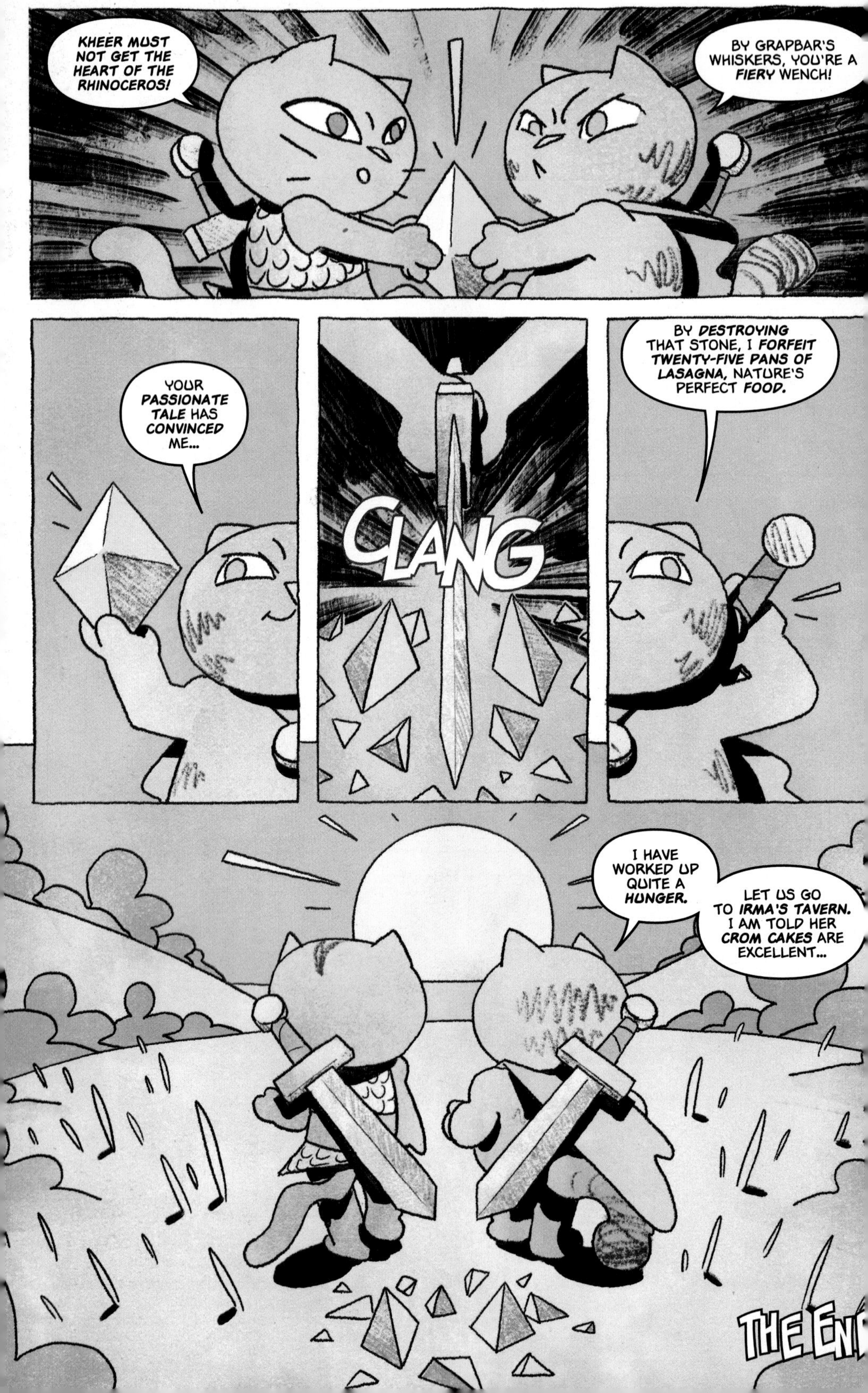
KHEER MUST NOT GET THE HEART OF THE RHINOCEROS!
BY GRAPBAR'S WHISKERS, YOU'RE A FIERY WENCH!
YOUR PASSIONATE TALE HAS CONVINCED ME...
CLANG
BY DESTROYING THAT STONE, I FORFEIT TWENTY-FIVE PANS OF LASAGNA, NATURE'S PERFECT FOOD.
I HAVE WORKED UP QUITE A HUNGER.
LET US GO TO IRMA'S TAVERN. I AM TOLD HER CROM CAKES ARE EXCELLENT...

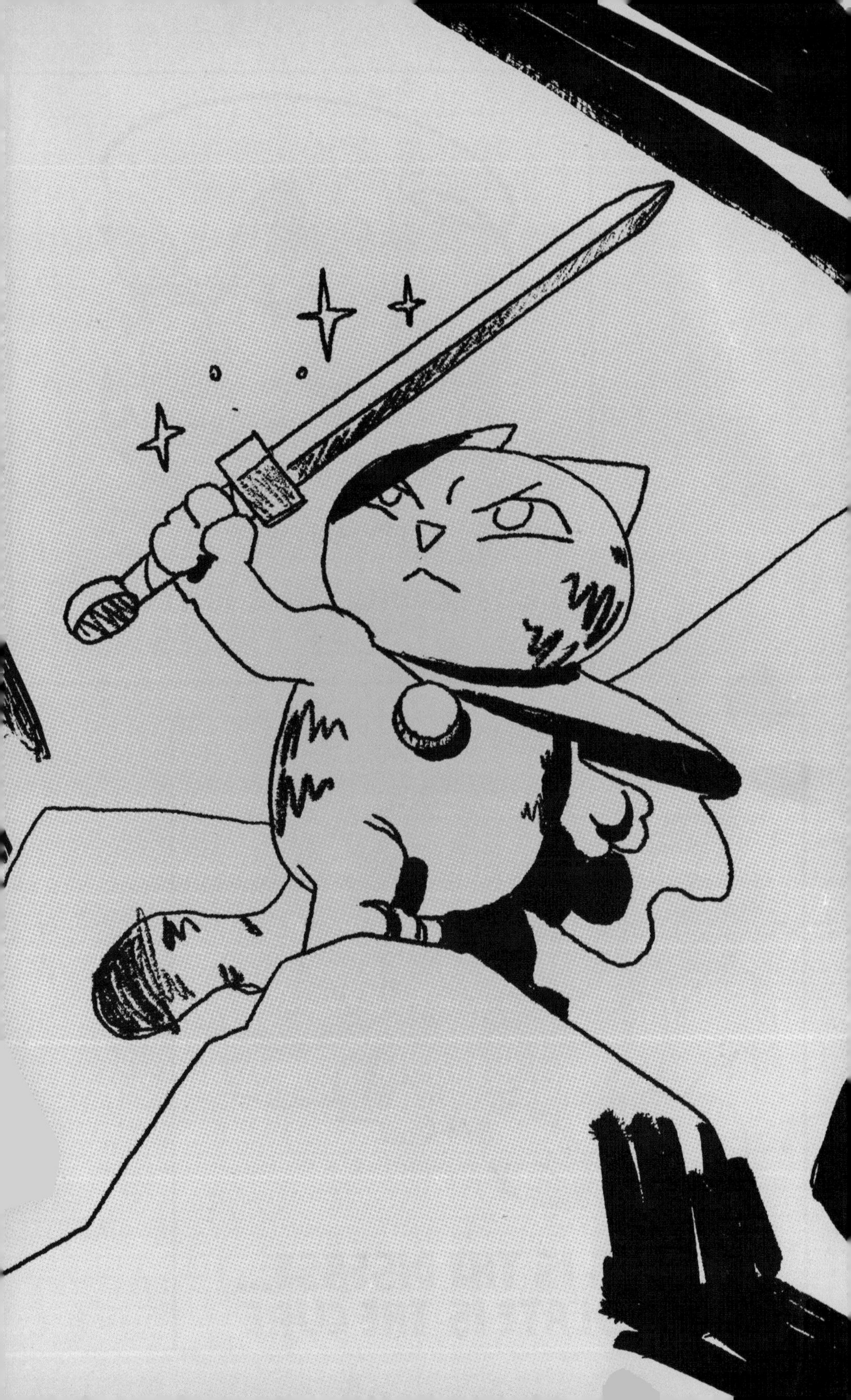

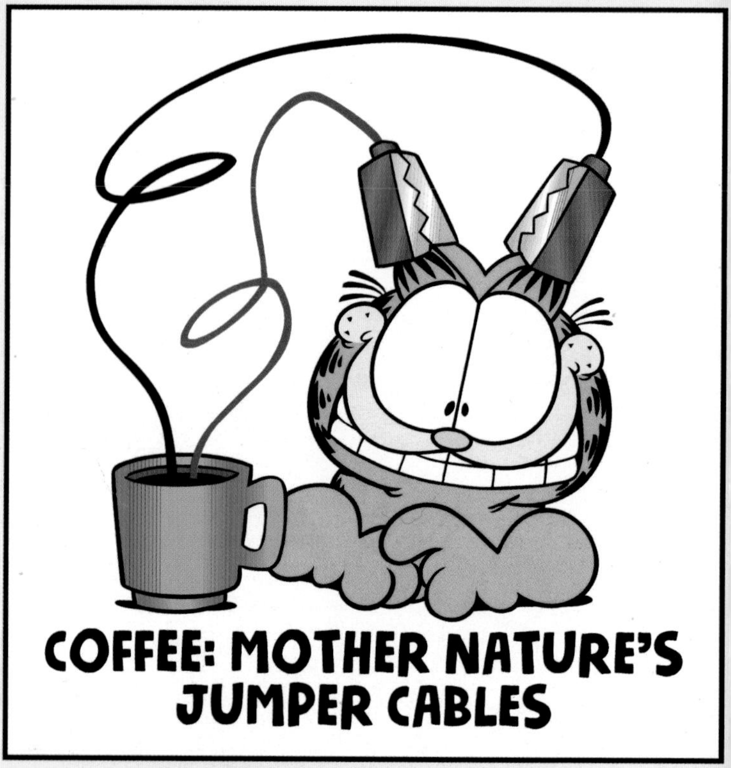
COFFEE: MOTHER NATURE'S JUMPER CABLES

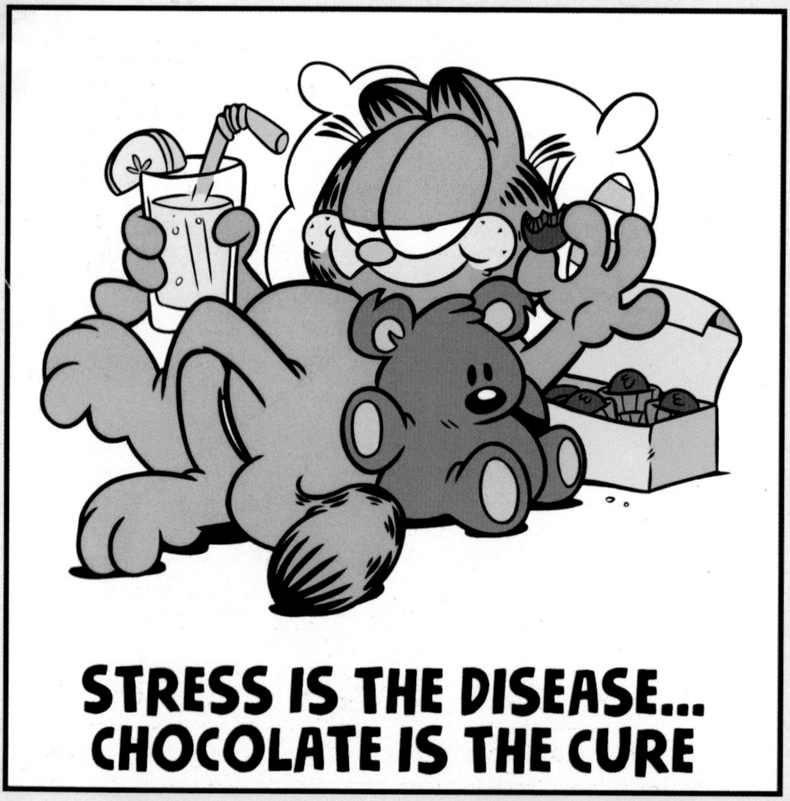
STRESS IS THE DISEASE...
CHOCOLATE IS THE CURE

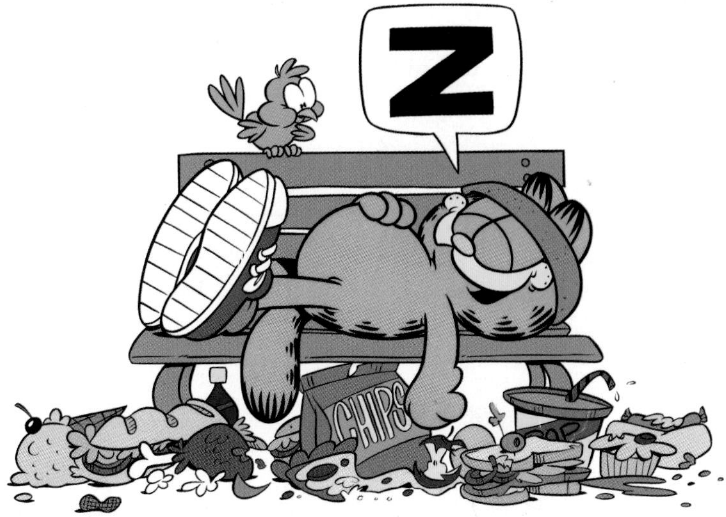
Z
CHIPS

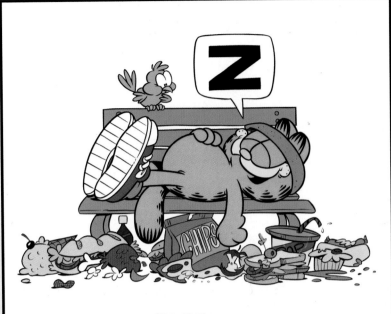

**SLEEP...
THE PERFECT EXERCISE**

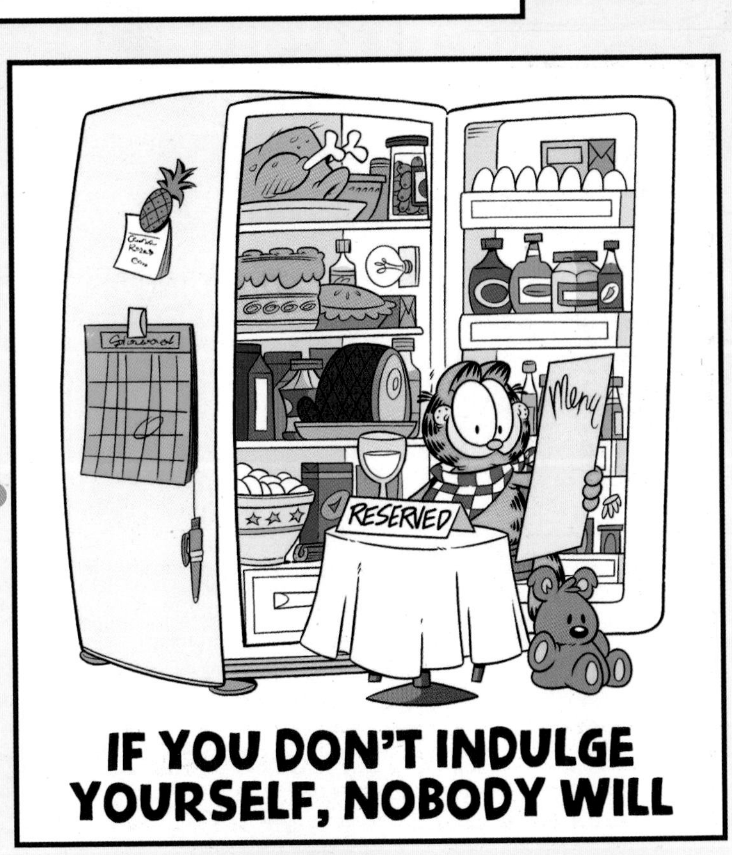
RESERVED
Menu

**IF YOU DON'T INDULGE
YOURSELF, NOBODY WILL**

Life's a Beach!

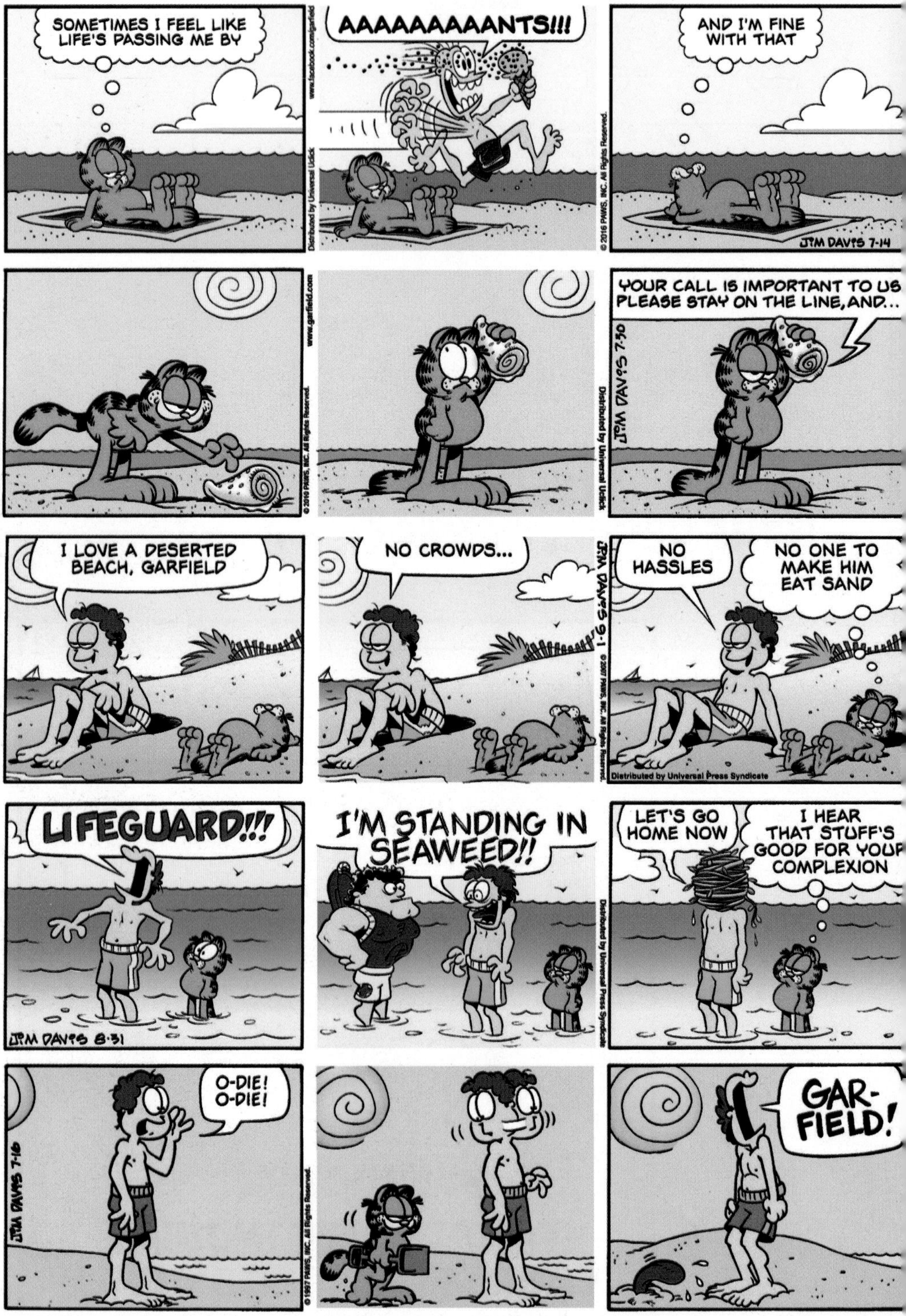

SOMETIMES I FEEL LIKE LIFE'S PASSING ME BY
AAAAAAAAANTS!!!
AND I'M FINE WITH THAT
JIM DAVIS 7-14
© 2016 PAWS, INC. All Rights Reserved.
Distributed by Universal Uclick
www.facebook.com/garfield
YOUR CALL IS IMPORTANT TO US PLEASE STAY ON THE LINE, AND...
JIM DAVIS 7-30
© 2016 PAWS, INC. All Rights Reserved.
Distributed by Universal Uclick
www.garfield.com
I LOVE A DESERTED BEACH, GARFIELD
NO CROWDS...
NO HASSLES
NO ONE TO MAKE HIM EAT SAND
JIM DAVIS 9-1
© 2007 PAWS, INC. All Rights Reserved.
Distributed by Universal Press Syndicate
LIFEGUARD!!!
I'M STANDING IN SEAWEED!!
LET'S GO HOME NOW
I HEAR THAT STUFF'S GOOD FOR YOUR COMPLEXION
JIM DAVIS 8-31
Distributed by Universal Press Syndicate
O-DIE! O-DIE!
GAR-FIELD!
JIM DAVIS 7-16
© 1997 PAWS, INC. All Rights Reserved.

GARFIELD TRIVIA QUIZ

Test your knowledge of the famous fat cat and his friends!

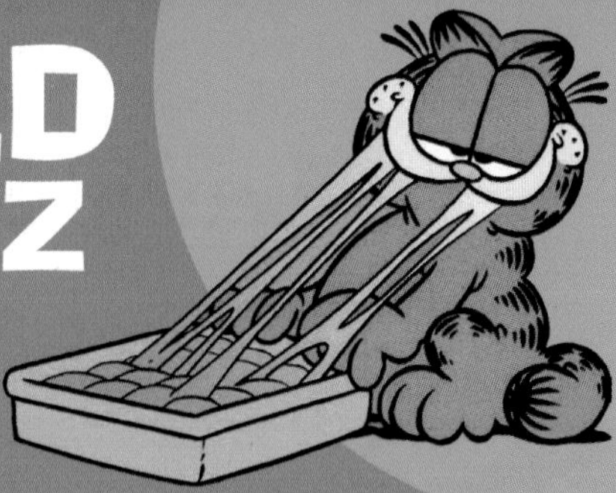

1
What is Garfield's favorite food?
A. Tofu Stew
B. Eel Curry
C. Blackened Brussel Sprouts
D. Lasagna

2
Where did Garfield find his teddy bear Pooky?
A. In a Dumpster
B. In a dresser drawer
C. In 'Nam
D. In Graceland

3
What does Garfield need to drink first thing in the morning?
A. Organic almond milk
B. Toilet water
C. Metamucil
D. Coffee

4
What did Garfield have tattooed on his chest?
A. "Born to Eat Bacon"
B. "My Owner's a Dork"
C. "Caution: Wide Load"
D. "USDA Choice"

5
According to Garfield, what would NOT be a good nickname for Odie?
A. Bouncy
B. Swifty
C. Sweetcheeks
D. Brainiac

6
What does Nermal call himself?
A. The Master of Disaster
B. The Ayatollah of Rock 'n' Rolla
C. The Real Slim Shady
D. The Worlds' Cutest Kitten

7
What is Binky's job?
A. Clown
B. Brain surgeon
C. TSA Inspector
D. Stunt double for Jackie Chan

8
What did Jon NOT get on Customer Appreciation Day at Irma's Diner?
A. "I ♥ Mystery Meat" T-shirt
B. "We passed our health inspection" balloon
C. All-day antacid
D. Solid gold monogrammed gravy boat

9
In the comic strip, what is Garfield's superhero name?
A. The Incredible Bulk
B. The Caped Avenger
C. Super-Size Man
D. The Masked Muncher

10
Which is the name of a real Garfield book?
A. Garfield Switches to Herbal Tea
B. Garfield Pulls His Hammy
C. Garfield Pulls His Weight
D. Garfield Maxes out His Data Plan

ANSWERS: 1.D, 2.B, 3.D, 4.B, 5.A, 6.D, 7.A, 8.D, 9.B, 10.C

Lazy Does It

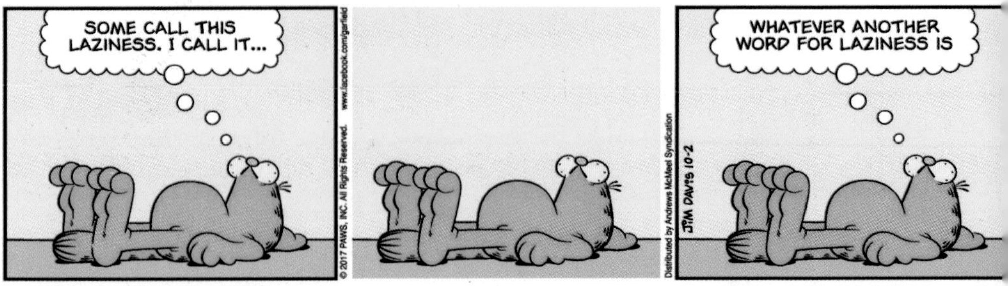
SOME CALL THIS LAZINESS. I CALL IT...
WHATEVER ANOTHER WORD FOR LAZINESS IS
© 2017 PAWS, INC. All Rights Reserved. www.facebook.com/garfield
Distributed by Andrews McMeel Syndication
JIM DAVIS 10-2

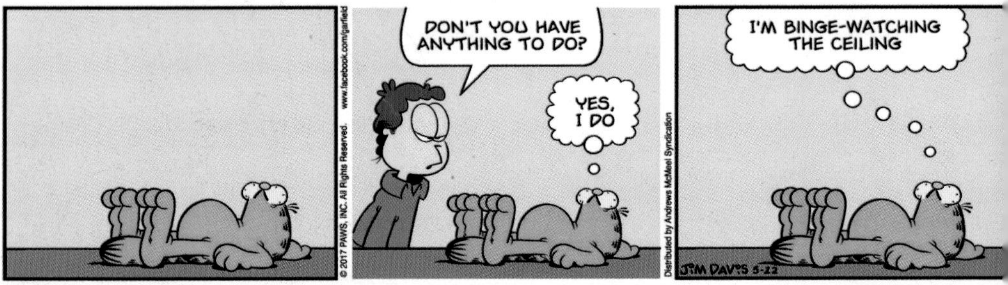
DON'T YOU HAVE ANYTHING TO DO?
YES, I DO
I'M BINGE-WATCHING THE CEILING
© 2017 PAWS, INC. All Rights Reserved. www.facebook.com/garfield
Distributed by Andrews McMeel Syndication
JIM DAVIS 5-22

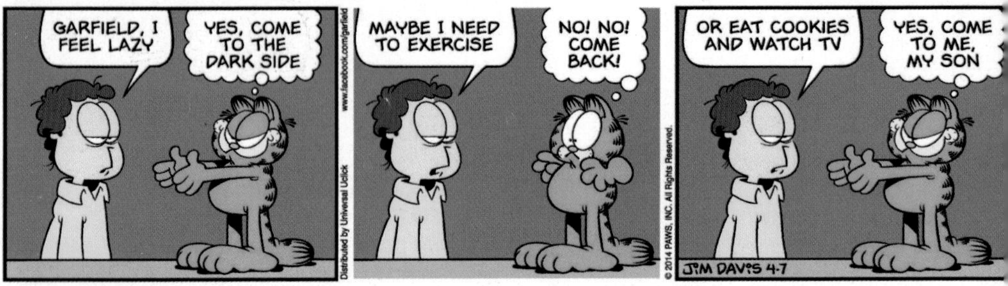
GARFIELD, I FEEL LAZY
YES, COME TO THE DARK SIDE
MAYBE I NEED TO EXERCISE
NO! NO! COME BACK!
OR EAT COOKIES AND WATCH TV
YES, COME TO ME, MY SON
www.facebook.com/garfield
Distributed by Universal Uclick
© 2014 PAWS, INC. All Rights Reserved.
JIM DAVIS 4-7

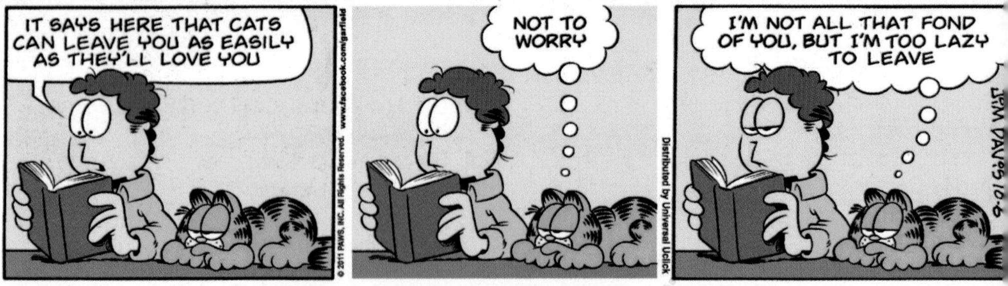
IT SAYS HERE THAT CATS CAN LEAVE YOU AS EASILY AS THEY'LL LOVE YOU
NOT TO WORRY
I'M NOT ALL THAT FOND OF YOU, BUT I'M TOO LAZY TO LEAVE
© 2011 PAWS, INC. All Rights Reserved. www.facebook.com/garfield
Distributed by Universal Uclick
JIM DAVIS 10-6

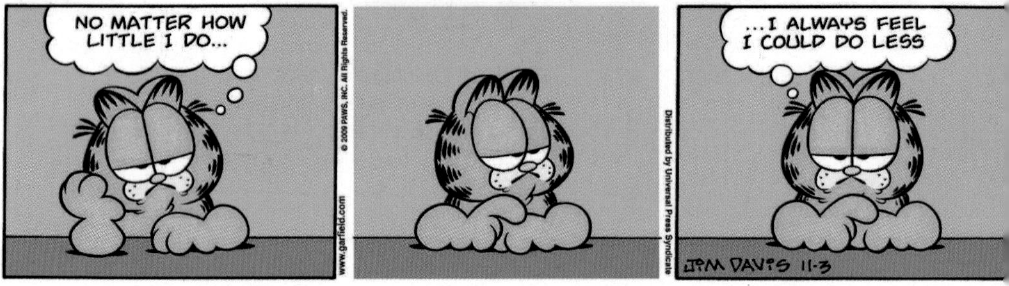
NO MATTER HOW LITTLE I DO...
...I ALWAYS FEEL I COULD DO LESS
www.garfield.com
© 2009 PAWS, INC. All Rights Reserved.
Distributed by Universal Press Syndicate
JIM DAVIS 11-3

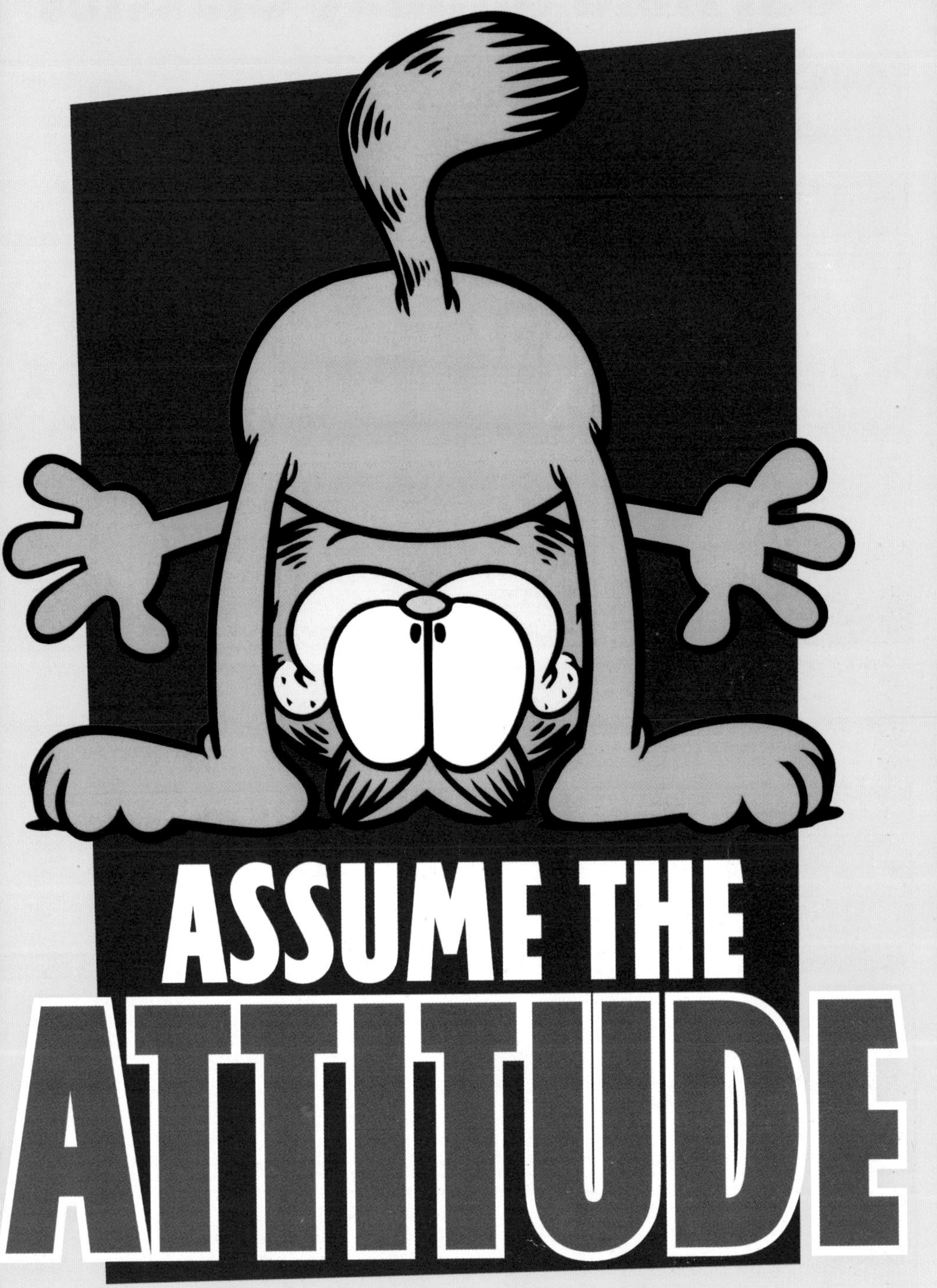
ASSUME THE
ATTITUDE

Garfield Sunday Classics

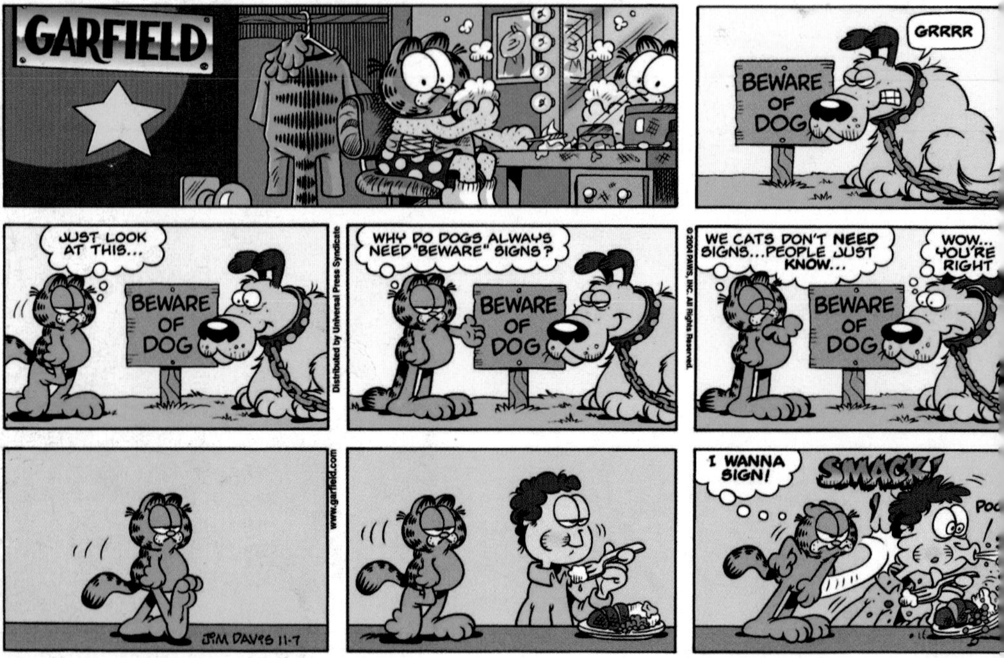

GARFIELD
GRRRR
BEWARE OF DOG
JUST LOOK AT THIS...
WHY DO DOGS ALWAYS NEED "BEWARE" SIGNS?
WE CATS DON'T NEED SIGNS...PEOPLE JUST KNOW...
WOW... YOU'RE RIGHT
Distributed by Universal Press Syndicate
© 2004 PAWS, INC. All Rights Reserved.
www.garfield.com
JIM DAVIS 11-7
I WANNA SIGN!
SMACK!

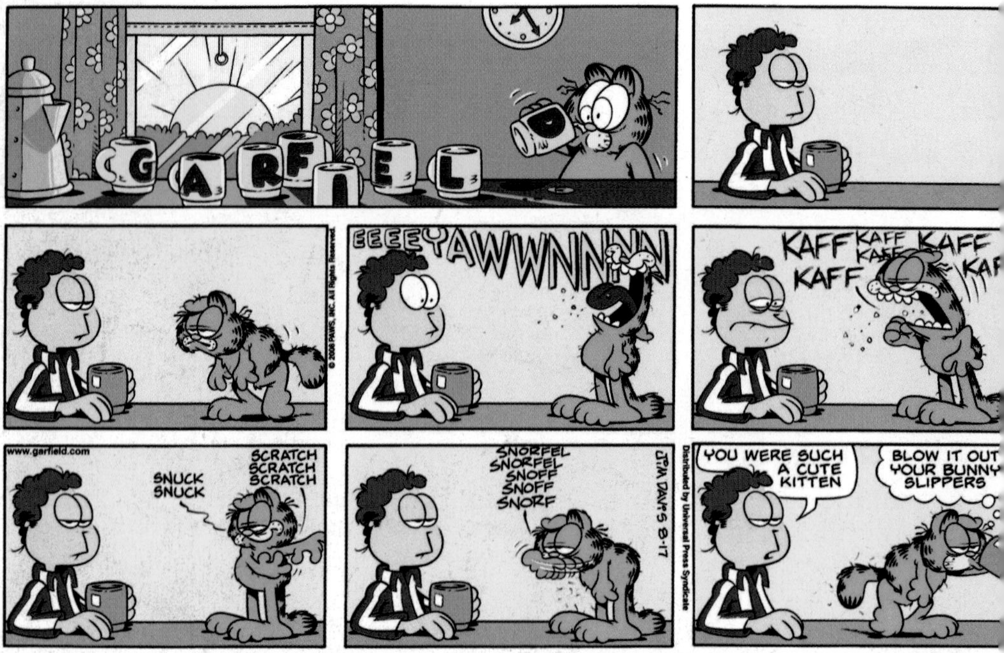

G A R F I E L
D
© 2006 PAWS, INC. All Rights Reserved.
EEEEYAWWNNNN
KAFF KAFF KAFF KAFF KAFF
www.garfield.com
SNUCK SNUCK
SCRATCH SCRATCH SCRATCH
SNORFEL SNORFEL SNOFF SNOFF SNORF
JIM DAVIS 8-17
Distributed by Universal Press Syndicate
YOU WERE SUCH A CUTE KITTEN
BLOW IT OUT YOUR BUNNY SLIPPERS